THE TURNING

Other books by Tim Winton

NOVELS
An Open Swimmer
Shallows
That Eye, the Sky
In the Winter Dark
Cloudstreet
The Riders
Dirt Music

STORIES
Scission
Minimum of Two

FOR YOUNGER READERS
Jesse
Lockie Leonard, Human Torpedo
The Bugalugs Bum Thief
Lockie Leonard, Scumbuster
Lockie Leonard, Legend
Blueback
The Deep

NON-FICTION
Land's Edge
Down to Earth (with Richard Woldendorp)

TIM
WINTON
THE TURNING

PICADOR

Pan Macmillan Australia

First published 2004 in Picador by Pan Macmillan Australia Pty Limited
St Martins Tower, 31 Market Street, Sydney

First deckled-edged edition

A CIP catalogue for this book is available from the National Library of Australia

ISBN 0 330 42139 5

Typeset in 11/16 pt Sabon by Post Pre-press Group, Brisbane
Printed by McPherson's Printing Group, Maryborough, Victoria

Papers used by Pan Macmillan Australia Pty Ltd are natural, recyclable products made
from wood grown in sustainable forests. The manufacturing processes conform to the
environmental regulations of the country of origin.

for Ken Kelso

And I pray that I may forget
These matters that with myself I too much discuss
Too much explain
Because I do not hope to turn again
Let these words answer
For what is done, not to be done again

T.S. Eliot
'Ash Wednesday'

Contents

Big World

AFTER FIVE YEARS of high school the final November arrives
and leaves as suddenly as a spring storm. Exams. Graduation.
Huge beach parties. Biggie and me, we're feverish with anticipation; we steel ourselves for a season of pandemonium. But
after the initial celebrations, nothing really happens, not even
summer itself. Week after week an endless misting drizzle
wafts in from the sea. It beads in our hair and hangs from the
tips of our noses while we trudge around town in the vain
hope of scaring up some action. The southern sky presses
down and the beaches and bays turn the colour of dirty tin.
Somehow our crappy Saturday job at the meatworks becomes
full-time and then Christmas comes and so do the dreaded
exam results. The news is not good. A few of our classmates
pack their bags for university and shoot through. Cheryl

Button gets into Medicine. Vic Lang, the copper's kid, is dux of the school and doesn't even stay for graduation. And suddenly there we are, Biggie and me, heading to work every morning in a frigid wind in the January of our new lives, still in jeans and boots and flannel shirts, with beanies on our heads and the horizon around our ears.

The job mostly consists of hosing blood off the floors. Plumes of the stuff go into the harbour and old men sit in dinghies offshore to catch herring in the slick. Some days I can see me and Biggie out there as old codgers, anchored to the friggin place, stuck forever. Our time at the meatworks is supposed to be temporary. We're saving for a car, the V-8 Sandman we've been promising ourselves since we were fourteen. Mag wheels, a lurid spray job like something off a Yes album and a filthy great mattress in the back. A chick magnet, that's what we want. Until now we've had a biscuit tin full of twos and fivers but now we're making real money.

Trouble is, I can't stand it. I just know I won't last long enough to get that car. There's something I've never told Biggie in all our years of being mates. That I dream of escaping, of pissing off north to find some blue sky. Unlike him I'm not really *from* here. It's not hosing blood that shits me off – it's Angelus itself; I'm going nuts here. Until now, out of loyalty, I've kept it to myself, but by the beginning of February I'm chipping away at our old fantasy, talking instead about sitting under a mango tree with a cold beer, walking in a shady banana plantation with a girl in a cheesecloth dress. On our long walks home I bang on about cutting our own pineapples and climbing for coconuts. Mate, I say, can't you see yourself rubbing baby oil into a girl's strapless back on Cable Beach? Up north, mate, think north! I know Biggie loves this town and he's committed to the shared vision of the panel van, but I white-ant him day after day until it starts to pay off.

By the last weeks of February Biggie's starting to come around. He's talking wide open spaces now, trails to adventure, and I'm like this little urger in his ear. Then one grey day he crosses the line. We've been deputised to help pack skins. For eight hours we stand on the line fighting slippery chunks of cow hide into boxes so they can be sold as craybait. Our arms are slick with gore and pasted with orange and black beef-hairs. The smell isn't good but that's nothing compared with the feel of all those severed nostrils and lips and ears between your fingers. I don't make a sound, don't even stop for lunch, can't think about it. I'm just glad all those chunks are fresh because at least my hands are warm. Beside me Biggie's face gets darker and darker, and when the shift horn sounds he lurches away, his last carton half-empty. Fuck it, he says. We're outta here. That afternoon we ditch the Sandman idea and buy a Kombi from a hippy on the wharf. Two hundred bucks each.

We put in two last weeks at the meatworks and collect our pay. We fill the ancient VW with tinned food and all our camping junk and rack off without telling a soul. Monday morning everyone thinks we're off to work as usual, but in ten minutes we're out past the town limits going like hell. Well, going the way a 1967 Kombi will go. Our getaway vehicle is a garden shed on wheels.

It's a mad feeling, sitting up so high like that with the road flashing under your feet. For a couple of hours we're laughing and pointing and shoving and farting and then we settle down a bit. We go quiet and just listen to the Volkswagen's engine threshing away behind us. I can't believe we've done it. If either of us had let on to anybody these past couple of weeks we'd never have gone through with it; we'd have piked for sure. We'd be like all the other poor stranded failures who stayed in Angelus. But now we're on the road, it's time for second thoughts. Nothing said, but I can feel it.

The plan is to call from somewhere the other side of Perth when we're out of reach. I want to be safe from the guilts – the old girl will crack a sad on me – but Biggie has bigger things to fear. His old man will beat the shit out of him when he finds out. We can't change our minds now.

The longer we drive the more the sky and the bush open up. Now and then Biggie looks at me and leers. He's got a face only a mother could love. One eye's looking at you and the other eye's looking *for* you. He's kind of pear-shaped, but you'd be a brave bugger calling him a barge-arse. The fists on him. To be honest he's not really my sort of bloke at all, but somehow he's my best mate.

We buzz north through hours of good farm country. The big, neat paddocks get browner and drier all the while and the air feels thick and warm. Biggie drives. He has the habit of punctuating his sentences with jabs on the accelerator and although the gutless old Volksie doesn't exactly give you whiplash at every flourish, it's enough to give a bloke a headache. We wind through the remnant jarrah forest, and the sickly-looking regrowth is so rain-parched it almost crackles when you look at it.

When Perth comes into view, its dun plain shimmering with heat and distant towers ablaze with midday sun, we get all nervous and giggly, like a pair of tipsy netballers. The big city. We give each other the full Groucho Marx eyebrow routine but we're not stopping. Biggie's a country boy through and through. Cities confound him, he can't see the point of them. He honestly wonders how people can live in each other's pockets like that. He's revolted and a little frightened at the thought. Me, I love the city, I'm from there originally. I really thought I'd be moving back this month. But I won't, of course. Not after blowing my exams. I'm glad we're not stopping. It'd be like having your nose rubbed in it. Failure, that is. I can't tell Biggie this but missing out on uni really stings. When the results came I cried my eyes out. I thought about killing myself.

To get past Perth we navigate the blowsy strips of caryards and showrooms and crappy subdivisions on the outskirts. Soon we're out the other side into vineyards and horse paddocks with the sky blue as mouthwash ahead. Then finally, open road. We've reached a world where it isn't bloody raining all the time, where nobody knows us and nobody cares. There's just us and the Love Machine. We get the giggles. We go off; we blat the horn and hoot and chuck maps and burger wrappers around the cabin. Two mad southern boys still wearing beanies in March.

I'm laughing. I'm kicking the dash. That ache is still there inside me but this is the best I've felt since the news about the exams. For once I'm not faking it. I look across at Biggie. His huge, unlovely face is creased with merriment. I just know I'll never be able to tell him about the hopes I had for myself and for a little while I don't care about any of it; I'm almost as happy as him. Biggie's results were even worse than mine – he really fried – but he didn't have his heart set on doing well; he couldn't give a rat's ring. For him, our bombing out is a huge joke. In his head he's always seen himself at the meatworks or the cannery until he inherits the salmon-netting licence from his old man. He's content, he belongs. His outlook drives my mother wild with frustration but in a way I envy him. My mother calls us Lenny and George. She teaches English; she thinks that's funny. She's trying to wean me off Biggie Botson.

In fact she's got a program all mapped out to get me back on track, to take the year again and re-sit the exams. But I've blown all that off now. Biggie's not the brightest crayon in the box but he's the most loyal person I know. He's the real deal and you can't say that about many people.

My mother won't chase me up; she's kind of preoccupied. She's in love with the deputy principal. He's married. He uses the school office to sell Amway. Both of them believe that Civics should be reintroduced as a compulsory course.

We get out into rolling pasture and granite country and then wheat-lands where the ground is freshly torn up in the hope of rain. The VW shakes like a boiling billy and we've finally woken up to ourselves and sheepishly dragged our beanies off. The windows are down and the hot wind rips through our hair.

Biggie must have secrets. Everyone dreams of things in private. There must be stuff he doesn't tell me. I know about the floggings he and his mum get, but I don't know what he wants deep down. He won't say. But then I don't say either. I never tell him about the Skeleton Coast in Africa where ships come aground on surf beaches and lie there broken-bellied until the dunes bury them. And the picture I have of myself in a café on the Piazza San Marco leaving a tip so big that the waiter inhales his moustache. Dreams of the big world beyond. Manila. Monterey. Places in books. In all these years I never let on. But then Biggie's never there in the picture with me. In those daydreams he doesn't figure, and maybe I'm guilty about that.

After a while we pull over for a leak. The sunlight is creamy up here. Standing at the roadside with it roasting my back and arms through the heavy shirt, I don't care that picking guavas and papaya doesn't pay much more than hosing the floor of an abattoir. If it's outside in the sun, that's fine by me. We'll be growing things, not killing them. We'll move with the seasons. We'll be free.

Mum thinks Biggie's an oaf, that he's holding me back. She doesn't know that without Biggie there'd be nothing left of me to hold back. It sounds weak, but he saved my life.

We didn't meet until the second week of high school. I was new in town and right from the start a kid called Tony Macoli became fixated on me. He was very short with a rodent's big eyes and narrow teeth. He sat behind me every class he could and whispered weird threats under the uncomprehending gaze of the teachers, especially my mother. He liked to jab me in the back with the point of his compass and lob spitballs into my hair. He trod on my feet in passing and gleefully broke my pencils. I'd never been a brawler but I was confident that I could knock him down. Trouble was, my parents were new to the school – this was before the old man pissed off – and I didn't want to make trouble. I already sensed their mutual misery and I felt responsible somehow. So I put up with it. I hadn't even spoken to Tony Macoli. I was shocked by the hatred in his wan little face. I couldn't imagine how I'd put him out so thoroughly. It seemed that my very existence offended him.

The little bastard kept at me but I didn't touch him. After a week I didn't even react. I wasn't scared. It wasn't passive resistance or anything. I just got all weird and listless. I reckon I was depressed. But the less I responded the more Tony Macoli paid out on me.

On the second Monday of term I was shoved into a hedge, tripped in the corridor so that my books sprayed across the linoleum, and had my fingers slammed in a desk – all this before morning recess. Each little coup brought out Macoli's wheezy little laugh. It rocked his body and tilted his head back on his neck so that the whites of his eyes showed. At morning recess I was wiping mud from my pants while he gave in to that convulsive laugh. The wind blew his tie over his left shoulder and my pulse felt shallow, as though I was only barely alive. As I got wearily back to my feet, a shambling figure passed me and I saw the flash of a fist. One second Tony Macoli was laughing himself sick, and the next his nose was pointed over his shoulder in the same direction as his windblown tie. Blood spurted, Macoli went down and I can still hear the sweet melon sound of his head hitting the path. Macoli went to the district hospital and Biggie Botson began two weeks' suspension.

That's how it started. A single decisive act of violence that joined me to Biggie forever. If you believe him on the subject he acted more out of animal irritation than charity. But I felt like somebody ransomed and set free. Until that moment I was disappearing. School, home, the new town, they were all misery. If Biggie hadn't come along I don't know what would have become of me. Exam week, five years later, wasn't the first time I thought of necking myself. Biggie became my mate, my constant companion, and Tony Macoli was suddenly landscape.

For a while my mother thought Biggie and me were gay. She did a big *tolerance* routine that dried up when she realized we weren't poofs.

Back on the road again I'm thinking boab trees and red dirt, girls in sarongs, cold beer, parking the Vee Dub on some endless beach to sleep. And mangoes. Is there anything sexier than a mango?

I suppose we're all wrong for each other, Biggie and me. He's not a very introspective bloke. Sometimes he makes me restless. But we get along pretty well most of the time. We go camping a lot, hike out to all sorts of places and set up on our own. Biggie loves all the practical stuff, reading maps, trying survival techniques, learning bushcraft. I'm more into the birds and plants and stars and things. Some mornings out in the misty ranges the world looks like it means something, some simple thing just out of my reach, but there anyway. That's why I go. And both of us dig the fact that nobody else is out there pursing their lips at us or taking a swing.

Biggie truly is a funny bugger. He can do Elvis with his belly-button – *thank you very much* – a toothless King sprouting manky black hairs in a face made of fat. He can fart whole sentences, a skill St Augustine admired in others. He's not much for hygiene. His hair's always greasy and that navel smells like toejam. He doesn't swim. He couldn't carry a tune in a bucket but he can find true north by instinct. On his day he's a frightening fast bowler but most days he can't hit the pitch for love or money. He once surfed a school bus thirty miles. He caught nineteen herring with the same single green pea and an unweighted hook. And he was the only one in the class brave enough to hold the bin for the student teacher while she puked so hard it came out her nose. His sole academic success was his essay on the demise of Led Zeppelin, but then I wrote that for him.

Friendship, I suppose, comes at a price. There have been girls I've disqualified myself from because of Biggie. Not everyone wants to have him tagging along everywhere, though in the days before we get our licences there are those who don't mind walking out with us to the drive-ins. I figure we're not glamorous but we're entertaining in our way. Right through high school I have occasional moments, evenings, encounters with girls but no real girlfriend and mostly I don't regret it. Except for Briony Nevis. For two years we're sort of watching each other from a distance. Sidelong glances. She's flat-out beautiful, long black hair like some kind of Indian. Glossy skin, dark eyes. She's funny in a wry, hurt kind of way, and smart. In class she goads me, says I'm not as stupid as I make out. I kiss her once at a party. Well, maybe she kisses me. Hair like a satin pillowslip. Body all sprung as though she's ready to bolt. A long, long kiss, deep and playful as a conversation. But there at the corner of my eye is Biggie alone on the smoky verandah, waiting to go home. I don't go to him straight up. I do make him wait a fair old while but I don't go on with Briony Nevis the way I badly want to because I know Biggie will be left behind for good. Not that I don't think about her. Hell, I write poems to her, draw pictures of her, construct filthy elaborate fantasies she'll never know about. But I never touch her again. Out of loyalty. Briony isn't exactly crushed. If anything she seems amused. She sees how things are.

And she's right, you know, I'm not as stupid as I make out. It's a survival thing, making yourself a small target. But even now, feeling kind of euphoric, buzzing up the highway, I know I'm stuck in something that I can't figure my way out of.

You see, back in first year, right at the beginning when Biggie was my saviour and still doing his two weeks' suspension for busting Tony Macoli's nose, I kept notes for the full fortnight and more or less wrote Biggie's essays for him when he got back. He didn't care if he passed or failed but I wanted to do it for him, and so what began as a gesture of gratitude became a pattern for the rest of our schooling. I made him look brighter than he was and me a little dimmer. His old man preferred him to be a dolt. My mother expected me to be an academic suckhole. Most of the time Biggie couldn't give a damn but sometimes I think he really got his hopes up. I feel responsible, like my ghost work stopped him from learning. In a way I ruined his chances. For five years I worked my arse off. I really did all our work. Out of loyalty, yeah, but also from sheer vanity. And the fact is, I blew it. I got us both to the finish line but ensured that neither of us got across it. Biggie hadn't learnt anything that he could display in an exam and I was too worn out and cocky to make sense. We fried. We're idiots of a different species but we are both bloody idiots.

At New Norcia we pull in to fuel up and use the phone. Biggie decides that he's not calling home so he sits in the VW while I reverse the charges and get an earful. My mother wails and cries. I'm vague about my whereabouts and look out at the monastery and church spires and whitewashed walls of the town while she tells me I'm throwing my future away. I hang up and find Biggie talking to a chick with a backpack the size of an elephant saddle. She's tall and not very beautiful with long, shiny brown hair and big knees. She thinks she's on the coast road north and she's mortified to discover otherwise. Biggie explains that this is the inland route, shows her on the map. She wants to get to Exmouth, she says. I can see Biggie falling in love with her moment by moment. My heart sinks.

There isn't really even much consultation. We just pull out with this chick in the back. Meg is her name. I know it's hot and she's had a tough day but she's on the nose. She's got a purple tanktop on and every time she lifts an arm there's a blast of BO that could kill a wildebeest. Biggie doesn't seem to notice. He's twisted around in his seat laughing and chatting and pointing and listening while I drive in something close to a sullen silence.

Meg is as thick as a box of hammers. It's alarming to see how enthralled Biggie is. He goes right ahead and tells her about life in the salmon camp every season when all the huts are full and the tractors are hauling nets up the beach and trucks pull down to the water's edge to load up for the cannery. All the drinking and fighting, the sharks and the jetboats, the great green masses of fish pressed inside the headlands. He doesn't tell Meg that it's all for petfood, that his mother cries every night, that he's given up defending her, not even urging her to leave now, but nobody could hold that against him. Meg, this mouth-breathing moron, is staring at Biggie like he's a guru, and I just drive and try to avoid the rear-view mirror.

I get to thinking about the last night of school and the bonfire at Massacre Point, the beginning of that short period of grace when my very limbs tingled with relief and the dread of failure had yet to set in. Someone had a kite in the air and its tail was on fire, looping and spiralling orange and pink against the night sky, so beautiful I almost cried. I was smashed and exhausted; I suppose any little thing would have seemed poignant and beautiful. But I really felt that I'd reached the edge of something. I had a power and a promise I'd never sensed before. The fact that the burning kite consumed its own tail and fluttered down into the sea didn't really register. I didn't see it as an omen. Biggie and I drank Bacardi and Coke and watched some lunatic fishing for sharks with a Land Rover. Briony Nevis was there, teeth flashing in the firelight. I was too pissed to go over to her. I fell asleep trying to work up the nerve.

We woke by a huge lake of glowing embers, our sleeping bags damp, the tide out and our heads pounding, but it was the smiling that hurt the most. Biggie wanted to stay a while in that tangle of blankets and swags but I convinced him to get up with me and swim bare-arsed in the cold clear water inside the rocky promontory before we stole back through the sleeping crowd towards my mother's car. That was a great feeling, tingling, awake, up first, seeing everybody sprawled in hilarious and unlikely pairings and postures. The air was soupy, salty, and as we padded up the sand track with birds in the mint-scented scrub all round, I just couldn't imagine disappointment. The world felt new, specially made for us. It was only on the drive back to town that our hangovers caught up.

While I'm thinking about all of this Biggie's gone and climbed over into the back and Meg's lit up a number and they're toking away on it with their feet up like I'm some kind of chauffeur. The country is all low and spare now and the further we go the redder it gets. Biggie's never had much luck with girls. I should be glad for him. But I'm totally pissed off.

In the mirror Biggie has this big wonky grin going. He sits back with his legs stretched out and crossed at the ankles, his Blundstones poking through the gap in the seats at my elbow. Meg murmurs and exclaims at the beauty of the country and Biggie just nods slit-eyed with smoke and anticipation while I boil.

Late in the day, when Biggie and Meg are quizzing each other on the theme tunes to TV sitcoms, we come upon a maze of salt lakes that blaze silver and pearly in the sun and stretch to the horizon in every direction. I begin to have the panicky feeling that the land and this very afternoon might go on forever. Biggie's really enjoying himself back there and I slowly understand why. There's the obvious thing of course, the fact that he's in with a big chance with Meg come nightfall. But something else, the thing that eats at me, is the way he's enjoying being brighter than her, being a step ahead, feeling somehow senior and secure in himself. It's me all over. It's how I am with him and it's not pretty.

The Kombi fills with smoke again but this time it's bitter and metallic and I'm halfway to asking them to leave off and open a bloody window when I see the plume trailing us down the highway and I understand that we're on fire. I pull over into a tottery skid in the gravel at the roadside and jump out to see just how much grey smoke is pouring out of the rear grille. When Biggie and Meg join me we stand there a few moments before it dawns on us that the whole thing could blow at any moment and everything we own is inside. So we fall over each other digging our stuff free, tossing it as far into the samphire edges of the saltpan as we can. Without an extinguisher there's not much else we can do once we're standing back out there in the litter of our belongings waiting for the VW to explode. But it just smoulders and hisses a while as the sun sinks behind us. In the end, with the smoke almost gone and the wiring cooked, it's obvious we're not going anywhere. We turn our attention to the sunset. Meg rolls another spliff and we share it standing there taking in the vast, shimmering pink lake that suddenly looks full of rippling water. We don't say anything. The sun flattens itself against the saltpan and disappears. The sky goes all acid blue and there's just this huge silence. It's like the world's stopped.

Right then I can't imagine an end to the quiet. The horizon fades. Everything looks impossibly far off. In two hours I'll hear Biggie and Meg in his sleeping bag and she'll cry out like a bird and become so beautiful, so desirable in the total dark that I'll begin to cry. In a week Biggie and Meg will blow me off in Broome and I'll be on the bus south for a second chance at the exams. In a year Biggie will be dead in a mining accident in the Pilbara and I'll be reading Robert Louis Stevenson at his funeral while his relatives shuffle and mutter with contempt. Meg won't show. I'll grow up and have a family of my own and see Briony Nevis, tired and lined in a supermarket queue, and wonder what all the fuss was about. And one night I'll turn on the TV to discover the fact that Tony Macoli, the little man with the nose that could sniff round corners, is Australia's richest merchant banker. All of it unimaginable. Right now, standing with Biggie on the salt lake at sunset, each of us still in our southern-boy uniform of boots, jeans and flannel shirt, I don't care what happens beyond this moment. In the hot northern dusk, the world suddenly gets big around us, so big we just give in and watch.

Abbreviation

IT WAS DARK when the Langs rolled into White Point and nobody had anything to say. They were hours late and everyone knew why but with Nanna in the Jeep nobody was game to say a thing. Vic squirmed in his seat and sighed again, despite himself.

You must have worms, said his grandmother sternly.

I always bring my own bait, he said.

Vic, said his mother with a note of warning.

Sorry, he mumbled.

But he wasn't sorry. If the others hadn't kept them waiting half the afternoon they'd be there by now. They'd be set up on the beach with a fire going. It was the usual Uncle Ernie balls-up. When they arrived at his place at noon all Vic's girl-cousins were packed and ready in the Land Rover out on the hot street, their faces as red as their hair, while their parents were inside having a blue. The Landy's motor was running, the dinghy was hitched to it with the rods and mattresses and eskies strapped aboard in a bristling pile, but Ernie and Cleo were still in the house with the door locked. When Vic's old man banged on the window, nothing happened. He rattled the door, rang the bell. He got Vic's cousins out of the vehicle and sat them in the shade. They were the sorriest-looking bunch of girls you'd ever see, freckly as all get-out, with needle teeth and big nostrils. He'd seen carpet sharks prettier than them. Uncle Ernie was a ginger banty-rooster of a bloke and Auntie Cleo let everyone know she was too good for him. She was blonde. She had the looks of an old-timey movie star gone to fat. She had cleavage that damn-near made an echo when she spoke.

Everybody sat out in the street until Vic's baby sister began to scream in the heat and his grandmother yanked the keys from Ernie's idling Landy and opened the front door of the house herself. Ernie and Cleo came out pushing and shoving and swearing like sailors and all the wobbegong cousins began to bawl and then Ernie's Land Rover wouldn't start because it had overheated chugging out there in the street for God knows how long, and there was more bitching and backbiting while they waited for it to cool, but Nanna wouldn't hear a word against her favoured son.

So here they were now in the hot night, the Jeep and the Landy winding down the hill to White Point. The streets were empty. They drove on through to where the road ended and the white dunes banked up like a snowfield in the moonlight. Not that Vic had ever seen snow; it's just how he imagined it going on white forever.

They climbed into the dunes, motors grinding and whinny-ing. Vic rode the rolls and jerks and tried not to think about food. When the going was smooth the rumble of the diffs lulled him close to sleep and several times he stirred to see that Uncle Ernie was bogged to the axles and Vic had to get out with his father and grandmother to dig or set a tow rope.

It's the boat he's pulling, said Nanna, in defence of Ernie's driving. It's the load and all those kids.

Vic's mother pressed her lips together in the bright moon-light and nursed his baby sister. She knew as well as Vic that Ernie was careless, that he approached every hill in top gear, that his tyres were pumped too hard.

Nanna directed vehicle recovery. She rode out on the side step and talked through the open window, barking the kind of instructions that only a non-driver could give. After a long time they came into saltbush country and down into firm tracks that were steady going. The red eyes of the boat trailer up ahead mesmerized Vic until he slept again. When he woke they were down on wide, white beach that was as hard as a highway. For miles they drove fast and easy until they came to a spit where several campfires burned already.

Vic put up poles and ropes and tarps with the rest of them and ate cold roast lamb and potatoes in a stupor of fatigue. He fell onto a mattress and wound himself in a sheet and slept with the surf roaring all around him. He woke in the night, certain the sea had overrun them, but it was only the cool breeze rolling over him in waves and he slept on dreamless.

At first light the wind off the land was already hot and it smelt of saltbush and desert. When Vic woke, his grandmother was frying eggs over a driftwood fire. His father and uncle had the dinghy at the water's edge and were loading it with big cane craypots. Vic sat at the trestle table beneath the billowing tarp and ate eggs and drank tea from an enamel cup. The girls were only just stirring now and the other women were still asleep. The men came and ate breakfast and when they were finished Vic helped them push the boat into the shorebreak and jumped in when the outboard fired.

Ernie throttled them out into calm water and Vic looked back at the other cluster of tents and tarps not far from their own camp. He saw a truck and a tractor and a striped tent big as a circus marquee. The sun was low on the rolling dunes and he felt tired and strangely old. Today was the last day of the year. He wished there'd been room for a mate on this trip, someone to see 1973 in with, but the only spare seat had gone to Nanna; these days there was no escaping her. And now that the wind was rifling through his hair and the aluminium hull thrummed underfoot, he began to wish that it was his father at the tiller and not his uncle, because Ernie steered a boat as nonchalantly as he drove. The more confident Ernie was the less cause there was for anyone else to feel safe. But it was Ernie's boat not his father's. They didn't have a boat, couldn't afford one. Vic smiled gamely at the old man, reading the amusement in his raised eyebrows, and held on as they pounded out towards the reef. Beneath him the water flashed by, white, green, blue, yellow. When they got out over the mottled deep, swells rolled in smooth and oily while Vic's old man baited the pots with beef hocks and Ernie uncoiled ropes and floats. They tipped the craypots into sandy green holes and left the ropes snaking on the surface.

Back on the beach the carrot-top cousins squealed for a ride in the boat.

While they were tootled around the shallows Vic went up to the makeshift shelter between vehicles and saw that his mother was up. He rocked his baby sister while his mum ate breakfast and listened to Auntie Cleo talk about fingernails and cuticles. Vic's Auntie wasn't really a Cleo; she botted the name from the magazine with the horoscopes and male centrefolds. Her real name was Cloris. She bored his mum stupid. Vic's mum did her best to hide it from him but he knew it well enough. She must have been tired this morning because at one moment during Cleo's prattling monologue, at the very instant that Nanna happened to look their way, she rolled her eyes at him as if to say *give me strength*. Cleo didn't notice but Nanna's mouth was like a knife edge.

Vic didn't know why they were all stuck on this trip together but there was no doubt it was Nanna's idea. She had firm ideas about family, and when she was around everybody else's ideas went soft.

He wasn't quite thirteen but Vic knew a thing or two about Uncle Ernie. The oldies kept it quiet but he knew that with Nanna Ernie had protected status. It was as though he could do no wrong. Yet everything Ernie touched turned bad. He liked the nags. He played two-up and always knew a bloke who knew a bloke who had something or other on the highest authority. He was, therefore, always in trouble. It wasn't unusual to have men come knocking on the door for him as though Vic's old man was his father and not just his brother. Less than a year ago, just after his sister was born, Vic and his dad had to take Ernie's truck out in the wee hours to deliver milk for him. Nobody said where Ernie was. Nanna came along of course. She read out the orders by the light of a policeman's torch, and Vic ran until his throat was raw. The streets were dark and still. His father drove and ran and hardly said a word all night. Vic sensed that there'd been other nights he was spared. Now the milk round was gone in any case.

Vic was always uneasy around his uncle. Ernie *was* funny. There was always a joke on the boil, something to be kept from the women, but you'd never tell him anything important about yourself. He was always talking, never listening. One Christmas, when Vic was eight, Uncle Ernie arrived out of the blue with a brand new bike for him, a Stingray with a T-bar shift. It was redder than Ernie's face and seemed to please his uncle as much as him but Vic's parents were strangely subdued. As an eight-year-old he had wondered if it was too much, too big a gift. He suspected they were jealous or even ashamed of their own thrift. Now he suspected that the bike was hot. There'd never been any gifts since.

Ernie, Vic realized, was a live wire, an adventurer. That was his role in the family. Vic's father, on the other hand, was the one who tidied up after the excitement. You could see they'd been doing it all their lives.

Ernie and Cleo think they're irresistible, he overheard his mother say one Easter.

So, said his father, who gets to break the news to them?

Vic sat around with the others as long as he could stand it but when it grew hot even beneath the shade of the tarps he unstrapped his surfboard from the roof of the Jeep and struck off down the beach. He walked until their camp was just a solitary blot in the white distance.

The waves were only small but he wasn't much of a surfer yet so he didn't mind. After the hot walk the water was delicious. He paddled out excitedly and caught a few waves but either nosedived or tripped over himself. He even fell off trying to sit on the thing out beyond the break; it was like riding a greased pig. But you had to laugh at yourself. With mile after mile of deserted beach stretching out behind you there was nothing to be embarrassed about. He could have surfed in the nude if he wanted. Out in the calm he dived to the bottom and saw the ripples of the sandy seabed stretching out forever. The water travelled over his skin like a breeze. He felt free and happy.

When he surfaced he was startled to realize that someone was watching him. Up on the crest of the first dune somebody sat with their arms across their knees. He couldn't make out if it was a man or woman, boy or girl, and he hung in the water, holding his board, waiting for them to move off, but whoever it was stayed put. Vic grew a little nervous. He supposed he could lie here all day if need be; he could maybe paddle out if he felt really threatened but he didn't get the chance because a big set came through while he had his back to the sea. The first wave sent him bum over breakfast onto the sandbar and snatched the board from his grasp, and the four monsters that followed slammed him, tumbling, along the bottom, holding him down so long that when he finally surfaced, with his shorts halfway down his legs, he gave out a pathetic squeak more embarrassing than the fact of his bare arse. He dragged up his shorts and stumbled, coughing, along the shore to where his board lay washed up.

Over on the dune the stranger clapped. It was a girl and not one of his cousins. He wanted to snatch up the board and walk back to camp then and there but he was winded and weak at the knees, so he sat on the thing with his back to the girl and did his best to ignore her. Bitch. But he felt so stupid with his head sunk between his shoulders out in the middle of an empty beach like this. He was like a turtle trying to pull its head back into its shell. He hunched over, fuming. A stream of water gushed from his nose.

Well, you didn't see that one coming, said the girl, suddenly behind him.

Vic whirled around and a string of snot and saltwater landed on his arm. While he scrubbed at it with his knuckles, he saw the green polish on her toenails.

Sorry, she said. Didn't mean to sneak up on you.

Vic shrugged. The sun was right behind her head; he couldn't see her at all.

Nice in the water?

Yeah, he said. Nice.

I was wondering. If I could have a go on that thing.

She stepped over and put a toe on the board. She wore Levi's and a tee-shirt that said Phi Zappa Krappa. There was a picture of a naked man sitting on the toilet.

Okay, he said.

You sure?

He shrugged again.

Always wanted to try, she said. And Christ, I'm so bored. You know?

Vic smiled hesitantly and wiped his nose twice – once with each hand. He got up off the board. The girl reefed off her shirt and shucked down her jeans. She dropped her mirror shades onto the little pile they made on the sand. She wore a lime-green bikini with little plastic hoops at the hips like that Bond girl. Sunlight caught the fine down on her thighs. She had brown hair that swung across her back. She had real breasts. She was older, much older than him.

Any tips? she said, hoisting the board to her hip.

Um. Don't fall off?

She smiled kind of sideways at him and walked down to the water. He watched her go, alert to her calves and the way her bum moved. He wondered what it'd be like to have an older sister. How could you stand the sight of all that flesh without turning into some kind of sister-weirdo?

24

As a surfer the girl was no more a natural than he was. Her hopeless floundering came as sweet relief. When she came back she dropped the board at his feet and squeezed the water out of her hair. There was sand salted down the front of her legs. She was pretty. He didn't know where to look.

Thought you'd come out and help me, sport, she said, grabbing up her shirt and wiping her face on it.

Sorry, he mumbled, turning away from the sight of her dabbing at her chest with the damp shirt.

What's your name?

He told her.

From the city?

He shook his head. Not anymore, he said. We just moved down south. Angelus. It's pretty crap.

He looked at her green-painted fingernails as she flapped the shirt. Something wasn't right.

She sat on the sand and crossed her legs like a primary schooler or a hippy. She pulled on the mirror shades and then he saw it. There was a finger missing.

What? she said.

Sorry?

The finger?

No, he said.

Bullshit. Come on sport, own up. Here, look.

She held up her left hand. The third finger was little more than a stump.

Vic felt himself grimacing, tried to undo his face but she'd seen it.

Hay baler, she said.

Oh, he murmured, not knowing what a hay baler was. It sounded like a farm thing.

You on a farm?

Kind of. Boarding school, really.

Did it. Hurt?

Like a total bastard, she said. But, you know, all the big things hurt, the things you remember. If it doesn't hurt it's not important.

You really think?

She grabbed him by the ear, pinched his lobe so hard he saw spots, and the more he tried to squirm free the tighter she gripped him. It felt like his whole ear would be uprooted from his head. She was a psycho; he was stuck out here with a psycho and he had tears in his eyes now and she had her mouth on his, kissing him soft and slow until his mouth slackened, and all the time, even while her tongue slid across his teeth and he snorted like a frightened horse through his nose, she squeezed his ear without relenting until the long hot kiss was over.

She let go. He gasped.

See?

See *what*? he said, grabbing his ear.

You won't forget your first real kiss.

You're nuts!

Wrong choice of words, sport, she said, looking down at the stiffy in his shorts.

Vic hunched away from her.

Just trying to make a point, she said with a grin.

Fuck you, he said.

My mother's worried about my wedding day. Says it'll be awkward when my husband goes to put the ring on in front of all the dearly beloved.

Does it worry you? he asked, despite himself.

Nah. Weddings are bourgeois. Marriage is over. Who the hell wants to get married?

Your mum did.

She's a farmer's wife. She doesn't know any better.

Vic looked at her hands. He was appalled and fascinated by her.

I call it my abbreviation, she said, lying back on her jeans, holding out her damaged hand like a starlet admiring the ring Rock Hudson or somebody had just bought her.

Sorry?

The finger. My abbreviation. Drives the old man spare. He can't even look at it.

Vic couldn't take his eyes off it.

Guilty, I spose. I was six years old. Thinks he should have been more careful.

Maybe he should have.

Nah. Wasn't his fault. Wasn't even an accident. I just stuck my hand in because I was curious.

Curious?

To see how it all worked.

Far out, he murmured.

And the lesson is that it all works too quickly to see, she said with a laugh. But I remember everything about that day. What everyone was wearing, all the daggy things people said in the car on the way into town. The smell of stubble, upholstery. The taste of tomato in my throat from lunch.

What's your school like? he said.

A battery farm. A thousand girls trying to lay an egg.

How old are you? he asked, emboldened.

Sixteen. And bloody bored.

Can I see your finger? Close up, I mean?

I don't care, she said, holding out her hand from where she lay.

The whole time they'd been speaking it wasn't the girl's shaved legs he was watching, not even the wedge of cloth over the mound between them, but her hand raking the sand at her side. Her knuckles were frosted with tiny white grains; he hadn't been able to look away and now, as he shuffled over on his knees to get a closer look, he felt a flutter in his throat. She turned the hand one way and then the other for his benefit. He leaned down and blew sand from her finger and the quartzy grains settled on her belly.

She tilted her hand down the way posh ladies did on the movies when they wanted their hand kissed. Without thinking, he kissed it.

Kiss my aura, Dora.

What?

Frank Zappa. It's a quote.

Oh.

This sun's a bugger. I need some blockout. And I'm hungry.

She grabbed his face the way an auntie would, then let him go.

They walked back up the beach in no great hurry, talking a bit as they went. Her name was Melanie and her family had the big blitz truck and the circus tent. They were here for a few days' break before harvesting. There was a big low in the north and they were keeping an ear on the weather reports on radio. Neighbours and cousins were with them but she was the only one her age.

We're in the same boat, he said.

She laughed sceptically.

We're having a bonfire, he said. For New Year's.

Uh-huh.

He sensed that she'd grown bored with him now.

He caught sight of himself in Melanie's mirror shades. His lips were white with sand where he'd kissed her hand. He looked like a nine-year-old.

I'm hot, he said, flushing.

Okay.

I'm gunna swim a bit.

Right.

See ya, then.

Vic's skin all but sizzled when he hit the water. He lay there watching Melanie walk back into camp. The excitement of being with her had lapsed into a sudden sense of failure. The sea sucked at him. He tingled all over.

That afternoon Vic sat out in the dinghy catching flathead and whiting with the men. Uncle Ernie bitched about traffic fines and summonses and the tax man and Vic's old man let it go. One of Ernie's balls kept peeking out of his tiny shorts like a dangling gingernut and both Vic and his father struggled to keep a straight face. Now and then, in lulls in the bite, Vic rubbed the tender lobe of his ear.

When they came in at dusk the women and the wobbegong girls were in the water, splashing and screaming. Nanna had the baby on her hip, searching the water for unseen perils.

Later they lit the bonfire and while it got going they ate fish and potato salad and green beans. A big tangerine moon rose from the dunes and the breeze died out altogether. The girls rooted through the icebox for bottles of Passiona. Vic drank Cottee's cola with his mother and felt his skin tight with sunburn. Nanna had her icewater and the other adults had beer. Soon there were empty king browns all over the trestle.

When the fire was really crackling Vic walked down to the water in search of more driftwood. Up the beach a little way, out in front of the big old army truck and the striped circus tent, there was a fire burning twenty feet high. It was a real monster. He walked up into the dunes so he could come up behind Melanie's camp and look on without being seen.

He crouched in a bit of saltbush and gazed down on the fire and the pile of mallee roots beside the truck. There were people laughing down there, big men's voices and squeaking kids and the titter of women. He smelled meat grilling and onions frying.

Like a peasant feast, said a familiar voice beside him.

Vic nearly cried out in fright. Melanie was tucked into another clump of saltbush, a bottle glinting in her hand.

Scared you again.

No, he lied.

Bored, too, eh?

A bit.

Want some?

What is it?

New Year's Eve.

Very funny.

Feel like a swim?

No, said Vic. A walk maybe.

Okay, a walk.

As the moon dragged itself back into shape, they walked out into the rolling, white sandhills until they came to a valley whose wind-ribbed contours reminded Vic of the ocean floor; the fluted ripples went on forever.

Cheer me up, sport, said Melanie.

Vic told her about Ernie's dangling gingernut and the jugs on his Auntie Cleo. He told her about his cousins, their needle teeth and wobbegong skin.

Woebegone, said Melanie.

Wobbegong. It's a carpet shark.

I know this. Sport, I'm with you.

They sat down in a hollow to rest a moment. Melanie pulled the lid off her bottle and drank.

Happy New Year, she said, passing it to him.

Ginger, he murmured, sniffing.

Stone's Green Ginger Wine. Made from the little ginger balls of strange uncles.

Vic laughed. He took a sip but didn't like it. The stuff tasted like ginger beer mixed with diesel.

How's your ear? Melanie said, reaching over and giggling as he drew away warily.

Orright, he said.

Let me see, then.

Vic didn't trust her but he couldn't resist the idea of her touching him. She took his earlobe tenderly and rubbed it between two fingertips.

You'll remember that, I reckon.

Yes.

Mean old trick, she said, grabbing his chin like an auntie again.

How come you're sad? he said with her still holding his face.

It's nothing, sport.

You really seem sad.

New Year's Eve.

School's not for another month.

Not for me, sport.

Posh school, then.

No, she said. I'm not going back. A few months on the farm.

She put a finger over his mouth to stop him talking and she held him like that while she socked back another drink. He closed his lips over her finger.

Ah, she said. A kiss. But what about this one?

She held up the stub of her ring finger in the moonlight

31

before him and Vic took her wrist and drew it to him. He felt her whole hand across his face as he took the stump into his mouth. It blotted out the sky, it blacked the glare of moonlight and tasted of salt and ginger and sugar all at once. There was no texture of a fingerprint against his tongue, just a slick smoothness that made his blood bubble.

Come here, she said. What the hell. Auld Lang Syne.

She kissed him and her mouth was soft and hungry as she bent down to reach him and he heard the bottle gurgle out into the sand where their knees had knocked it while her tongue found his and he shaped his mouth to hers. He let his hands settle on her hips, felt his head cradled in her fingers and he swam up into her, happy and awake as he'd ever been. When she broke off and kissed the top of his head he was bereft. He pressed his brow to her throat and she dug her fingers in his hair and drew up her shirt so that her breasts shone in the moonlight. She guided him down and he kissed them. They were full against his face and when he drew the nipple into his mouth she murmured and gasped and finally, confoundingly, began to cry.

It was midnight when he got back to the bonfire. The others were singing and kissing and nobody asked him where he'd been. They were Langs singing 'Auld Lang Syne' and the cousins were asleep on their feet.

Vic woke in the night to the sound of puffing and moaning. Everyone was in bed now but a camp stretcher was grinding and squeaking. He felt his mother stir beside him. It was Auntie Cleo panting over there. Vic saw her legs up in the moonlight.

Oh, for God's sake, whispered his mother.

He listened until his lap was wet and the sheet clammy around him. Ernie gave one sharp grunt, like a man who'd suddenly remembered something, and in the quiet that followed, while the sea crawled against the shore and the moon spilled through holes in the tarp overhead, Vic thought of Melanie and the strangeness of her tears and the long, silent walk back to camp. He hadn't hurt her, he knew that much, but he sensed she was in some kind of pain, something important that was out of his reach, the way everything is when you're just a stupid kid and all the talk is over your head. He thought of the hollow between her breasts, pressed his face to the pillow and slept.

His father woke him at dawn. The boat was already afloat in the shallows. Ernie yanked at the outboard's starter rope.

They were out in deep water before Vic was properly awake. The water was clear; you could see sandy bottom in the green holes in the reef. Kelp rose yellow and brown from jagged lumps and fish sprayed in all directions.

When they came upon their first float, Vic's old man gaffed it aboard and hauled on the rope. The boat wallowed between swells and tipped precariously as the pot came over the side all clicking and slapping with tails and feelers and dropping legs.

Happy New Year, said the old man, dragging crays out and dropping them into the bucket.

Shit! said Ernie. Hang on!

The engine roared and the boat surged and the old man all but fell onto Vic who saw the wave looming beyond him. The bow rose. The old man's head was on the seat beside him, one hand gripping Vic's leg as they speared up, freefalling from the back of the wave. They slammed back onto the water and the old man laughed but Vic could already see the next wave coming.

Go! he screamed. Go!

Ernie throttled up and the old man crawled out of a nest of rope to sit up in the bow, head swivelling. This wave was much bigger. It was beginning to break already and in its path the water was dimpled and lumpy with the contours of the reef beneath them.

The old man pointed one way. Ernie steered in the opposite direction. And just as the wave broke on their beam a few yards out, he turned the boat shoreward and tried to outrun the thing.

Vic felt the wave bear down on them, a spitting, roaring draught behind his ears, before it snatched them up and left them, for two or three seconds at most, actually surfing down the face the way he'd never dreamt possible. The motor snarling. Sea and air thundering in his head.

And then it was quiet. Bubbles danced before his face and his hands were pearly and his hair swooning all in one direction. His head hit something sharp and hard before he realized he was beneath the boat. The water was crowded with rope and lines. Something bit his leg. He was bursting and the grey shell of the boat held him under till the water pressed at his lips.

Something collared him, dragged him down and sideways. Vic felt the water against his teeth. He screamed out the last of his air and then he was up.

He's snagged, said his father.

Except for the fading carpet of bubbles the sea was smooth again. The air was raw in his lungs. He began to cry. The old man dived and came up pulling line so Vic could move, but every time he kicked as he trod water something bit deep in his calf.

It's a hook, said the old man. Can you swim?

Vic nodded, still bawling.

It's okay, said the old man. Vic, son, we're orright.

He floated and sculled the best he could with the hook and heavy line dragging on his leg. Ernie climbed onto the over-turned hull, the cheeks of his arse bare to the morning sun. Together the men righted the boat and while Ernie bailed it the old man swam back with a knife to cut him free.

Then they caught the floating oars and climbed into the boat. Ernie was naked. His shorts were gone. The three of them had a jittery laugh and started bailing with their hands.

The motor was dead. It took a long time to row in against the breeze. Women and girls cried on the beach. Vic's cousins looked uglier than something dragged from a reeking craypot. Nanna fetched Ernie some shorts.

In the shade of the tarp the women held him down while Ernie and his father pushed the big hook through his leg until the barb broke free of the skin and then they cut it off with pliers and dragged it back out. The whole time they worked, through every blast of pain, he thought of Melanie. Her finger, her swinging breasts, a puddle of sand on her belly. He didn't give a bugger about the cousins; let them see him writhe and blubber. He was thinking of her. He was immune; nothing could touch him. And afterwards, in the long calm on the other side of the pain, when he felt spent and sleepy and silky-skinned, he let the women douse him with Mercurochrome and ply him with eggs and sugary tea, and pat his tears dry, and when they finally left off he took the barbless hook and limped up the beach to give it to her. Melanie would under-stand; she'd know what he meant by it.

But the blitz truck was gone and the tractor, too. A great mound of coals smouldered on the sand. Where the big tent had been there were bottles and cans and the smooth imprints of mattresses and bodies. The harvest, he thought. There must be rain on the way. He took the hook from his pocket. It looked blunt and misshapen. It shone in the sun. Vic's leg throbbed and burned. He looked out across the sea for the first sign of cloud, for any kind of signal of a change in the weather, but the sea and the sky were as pale and blue and blank as sleep, as empty as he felt standing there on the lapping shore.

Aquifer

VERY LATE ONE EVENING not long ago I stirred from a television stupor at the sound of a familiar street name and saw a police forensic team in waders carry bones from the edge of a lake. Four femurs and a skull, to be precise. The view widened and I saw a shabby clump of melaleucas and knew exactly where it was that this macabre discovery had taken place. I switched the TV off. My wife had long gone to bed. Through the open window I smelt wild lupins and estuary mud and for a time I forgot where I was. Life moves on, people say, but I doubt that. Moves in, more like it.

I went to bed. But I lay awake all night. I thought of the dullards I would face in the morning, the smell of their dirty hair, the stiffness of their hands on the instruments, the Mariah Carey tunes they'd bleat at me. In flickering bursts I thought about the war but I knew that I was only trying to think about it, because my mind was elsewhere, travelling in loops and ellipses away from middle age on the all-night sound of the moving tide.

Before dawn and without waking my wife or even leaving her a note, I rose, made myself coffee and began the five-hour drive back from Angelus to the suburbs where I grew up.

The battlers' blocks. In the early sixties, that's what they called the meagre grid of limestone streets of my childhood. Suburban lots scoured from bushland so that immigrants from Holland, England and the Balkans, and freckly types like us, barely a generation off the farm, could build cheap houses. Our street wound down a long gully that gave on to a swamp. A few fences away the grey haze of banksia scrub and tuart trees resumed with its hiss of cicadas and crow song. Houses were of three basic designs and randomly jumbled along the way to lend an air of natural progression rather than reveal the entire suburb's origins in the smoky, fly-buzzing office of some bored government architect. Our homes were new; no one had ever lived in them before. They were as fresh as we imagined the country itself to be.

As they moved in, people planted buffalo grass and roses and put in rubber trees which brought havoc to the septics a decade later. From high on the ridge the city could be seen forming itself into a spearhead. It was coming our way and it travelled inexorably in straight lines. The bush rolled and twisted like an unmade bed. It was, in the beginning, only a fence away.

The men of our street went to work and left the driveways empty. They came home from the city tired, often silent. They scattered blood and bone on their garden beds and retired to their sheds. All day the women of the street cleaned and cooked and moved sprinklers around the garden to keep things alive. Late in the morning the baker arrived in his van, red-cheeked from civilization, and after him the man with the vegie truck. At the sound of their bells kids spilled out into the dusty street and their mothers emerged in housecoats and pedal pushers with rollers in their hair. Everyone was working class, even the Aborigines around the corner whose name was Jones, though it seemed that these were Joneses who didn't need much keeping up with. We were new. It was all new.

At night when I was a baby my parents went walking to get me to sleep and while they were out they foraged for building materials in the streets beyond where raw sandy lots lay pegged out between brickies' sheds and piles of rough-sawn jarrah.

The old man built a retaining wall from bricks he loaded into the pram that first summer. A lot of sheds went up quickly in our street. All those jarrah planks, all that asbestos sheeting, those bags of Portland cement. It was all taxpayers' property anyway. Great evening strollers, the locals.

I grew up in a boxy double brick house with roses and a let-terbox, like anyone else. My parents were always struggling to get me inside something, into shirts and shoes, inside the fence, the neighbourhood, the house, out of the sun or the rain, out of the world itself it often seemed to me. I climbed the jacaranda and played with the kids across the street and came in ghosted with limestone dust. I sat on the fence and stared at the noisy blue bush and in time I was allowed to roam there.

When the road crew arrived and the lumpy limestone was tarred the street seemed subdued. The easterly wind was no longer chalky. In July and August when it finally rained the water ran down the hill towards the reedy recess of the swamp. A little way from our place, outside the Dutchies' house with its window full of ornaments, a broad puddle formed and drew small children to its ochre sheen. The swamp was where we wanted to be, down there where the melaleucas seemed to stumble and the ducks skated, but our parents forbade it; they talked of quicksand and tiger snakes, wild roots and sub-merged logs so we made do with the winter puddle outside the van Gelders'. I remember my mother standing exasperated in the rain with the brolly over her head at dusk while I frog-kicked around in my speedos.

Eventually the road crew returned to put a drain in and my puddle became less impressive. Then a red telephone box appeared beside it. I suppose I was five or six when I learned to go in and stand on tiptoe to reach up and dial 1194 to hear a man with a BBC voice announce the exact time. I did that for years, alone and in company, listening to the authority in the man's voice. He sounded like he knew what he was on about, that at the stroke it would indeed be the time he said it was. It was a delicious thing to know, that at any moment of the day, when adults weren't about, you could dial yourself some-thing worth knowing, something irrefutable, and not need to pay.

When I was old enough I walked to school with the ragged column of kids who made the mile-long journey up the hill. From the high ground of the schoolyard you could see the city and the real suburbs in the distance. You could even smell the sea. In the afternoons the blue bush plain was hazy with smoke and the dust churned up by bulldozers. At home on winter nights great bonfires of fallen trees flickered in the sky above the yard. Beyond the fence cicadas and birds whirred. Now and then the hard laughter of ducks washed up the street; they sounded like mechanical clowns in a sideshow. When summer came and the windows lay open all night the noise of frogs and crickets and mosquitoes pressed in as though the swamp had swelled in the dark.

The smallest of us talked about the swamp. Down at the turnaround where the lupins and wild oats took over, we climbed the peppermint to look out across that wild expanse, but for the longest time we didn't dare go further.

Bruno the Yugo went to the swamp. He had a flat head and he was twelve. He ranged down through the reeds until dark, even though his oldies flogged him for it. Across from Bruno lived the Mannerings. They were unhappy Poms whose house smelled of boiled cabbage. George the father had very long feet. He wore socks and plastic sandals. His son Alan waited for me after school some days to walk behind me and persecute me wordlessly the whole way home. He was twelve and scared of Bruno the Yugo. I never knew why he picked me from all the kids in our street. He never said a thing, just poked and prodded and shoved until we came down the hill to within sight of our homes. He was tall and fair, Alan Mannering, and though I dreaded him I don't think I ever hated him. When he spoke to someone else beyond me his voice was soft and full of menace, his accent broadly local as my own. Some days he threw his schoolbag up onto the verandah of his place and headed on down to the swamp without even stopping in and I watched him go in relief and envy. Mostly I played with the Box kids across the road. There were seven or eight of them. They were Catholics and most of them wet the bed though it was hard to say which ones because they all had the same ammonia and hot milk smell. I liked them, though they fought and cried a lot. We slipped through the bush together where there were no straight lines. Beyond the fence there were snarls and matted tangles. We hid behind grasstrees and twisted logs and gathered burrs in our shirts and seeds in our hair. Eventually the Boxes began to slip off to the swamp. I always pulled up short, though, and went back to dial 1194 for reassurance.

Another Pom moved in next door. I saw him digging and stood on the fence to watch, my shadow the only greeting. I watched him dig until only his balding head showed. He winked and pointed until I climbed down into his yard. I shuffled over to the lip of his hole and saw the wet earth beneath his sandals. A puddle began to form around his feet.

The water table, he said in a chirpy accent. It's high here, see. Half these fence posts are in it, you know.

The rank, dark stink of blood and bone hung in the air. I climbed back over the fence but kept watching him dig.

Looks dry this country, it does, but underground there's water. Caves of it. Drilling, that's what this country needs.

I went indoors.

Someone hung a snake from our jacaranda out front. It was a dugite, headless and oozing. My mother went spare.

Across the road one night, Mr Box left his kids asleep in the Holden and went indoors with his wife. It was for a moment's peace, my oldies said, but a moment was all they had. The station wagon rolled across the road, bulldozed the letterbox and mowed down our roses.

George Mannering with the long feet trimmed his buffalo grass every week with a push mower. He liked grass; it was the one thing he'd not had in England though he reminded us that English grass was better, finer. My mother rolled her eyes. George Mannering bought a Victa power mower and I stood out front to watch his first cut. I was there when two-year-old Charlie lurched up between his father's legs and lost some toes in a bright pink blur. All the way back inside to my room I heard his voice above the whine of the two-stroke which sputtered alone out there until the ambulance came.

I forget how old I was when I gave in and went to the swamp. It felt bad to be cheating on my parents but the wild beyond the fences and the lawns and sprinklers was too much for me. By this time I was beginning to have second thoughts about the 1194 man. My parents bought a kitchen clock which seemed to cheat with time. A minute was longer some days than others. An hour beyond the fence travelled differently across your skin compared with an hour of television. I felt time turn off. Time wasn't straight and neither was the man with the BBC voice. I discovered that you could say anything you liked to him, shocking things you'd only say to prove a point, and the man never said a thing except declare the plodding time. I surrendered to the swamp without warning. Every wrinkle, every hollow in the landscape led to the hissing maze down there. It was December, I remember. I got off my bike and stepped down into dried lupins like a man striding through a crowd. Seed pods rattled behind me. A black swan rose from the water. I went on until the ground hardened with moisture and then went spongy with saturation. Scaly paperbarks keeled away in trains of black shadow. Reeds bristled like venetian blinds in the breeze. Black water bled from the ground with a linoleum gleam.

From the water's edge you couldn't even see our street. The crowns of tuart trees were all I saw those early years before jacarandas, flame trees, and cape lilacs found their way to water and rose from yards like flags. I found eggs in the reeds, skinks in a fallen log, a bluetongue lizard jawing at me with its hard scales shining amidst the sighing wild oats. I sat in the hot shade of a melaleuca in a daze.

After that I went back alone or in the company of the Box kids or even Bruno. We dug hideouts and lit fires, came upon snakes real and imagined. I trekked to the swamp's farthest limits where the market gardens began. Italian men in ragged hats worked on sprinklers, lifted melons, turned the black earth. Water rose in rainbows across their land. I went home before dark, amazed that my parents still believed me when I swore solemnly that I hadn't been down the swamp.

At school I learned about the wide brown land, the dry country. Summer after summer we recited the imperatives of water conservation. Sprinklers were banned in daylight hours and our parents watered glumly by hand.

One summer my mother announced that she'd come upon some Cape Coloureds at the nearest market garden. I thought she meant poultry of some kind. I met them on my own one day and was confused by their accents. We threw a ball for a while, two girls and me. Their skin had a mildness about it. They didn't seem as angry as the Joneses. The Joneses were dark and loud. Even their laughter seemed angry. I never had much to do with any of them. I rode past their house careful not to provoke them. They gave my little brother a hiding once. I never knew why. His nose swelled like a turnip and he nursed this grievance for the rest of his life. It made his mind up about them, he said. I kept clear. I already had Alan Mannering to worry about.

The Joneses never went near the swamp. I heard they were frightened of the dark. Their dad worked in a mine. Bruno said vile things to them and bolted into the swamp for sanctuary. It was his favourite game the year Americans went to the moon.

One sunny winter day I sat in a hummock of soft weeds to stare at the tadpoles I had in my coffee jar. Billy Box said we all begin as tadpoles, that the Pope didn't want us to waste even one of them. I fell asleep pondering this assertion and when I woke Alan Mannering stood over me, his face without expression. I said nothing. He looked around for a moment before pulling his dick out of his shorts and pissing over me. He didn't wet me; he pissed around me in a huge circle. I saw sunlight in his pale stream and lay still lest I disturb his aim. When he was finished he reeled himself back into his shorts and walked off. I emptied my tadpoles back into the lake.

What did he want? What did he ever want from me?

I was ten when people started dumping cars down at the swamp. Wrecks would just appear, driven in the back way from behind the market gardens, stripped or burned, left near the water on soft ground where the dirt tracks gave out.

Alan Mannering was the first to hack the roof off a car and use it upturned as a canoe. That's what kids said, though Bruno claimed it was his own idea.

I was with half a dozen Box kids when I saw Alan and Bruno out on the lake a hundred yards apart sculling along with fence pickets. Those Box kids crowded against me, straining, big and small, to see. I can still remember the smell of them pressed in like that, their scent of warm milk and wet sheets. The two bigger boys drifted in silhouette out on the ruffled water. One of the Boxes went back for their old man's axe and we went to work on the scorched remains of an old FJ Holden with nasty green upholstery. One of them came upon a used condom. The entire Box posse was horrified. I had no idea what it was and figured that you needed to be a Catholic to understand. Before dark we had our roof on the water. We kept close to shore and quickly discovered that two passengers was all it could carry. Several Boxes went home wet. I doubt that anybody noticed. They were always wet.

Next day was Saturday. I got down to the swamp early in order to have the raft to myself a while and had only pulled it from its nest of reeds when Alan Mannering appeared beside me. He never said a word. I actually cannot remember that boy ever uttering a word meant for me. He lived over the road for ten years. He all but walked me home from school for five of those, poking me from behind, sometimes peppering my calves with gravel. I was in his house once, I remember the airless indoor smell. But he never spoke to me at any time.

Alan Mannering lifted the jarrah picket he'd ripped from someone's fence and pressed the point of it into my chest. I tried to bat it away but he managed to twist it into my shirt and catch the flesh beneath so that I yielded a few steps. He stepped toward me casually, his downy legs graceful.

You're shit, I said, surprising myself.

Alan Mannering smiled. I saw cavities in his teeth and a hot rush of gratitude burned my cheeks, my fingertips. Somehow the glimpse of his teeth made it bearable to see him drag our FJ Holden roof to the water and pole out into the shimmering distance without even a growl of triumph, let alone a word. I lifted my tee-shirt to inspect the little graze on my chest and when I looked up again he was in trouble.

When he went down, sliding sideways like a banking aircraft out there in the ruffled shimmer of the swamp's eye, I really didn't think that my smug feeling, my satisfied pity about his English teeth, had caused the capsize. He didn't come up. I never even hated him, though I'd never called anyone shit before. After the water settled back and shook itself smooth again like hung washing, there wasn't a movement. No sign.

I went home and said nothing.

Police dragged the swamp, found the car roof but no body. Across the road the Mannerings' lawn grew long and cries louder than any mower drifted over day and night.

That Christmas we drove the Falcon across the Nullarbor Plain to visit the Eastern States which is what we still call the remainder of Australia. The old man sealed the doors with masking tape and the four of us sat for days breathing white dust. The limestone road was marked only with blown tyres and blown roos. Near the South Australian border we stopped at the great blowhole that runs all the way to the distant sea. Its rising gorge made me queasy. I thought of things sucked in, of all that surging, sucking water beneath the crust of the wide brown land.

Back home, though they did not find his body, I knew that Alan Mannering was in the swamp. I thought of him silent, fair, awful, encased in the black cake-mix of sediment down there.

The next year, come winter, the night air was musky with smoke and sparks hung in the sky like eyes. Bulldozers towing great chains and steel balls mowed down tuart trees and banksias.

I learned to spell aquifer.

Three doors up, Wally Burniston came home drunk night after night. His wife Beryl locked him out and if he couldn't smash his way in he lay bawling on the verandah until he passed out. Some school mornings I passed his place and saw him lying there beside the delivered milk, his greasy rocker's haircut awry, his mouth open, shoes gone.

New streets appeared even while the bush burned. In the phone box, which stank of cigarettes, I listened to the man from 1194 and knew that he was making the time up as he went along.

I saw the rainbow mist of the market garden sprinklers and felt uneasy. I thought of Alan Mannering in that mist. He'd have been liquid long ago. I was eleven now, I knew this sort of thing.

As our neighbourhood became a suburb, and the bush was heaved back even further on itself, there was talk of using the swamp for landfill, making it a dump so that in time it could be reclaimed. But the market gardeners were furious. Their water came from the swamp, after all. Water was no longer cheap.

The van Gelders divorced. Wally Burniston was taken somewhere, I never found out where. One Sunday afternoon I found myself in the van Gelders' backyard scrounging for a companion when I came upon Mrs van Gelder at the back step. I coasted over to her on my Dragstar to ask where her son might be but the sight of her struck me dumb. She had kohl around her eyes and a haircut that made her look like Cleopatra as played by Elizabeth Taylor. Her dress was short and half her buttons were undone. I stared at the reservoir of shade between her breasts and she raised her chin at me, took a great drag on her cigarette with her eyes narrowed, and gave me a confounding smile. She blew smoke across my handle-bars. I popped an involuntary wheelstand in my hurry to get away. I hurtled back out into the street, didn't even see the car coming, but its slipstream tugged at my shirt as it swerved to miss me. Tyres bawled on the fresh-laid bitumen. When I wheeled around, someone threw open the car door and began to shout and cry. And then people came into the street. I ped-alled past them and coasted down our driveway to hide in the shed. Months later I woke from a dream in which Mrs van Gelder leant in towards me with her blouse undone and I peered into her cleavage as though into a well. Then I sat up in bed as wet as a Catholic.

From one summer to the next water restrictions grew more drastic and people in our neighbourhood began to sink bores to get water. The Englishman next door was the first and then everyone drilled and I thought of Alan Mannering raining silently down upon the lawns of our street. I thought of him in

lettuce and tomatoes, on our roses. Like blood and bone. I
considered him bearing mosquito larvae – even being *in*
mosquito larvae. I thought of him in frogs' blood, and of tadpoles toiling through the muddy depths of Alan Mannering.
On autumn evenings I sat outside for barbecues and felt the
unsettling chill of dew. At night I woke in a sweat and turned
on the bedside light to examine the moisture on my palm
where I wiped my brow. My neighbour had gotten into everything; he was artesian.

At the age of twelve I contemplated the others who might
have drowned in our swamp. Explorers, maybe. Car thieves
who drove too close to the edge. Even, startlingly, people like
the Joneses before they became working class like us. The
more I let myself think about it the less new everything seemed.
The houses weren't old but the remnants of the bush, the
swamp itself, that was another thing altogether. Sometimes the
land beyond the straight lines seemed not merely shabby but
grizzled. I imagined a hundred years, then a thousand and a
million. I surveyed the zeroes of a million. Birds, fish, animals,
plants were drowned in our swamp. On every zero I drew a
squiggly tadpole tail and shuddered. All those creatures living
and dying, born to be reclaimed, all sinking back into the earth
to rise again and again: evaporated, precipitated, percolated.
Every time a mosquito bit I thought involuntarily of some
queasy transaction with fair, silent, awful Alan Mannering. If
I'm honest about it, I think I still do even now.

I knew even at ten that I hadn't willed him to die, good teeth
or bad. I pulled down my tee-shirt and saw him slip sideways
and go without a sound, without a word. I faced the idea that
he did it deliberately to spite me but he looked neither casual
nor determined as he slipped into the dark. It was unexpected.

The brown land, I figured, wasn't just wide but deep too. All that dust on the surface, the powder of ash and bones, bark and skin. Out west here, when the easterly blows, the air sometimes turns pink with the flying dirt of the deserts, pink and corporeal. And beneath the crust, rising and falling with the tide, the soup, the juice of things filters down strong and pure and mobile as time itself finding its own level. I chewed on these things in classroom daydreams until the idea was no longer terrifying all of the time. In fact at moments it was strangely comforting. All the dead alive in the land, all the lost who bank up, mounting in layers of silt and humus, all the creatures and plants making thermoclines in seas and rivers and estuaries. I wasn't responsible for *their* coming and going either but I felt them in the lake and on the breeze. I have, boy and man, felt the dead in my very water. Maybe that's why my wife finds me so often staring across the Cockleshell mudflats at the end of a grim day's teaching.

Not long after my thirteenth birthday we left the neighbourhood. We sold the house to a man who soon married and then divorced Mrs van Gelder. News of the street trickled back to me over the years. I met people in malls, airports, waiting rooms. The man next door murdered his wife. Up the road, near the ridge, a man invented the orbital engine and the Americans tried to ruin him. Bruno went back to Serbia to burn Albanians out of their homes; someone saw him on television. One of the Box kids became a celebrity priest. Girls got pregnant. Families began to buy second cars and electrical appliances that stood like trophies on Formica shelves. The suburb straightened the bush out.

Years went by. So they say. For the past five the state has endured a historic drought. The metropolitan dams look like rockpools at ebb tide and it has long been forbidden to wash a car with a running hose. Unless they have sunk bores people's gardens have crisped and died. With all that pumping the water table has sunk and artesian water has begun to stink and leave gory stains on fences and walls. And our old swamp is all but dry. I saw it on the news because of the bones that have been revealed in the newly exposed mud. All around the swamp the ground is hardening in folds and wrinkles. The mud is veinous and cracks open to the sun. I saw it for myself when I pulled up, stunned from the long drive.

From the moment I arrived in my airconditioned Korean car I began to feel sheepish. Police were pulling down their tape barriers and a few news trucks wheeled away. The action was over. I sat behind the little steering wheel feeling the grit of fatigue in my eyes. I didn't even get out. What had I been expecting to see, more bones, *the* bones perhaps, have them handed over for my close inspection? Would that suddenly make me sanguine about Alan Mannering?

The swamp has a cycleway around it now and even a bird hide. Around the perimeter, where the wild oats are slashed flat, signs bristle with civic exhortations. Behind the pine log barriers the straight lines give way to the scruffiness of natural Australia. The sun drove in through the windscreen and the dash began to cook and give off a chemical smell. Down at the swamp's receding edge the scrofulous melaleucas looked fat and solid as though they'd see off another five years of drought. I pulled away and drove up our old street running a few laps of the neighbourhood in low gear. I took in the gardens whose European ornamentals were blanching. Only a few people were about, women and children I didn't recognize. They stood before bloody mineral stains on parapet walls with a kind of stunned look that I wondered about. A man with rounded shoulders stood in front of my old house. The jacaranda was gone. Somebody had paved where it stood to make room for a hulking great fibreglass boat. No one looked my way more than a moment and part of me, some reptilian piece of me, was disappointed that no one looked up, saw right through the tinted glass and recognized me as the kid who was with Alan Mannering the day he drowned down there on the swamp. It's as though I craved discovery, even accusation. There he is! He was there! No one said it when it happened and nobody mentioned it since. People were always oddly incurious about him. He was gone; time, as they say, moves on. They all went on without him while he rose and fell, came and went regardless. And they had no idea.

It's kind of plush-looking, the old neighbourhood, despite the drought: houses remodelled, exotic trees grown against second-storey extensions. Middle class, I suppose, which is a shock until you remember that everyone's middle class in this country now. Except for the unemployed and the dead. The city has swept past our old outpost. The bush has peeled back like the sea before Moses. Progress has made straight the way until terracotta roofs shimmer as far as the eye can see.

As I left I noticed furniture on the sandy roadside verge around the corner. Some black kids hauled things across the yard in Woolworths bags under the frank and hostile gaze of neighbours either side. An Aboriginal woman raised her fist at a man with a mobile phone and clipboard. I pulled over a moment, transfixed. Another man with a mobile phone and aviator glasses came over and asked me to move on. They were expecting a truck, he said; I complied, obedient as ever, but as I gathered speed and found the freeway entry I thought of the Joneses being evicted like that. I was right to doubt the 1194 man on the telephone. Time doesn't click on and on at the stroke. It comes and goes in waves and folds like water; it flutters and sifts like dust, rises, billows, falls back on itself.

When a wave breaks, the water is not moving. The swell has travelled great distances but only the energy is moving, not the water. Perhaps time moves through us and not us through it. Seeing the Joneses out on the street, the only people I recognized from the old days, just confirmed what I've thought since Alan Mannering circled me as his own, pointed me out with his jagged paling and left, that the past is in us, and not behind us. Things are never over.

Damaged Goods

MY HUSBAND HAD THIS THING about a girl with a birthmark. It began when he was almost fourteen and went on all through high school like a fever that wouldn't break. It's a story he used to tell against himself in a kind of wistful tone, and to be honest it was one of the things about him that charmed me, that and his earnest demeanour. He told the story so many times that I feel like I was there, that I lived it with him. He didn't just rattle these memories off – he's never been that kind of bore – I had to wheedle them out of him.

Vic refuses to visit the town he grew up in but lately I find myself driving down alone for two or three days at a time. I took a friend once but she was restless inside twenty-four hours. She said I'm like some biographer sniffing around in vain for one final, telling detail that will complete the psychological puzzle at the centre of Vic's life, but the truth is that I go out of loneliness and, pathetic as it is, I sometimes feel closer to him there knowing that it was the place that formed him. Anyway, it's a nice little harbour town and this winter I've acquired an unexpected passion for whale watching. Now I know the difference between a southern right whale and a humpback. Believe me, I've had plenty of weekends to fill.

I suppose the sources of obsession are at once mundane and mysterious. If it wasn't for my sister's own fixation I'd be less forgiving about Vic and the weight of his past. I wouldn't understand at all. I'd be long gone.

When she was six my sister won a doll in a school raffle. It was almost as big as her, the most ravishing thing we girls had ever seen, but it was a cause of great conflict and shame in our house because, like lotteries and cards and horseracing, raffles were a form of gambling and therefore the work of the Devil. Our father was furious. My sister couldn't even remember buying the ticket – she was a devout girl and no rebel – but when she came home with the prize she begged to be allowed to keep it. She already loved it like a woman smitten by her newborn. Even our mother saw this and pleaded her case, but when our father could convince neither my sister nor my mother to take the doll back to school, it was boxed up and consigned to the top of the linen press where it lay, like a child in a cardboard and cellophane coffin, for fifteen years. In rare moments when the coast was clear my sister snuck to the linen press and climbed the shelves to peer in at the bright, cherubic cheeks and the lace gown and the dimples. It became her lost child. It was the only thing she took with her when she grew up and left home and for the rest of her life it has stood between her and other people, a kind of solace, really, but also a barrier to human intimacy. She has a senior position in the tax office. She's a highly rational and competent person. Except when it comes to that doll which lies in state in her livingroom like an embalmed child bride.

I always assumed Vic's infatuation with Strawberry Alison was all in the past, just a mortifying memory, but only last week I found him in the workshop, weeping over an old photograph and a poem and it gave me a chill.

The first time he saw that girl Alison he was horrified. Her birthmark was lurid crimson; it covered half her face and neck, like a mask incompletely removed. Against that splash of colour her thick long hair was blonder, and her eyes bluer than seemed possible. She was newly arrived in town. At first glance her face looked burnt, as though she'd suffered a terrible scorching. Vic's imagination already brimmed with these flarings, for in those days the news was all napalm flashes and looming thermonuclear disaster. Standing speechless on the school verandah, with his bag sliding from his shoulder, Vic's horror turned to fascination as he saw that the passing girl's skin was not bubbled with scar-tissue but perfectly smooth. Her mark was all colour. It was obviously congenital yet he still thought of conflagration, as though she'd survived a fire whose heat had never left her face.

Vic says he loved Alison from that first encounter. Not only could he pick her out in a crowd but he sought glimpses of her all over town. The trouble was, she was a year older and therefore perpetually out of bounds. Any dealings between year-levels were socially forbidden, and to make things worse Alison soon became surrounded by tougher, plainer girls who worked out their repulsion and fascination by forming a protective posse around her. There was just no way past them. It wasn't as if there weren't spunky girls his own age but they became dim presences. All the pert, hair-flicking embodiments of perfection who had only days before caused him to sweat with lust and dread simply dropped from his mind.

When she first arrived, people talked about Strawberry Alison as a shop-soiled beauty. Such a pity, they said about her birthmark. If only. Could have been a stunner. What a shame she's damaged goods.

To Vic it was no shame at all. He wanted her, mark or no mark. He told himself he saw past it, that he was the only one who did. Though in time he came to admit to himself that he loved Alison because of the mark, not just despite it. This, when it came down to it, was the root of his obsession and he's never completely explained it to me. I doubt he understands it himself, least of all now. In any dispute Vic will instinctively seek out a victim to defend. That's his nature and it's become his work as a labour lawyer, but I wonder if this impulse can account for his adolescent attraction to the flawed and imperfect. You see, Strawberry Alison was not the only damaged specimen to catch his imagination. Vic's first love was also older – in fact, quite a lot older – a farm girl whose ring finger ended at the first joint, the result of an accident with a hay baler. The finger that her wedding ring would have to slide on to ended in a stump. At thirteen he was enchanted. By the finger as much as the girl herself. His first kiss. She let him touch her breasts. It only happened the once – the whole thing lasted less than a day, a holiday encounter – but the strange excitement lingered. The Alison business wasn't so shortlived; it went on for years. I fear it isn't over yet.

Perhaps you could put Vic's fascination down to the times, Vietnam in shrieking flames on TV every night. That naked burning girl running down the road over and over again. Or maybe it's just the ruin and wreckage you're privy to as a copper's kid in a country town, the horrible weight of knowledge, all those distorting secrets the rest of us are spared. I used to think he exaggerated this stuff but his mother Carol put me straight. That town, Angelus, wasn't such a quaint place in those days. It crushed her husband. Something happened there which caused him to lose his way. He began to drink. Bob Lang, the proverbial straightshooter, became a local joke. And then their infant daughter died of meningitis. Vic was fifteen. He never mentioned a sister, never once said a word. I couldn't believe it – I was incensed – and when I confronted him about it he told me that he'd forgotten. A sick look came over his face. I pressed him for details but he picked up his keys and backed towards the door. I let him go. Angry as I was, I believed him. He'd blocked her from his mind. He looked as appalled as I was.

For years Vic never even spoke to Strawberry Alison. Until he was sixteen the closest he ever got to her was the library window. One afternoon, while stuck in a carrel, he glanced up to see Alison peering in. She wasn't looking in at all; she'd just caught sight of herself in the reflective glass and paused a moment in passing. She came closer, right up to the sill, and he was struck by the sadness of her gaze. She was full of longing, anybody could see that, and she was barely an arm's length away. Vic wanted to touch her face, to tell her that she needn't pine for a perfection he didn't want anyway. Her breath fogged the glass. She stepped back, pulled her hair behind her ear and walked on.

Carol told me that Vic was an anxious boy. She was reluctant to blame his father but Bob saw menace at every turn. The cop thing. What Bob didn't realize was that in addition to keeping him safe, his attempts to protect Vic from accident and injury transmitted fear. Unspoken worries hung over him like the omnipresent stink of the harbour. As a child of rigid fundamentalists I can identify with this, for although God Himself was supposed to have made it and sustained it, and though it seemed so beautiful, the world around us was eternally dangerous. The price of spiritual freedom, we learnt, was eternal vigilance. Such a high price for so long.

Less than a year after the child died, Bob Lang did a runner, quit the Force and disappeared. Vic has a compensatory element to his character. When he talks about his pro bono clients you can see the earnest teenager in him. You can picture him battling on with his mother, feeling responsible for her as the only man, the only child in her life. And then I think of Strawberry Alison and his boyhood conviction that he alone understood her trouble, that only he saw the true face behind the mask. So endearing until you think of it turned your way. It's no fun wondering if your husband's love could be another act of kindness, whether there's something about you he feels you need to be compensated for, as if you too qualify as his sort of damaged goods. Trust me, these weekends aren't all whales and bracing sea-mist. Some days I stay in and get plastered. Several times now the motel manager has come to the door to ask me to keep the racket down.

During his school years Vic maintained a kind of adoring surveillance of Alison, though he made sure he only followed her brazenly once a week. More than this, he knew, would be creepy. He hated the way other girls finished her sentences for her, how they patronized her by pretending to be envious of her long, smooth legs and ran their fingers through her glossy hair until he wanted to shove them into the lockers and shout in their faces. Yet he had to concede that some of their envy might be genuine because Alison did have fantastic legs and her hair was lustrous to the point of causing physical pain. Although he loved her face above all else, Vic grew more and more aware of her body. He was just a stick, a boy, and day by day as she grew more womanly, she became less attainable. Yet something in him refused to let go. During the day he dreamt of piling her into a car and tearing out of town. They'd go north. He'd rescue her, love her, marry her. White dress. Definitely no veil. He worked himself up into a romantic fantasy. But at night he got himself into far simpler turmoil thinking of her long legs around him and her breasts in his hands.

He found that the only legitimate way to watch Alison was on the netball court, where he could be part of a crowd, even if it struck some people as unusual. Here nobody patronized her. When she played centre she drew no pity; she was a fearsome thing, a cutthroat player with a temperament to match her face. In the exertion of the game both her cheeks and all of her neck grew red. Vic stood back a little or even watched through the chain-link fence as Alison cut them up. Whenever he stood near the half-time huddle he swore he felt the heat off her.

As a boy Vic was not the confiding sort. Nothing's changed in that regard. He never told his mates about his thing for Alison but his obsession must have been hard to conceal. The others were onto him. They thought it was funny. Who cares about the mantelpiece, they said, when you're busy stoking the fire? He didn't bother to explain himself. He just watched Alison and kept his ear to the ground. It was a small enough town for news to travel quickly and Vic knew who took her to the drive-ins and who claimed to have gone all the way, but he dismissed most of it as wishful thinking. Not every girl at the drives was like the legendary Slack Jackie. The stories about Alison didn't bear scrutiny.

You could say that Vic grew up in Alison's shadow. He had

a few girlfriends in high school but he was inattentive. The girls assumed his distraction was the usual male malaise but in his case it wasn't his mates who were constantly hovering at the edge of his mind.

In her final year of school as the netball captain, as a girl thought by most to have overcome a cruel twist of fate, Alison published a short but puzzling poem in the school magazine. As far as anybody could tell the poem was about two girls in flames. Vic overheard some teachers discussing the image in the library. What a shame it was, they said, that the girl hadn't conquered her defect after all. Despite everything we've done for her. It's indulgent. You just can't let yourself be defined by these things.

Indulgent or not, Vic liked the poem. The teachers' talk outraged him. He found himself suddenly emboldened. With a copy of the school magazine under his arm Vic marched down to the changerooms to confront Alison as she emerged for training. She looked startled. Right off the mark he declared that he loved her poem and then, to his own horror, he went on to testify to his love for her. She burst into tears and retreated to the changeroom. Vic stood there a moment before he thought of the posse of girls inside. He fled.

And then Alison graduated, got on the Westrail bus and headed for the city.

I'm ten years younger than Vic. I was brought up in the suburbs. So much of his youth seems to have taken place in an altogether different country – the teenage pregnancies, the roll-call of who died or went to jail before they reached majority – and the soundtrack of his youth is different from mine, but we do share a sense of having lived under siege. We each knew about the transmission of fear, and the fatigue associated with living in a circumscribed world. For me it was the church and for him the town, and for both of us the weird culture of family. When Vic and I met we were emerging from lives of vigilance and I think we liberated each other. Which is why I don't give up on him. We're part of each other's survival. But it's gone awry since his parents died. He's frozen over, shut down. And there's this unsettling reversion to thinking about Strawberry Alison, as though he's not just mourning his parents and his newly-remembered sister, but his whole boyhood, the gauche lad that he was. I'm always trying to convince him to come with me to the old place and face down a few ghosts. I keep thinking we should buy a panel van and cruise the beaches for a month. But he's not having any of it and I'm sick of waiting. I don't feel it but, for God sake, I'm still young. Some Fridays I'm tempted to quit him altogether. These past few weekends I've come close.

His mother died of cancer. His father was there for it. Out of the blue, after twenty-something years. Two days of family and then the old man went back out bush and fell down a disused mineshaft. I only met him the once at poor Carol's bedside. He was so thin and proud. And sober. Like a man from another era. His dying wife was incandescent. Rage, love, forgiveness. The feeling between them was so strong I could barely stay in the room.

In his last year of school Vic did what all country boys did. He rode around in cars and saved for one of his own. He went to parties and got smashed on Brandovino and Blackberry Nip. Out at salmon camps along the coast he smoked dope and lost his virginity. He felt what it was like to get a Holden airborne at a hundred miles an hour. He studied hard and thought about being a lawyer. He looked after his mother. He heard the rumours about Strawberry Alison at university and he tried to keep an open mind.

Word came back to town that Alison was a born-again

lesbian. It was something she picked up at uni, like vegetarianism. Vic found it hard to believe. For him she was still the epitome of regular sex, real sex, *normal* sex. Those long legs, her downy arms and white teeth, the swing of blonde hair and the crimson veil across her face. And yet, re-reading that old poem, he began to wonder. Two girls in flames. What longing had he really seen in Alison's eyes?

At year's end, with the final exams behind him, Vic drove out with his classmates to Massacre Point where somebody had a bonfire going and a keg open. He'd barely been there five minutes when a little green Renault pulled up and two girls got out. One of them had black curls thick and long as a cape and the other, the one with the crewcut, might have gone unrecognized if it hadn't been for the birthmark vivid in the firelight as she strode up. There was a moment of suspension. Music but no talk. Kids looked across the fire at each other as if gauging the mood, and then they all surged forward to greet Strawberry Alison. Except for Vic who was left with her girlfriend, the Italian beauty. For half an hour he drank beer and asked polite questions about university when all he wanted to know was what it was like to make love to Alison. What did it feel like to have her cheek against yours on the pillow? The dark-haired girl was witty and gorgeous. She made Alison finally impossible. But to his surprise he felt no envy.

When Alison joined them he jerked like a startled horse.

I still love your poem, he heard himself say.

And I still love you for loving it, said Strawberry Alison.

There was, for Vic, nothing else to say. He went home early and missed the best and worst of the party. When he woke, his mother told him that two girls had hit a tree out on the coastal highway. The car exploded on impact and incinerated them both.

Around noon Vic drove back out toward Massacre Point

and found the big gouged marri tree on the bend and he walked out with the others across the blackened paddock and thought of the crimson splash of flame Alison had sent forth and wondered if she had foreseen her own death.

I've been out there myself more than once. The tree is still scarred. The white crosses are gone. This winter the paddock is swimming with green hay. I've seen photos of the girl and read her poem and both seem unremarkable except for the fact that they entranced the boy who became my husband. I sit in a motel like a woman waiting for a man to show up. I go out to the cliffs with binoculars to see whales find their way in from the southern mist and I walk here in this paddock, stubbornly, wondering at the heat each of us leaves in our wake.

Small Mercies

PETER DYSON CAME HOME ONE DAY to find his wife dead in the garage. He'd only been gone an hour, kicking a ball in the park with their four-year-old son. The Ford's motor was still running, its doors locked, and even before he knew it for certain, before he put the sledge-hammer through the window, before the ambulance crew confirmed it, he was grateful to her for sparing the boy.

He held himself together until the funeral and then for a few weeks he lost his mind. His mates avoided him, but their wives rallied to save him. He drank alone until he blacked out. When he bothered to eat he forked up food straight from the casserole dishes his friends' wives left him when they dropped Ricky back in the evenings. One morning he woke beside one of those wives and she was weeping.

Thereafter Dyson endeavoured, for the sake of his son, to lead a decent, stable, predictable existence, something as close to normal as a ruined man could manage. Though he hated the house now and the city around it, he was determined to stay on in Fremantle for Ricky's sake, so that his year of kindergarten might proceed uninterrupted.

And somehow the better part of a year fell by. Ricky smiled, unbidden, and seemed to forget his mother for weeks at a time. It was a mercy. Dyson worked a couple of days a week. He did not see friends, he wasn't sure he had any left. His life was not joyless yet its pleasures were close to theoretical. He appreciated more than he felt. Still, he believed that he was making progress. He was not reconciled but he was recovering.

What undid him was not the approaching anniversary of his wife's death but the onset of winter. He was, quite suddenly, overtaken by disgust.

All it took was a change in the wind. He hated winter. The first major cold front of the season was heralded by the usual blustering nor'wester, a wind that always seemed used up and clammy, too eerily warm for what lay behind it, but this gusting breeze was especially dirty because Dyson woke early to the terrible stink of sheep. Being a country boy, he wasn't particularly sensitive to the smell of livestock. But this was the concentrated urinal stench of thousands of merinos being stacked in a floating high-rise. Down on the docks they were loading live cargo for the Saudis. Rising to pull down the window sash he found that the odour was in the curtains already. Outside on the line, the damp washing was tainted. The whole town was overtaken.

At breakfast Ricky wanted to know where the stink came

from. There was no point in keeping the sordid details from him. They'd have to pass the ships on the way to kindy anyway and he'd see for himself how they jammed them in tier upon tier. He told the boy about the weeks the animals spent at sea and the awful heat and the mortality rates and how the knives awaiting them at the other end must come as cruel relief after such an ordeal. Ricky grew silent. Dyson regretted his frankness. Neither of them could finish breakfast for the smell of death in the house. Dyson helped the boy dress and afterwards, trying to shave, he began to shake. He suddenly knew there was no way he was going down into that garage this morning. Even if he could make himself roll up the door and start the car, the smell of monoxide would set him off. You couldn't trust yourself to drive in that sort of state, not with a child in the car. The whole business was suddenly at the back of his throat; he was brimming.

Ricky enjoyed the taxi ride. Dyson smiled for him despite the sick smell of the driver's sweat and the oppressive babble of FM radio blasting into him from behind. When the boy was safely delivered, Dyson got out at the public pool whose sun-shades and pennants snapped and lurched in the mounting gale.

The pool was a grim morning ritual. The point was supposed to be to lose weight and regain some fitness but the real benefit lay in the monotony of swimming laps. For half an hour every morning, while he hauled himself through the water, he went mercifully blank. He preferred this time of day because the initial rush was over, the wiry execs and hairy machos were gone and the average lap speed was less frenetic. Mothers, retirees and a few shy students swam without hounding each other up the lanes.

But this morning the changerooms seemed unaccountably damp. Their pungent cocktail of bleach and mildew made his head spin. Even the pool water felt wrong; it was soupy and the chlorine made him gag. On his first lap every breath tasted of sheep piss. It was a relief to feel the distracting chill of wind-driven rain on his back.

He always liked the way the pool rendered the plainest body handsome. It cheered him to see the fat become stately and the aged graceful. Today, in an effort to break this dangerous mood, he concentrated on the feet kicking ahead of him and the pearly bubbles that trailed in their wake. Lap after lap he found himself behind a woman whose toenails were lacquered a kind of burgundy. It was the colour that initially caught his attention. There was something luscious about it. He became mesmerized by the symmetry of the woman's toes and then by the delicate veins that stood out in the high arches of her feet which, against the chemical blue of the pool, were as white and comely as those of any classical statue.

He crawled along, bewitched in the woman's wake. She was a good swimmer. Her legs were strong. As she churned through the water ahead of him he watched the movement of her calves, her working thighs and the mound of her buttocks. She was beautiful. He loved her belly in the nylon sheath of her Speedo suit and the way her breasts moulded to her. The water he swam in became turbulent. Without realizing it, he'd sped up until the woman's feet were almost striking him in the face and when he backed off he lost rhythm. Dyson tried to shift his attention from the swimmer ahead by taking an interest in people passing in other lanes, but it was no better. They were, all of them, lithe and delicious. He had a perilous urge to reach out and touch smooth limbs, to lay his cheek, his ear, his lips against every firm belly. Each new swimmer, male and female, was more beautiful than the one before and he swam without really breathing for fear of interrupting this view of perfection until his stroke became ragged and the air he was forced to gulp tasted foul. Blots and sparks rose behind his eyes and he blundered, gagging, against the lane rope to hang there like a piece of snagged trash.

When he had recovered somewhat, the sky was dirty-dark above him. As they climbed from the pool his fellow swimmers regained their varicose veins and moles and hanging guts. The sudden ugliness of everything was crushing. He felt a poisonous surge of revulsion towards everything around him but nothing disgusted him more than himself.

During his final punitive sprint to the wall, the water around him was all Band-Aids, floating scabs and hanks of hair. He was roiling through sweat and spit and other people's piss and when he hoisted himself out, the air was just as brothy.

On all fours, dripping and panting until he began to sob and cause people to step around him in consternation, he knew that things were wrong, that he had to make a change. Everything here was tainted now. Continuing to pretend otherwise was simply and finally beyond him.

In the spring Dyson packed up and moved south. He took possession of his mother's house on the hill above the harbour in Angelus. He knocked out a wall and painted the rest in colours that would have made his mother blanch. The roof was fair, the foundations good and being home gave him a sense of satisfaction that might once have alarmed him. He was not blind to the irony of starting over in a house and a community he'd long ago left behind, but it was a ready and practical option and it was the least disruptive for Ricky who seemed to love the place. Right at the outset Dyson sensed how much less force of will it took for him to be himself in front of his son and this new ease seemed to relax the boy. He'd never seen so clearly how this worked, how the boy took his emotional cues from him. He couldn't imagine what he'd done to the kid already without realizing it. He had to think of the future and to seem happy with their new start.

Although Ricky was enrolled at a kindergarten an easy walk from the house, Dyson kept him home for the first week of term so they could explore the old town together and he could give the kid his bearings. They walked the white beaches and hiked over the granite bluffs that dominated the harbour. From a windswept lookout, staring south across the whitecapped open ocean, they tried to picture the ice, the penguins, the very bottom of the world. Back at home Ricky passed nails while Dyson built him a cubbyhouse between the peppermints in the backyard. In the evenings, for as long as they could stand the cold, clean wind, they watched the lights of ships track through the narrow entrance to the encircling harbour. Rain chattered on the roof at night as father and son lay spooned together in bed.

For a day or so Ricky was fascinated by the idea that this was once his grandmother's house. He was so young when she died that he didn't really remember her but he insisted on seeing photographs, especially those few with him and his grandmother together. Dyson dreaded the photo albums but let the boy thumb through them, enthralled. Within the hour, Ricky had moved on to some fresh enthusiasm. He was small for his age, a serious dark-eyed child, curious and rarely fearful. Dyson himself had been, he gathered, much like him. He treasured the boy for selfish reasons. Ricky was the only thing that offered his life any meaning. He couldn't bear to think what damage the past year had done him.

In the days after poring over the photos, Ricky seemed more tender and solicitous. It was as though he finally understood that they were both motherless. Their Lego projects were quiet affairs. They sat at the table in the weak afternoon light with only the companionable scratch of pencils passing between them.

Dyson began to think about getting a job. For years he taught woodwork and outdoor ed, but after Ricky was born and the depression took hold of Sophie, he spent so much time on leave that he had to resign. So many emergencies, hospitalizations, sleepless nights. When things were stable he operated as a mobile handyman. The flexible hours allowed him to be around to pick up the debris when things unravelled at home. But it was fifteen months since he'd worked at all and he'd come south without any solid idea of what he might do for a job down here. It wasn't a matter of urgent concern. He owned this house and the place up in the city was let, so he didn't need much money. A job was more about adding some shape to his new life, meeting people he could start from scratch with, free from pity or recrimination. It would all have to be new. There was no point in seeking out people he'd gone to school with a decade ago. It was a small town but hopefully not so small that you couldn't choose your company.

The day he got Ricky settled into kindy, he took a walk down the main street with a view to wandering along the wharves to think about his prospects. He was barely halfway to the docks when a woman called his name.

Peter Dyson! cried a tall grey-haired woman in her sixties. It *is* you!

She stood in the doorway of a newsagency with a girl of seven or so whose lank blonde hair fretted in the wind.

Mrs Keenan?

Marjorie, she said with mock sternness. You're not a boy anymore.

How are you? he asked.

Gobsmacked. Don't just stand there, boy. Come and give me a hug. I don't believe it!

Dyson stepped up and embraced her for a moment. He'd almost forgotten what another adult body felt like. For a moment he found it difficult to speak.

Look at you, she said. Just look at you.

He managed to laugh. Marjorie Keenan was still sprightly but her face was lined. She seemed older than she was.

And what brings you back to town? she asked, composing herself and pulling the child gently into her hip.

Oh, life I spose. I've moved into Mum's place.

I don't believe it! she declared with delight.

Well, neither did I. But there we are.

Come for dinner. Don'd love to see you.

Maybe I will some time.

Bring your family.

That'd be nice.

You know that I'll keep you to it, she said with a smile.

I don't doubt it for a minute.

Dyson looked at the little girl who chewed her lip.

This is our Sky, said Marjorie Keenan.

Hello, said Dyson.

I'll chase you up, said the old woman.

Dyson laughed and stepped back into the street. He headed down to the town jetty with a creeping sense of disquiet. It was the child, Sky. Of course it was possible that she was a neighbour's daughter or one of the many strays of the sort he used to meet at the Keenans' himself when he was a schoolboy.

They were warm, kind people, Don and Marjorie, and their place was often a haven for runaways or foster kids, the beneficiaries of one church mission or other. Sky had the shop-soiled look of one of those children. But the dirty-blonde hair and the way she clung to Marjorie made him think that she was a grandchild. She had to be Fay's.

On the jetty old men jigged for squid with their heads lowered against the wind. Dyson stood out there looking across at the yacht club and the rusty roofs of Cockleshell on the farther shore.

Fay Keenan. He hadn't even considered that she might still be in town. Hadn't she left long before him? He had anticipated some awkward encounters. There would be the people he'd gone to school with, the ones who always talked of shooting through to the city at the first opportunity but never actually left. He prepared himself for their prickly defensiveness, consoling himself in the knowledge that after ten years these meetings would only be momentary. Most people would settle for a wave in the street, a brief greeting in Woolworths. But he hadn't considered folks like the Keenans. They were full-on people. They were salt of the earth. They would never settle for just a meeting on the main drag.

And Fay. With a daughter. He hadn't considered that at all.

For a few days Dyson kept to the house. He only went out to take Ricky to school and collect him afterwards. All day he absorbed himself in little projects of household repair and modification. He told himself it was the rain that kept him at bay but in truth he had the jitters. He was back to feeling that weird, diffuse guilt which had dogged him all his life. He'd given up teasing that one out years ago. The old man's early death, the disappointment he was to his mother, the business with Fay. And, God knows, the unravelling of Sophie. It was old news but ever fresh in him. The way he'd jumped, blushing already, when Marjorie Keenan called his name.

With Ricky beside him, he lay awake at night with real misgivings about coming home. Irony he could deal with, but the complications of history might be another matter.

On the third day, in the early afternoon, Marjorie Keenan came knocking as he knew she would. Come for dinner tonight, she told him. She had a lamb leg big as a guitar. There was no way out.

The Keenans lived down by the surf beach in a shabby art deco place beneath Norfolk Island pines. Dyson arrived at six and stood for a moment at the door, bracing himself for the necessary explanations about his status as a single parent. Ricky looped his fingers around Dyson's belt. Both looked up at the soughing pines before Dyson knocked.

Marjorie squeezed each of them on the doorstep and dragged them indoors. The house was unchanged since the days he'd come here to play pool and grope their daughter furtively in the garage. In the hallway a candle burned before an icon of a severe Russian Christ. There were seascapes on the walls and a portrait of the Pope. The place smelled of meat and potatoes and the strange lemony odour of old people. Somewhere in the house a television blared.

In the kitchen Don Keenan rose on sticks and met Dyson with a hand outstretched, copper bracelet gleaming. There were tears in his eyes.

Look at you, he said. Lord, just look at you.

Long time, Don.

The old man sat and wiped his face. Yeah, he said brightly. And time wounds all heels, eh?

Except that it's his knees that've given out, said Marjorie. That's a lifetime of football for you.

They beckoned him to sit and Ricky edged onto his lap, reserved but curious. Dyson saw that the boy was transfixed by the old man. The tears, the florid cheeks, the Brylcreemed hair, the walking sticks. Ricky curled against his father. Dyson smelled the sweetness of his scalp.

Mister Keenan was my coach, Rick. When I was a boy. He was a gun footballer, you know. Played for Claremont. Three hundred and twenty-two games for Railways – that's a team here.

You like footy, Ricky? the old man asked.

The boy nodded.

Who's your favourite player, then?

Ricky looked at his father.

Go on, said Dyson.

Leaper, said the boy.

Ah, said Don. Now *he* can play!

Lamb's ready, said Marjorie.

Still cooking on the woodstove, said Dyson admiringly. Look at the size of that thing.

It's the Rolls-Royce of ranges, that, she said.

Big as a blessed Rolls-Royce, too, said Don.

Just as their plates came and the old man was carving the meat, the thin blonde child came into the kitchen and took a seat.

You met Sky, said Marjorie.

Sky, said Dyson. This is Ricky.

Hi, the girl murmured.

Lo, said Ricky.

There was a brief moment of bewilderment when grace was

said. After all the crossing and amens Ricky glanced at Dyson for reassurance. Then hunger got the better of him and he ate unselfconsciously.

The talk was of the town, how the harbour had finally been cleaned up and the whales had returned and brought new tourists to the place. There are wineries now, said Don, and good wine like this one. Dyson didn't have the heart to tell him he'd given up the booze but he knew that Marjorie wouldn't have missed the fact that his glass was untouched. The food was simple and hearty and the kitchen sleepy-warm. It was nice to be with them again after all this time. The Keenans were good people and he felt bad that he'd left it so long to come and see them. After all, he'd been closer to them at one stage than he was to his own mother. A long time had passed since the business with him and Fay. He told himself he needn't have been so anxious.

Ricky pleased Marjorie by taking a second helping of every-thing. Rain lashed the windows and though he was sober Dyson felt as safe as a man with four drinks under his belt. Eventually the kids sloped off shyly to watch TV. Marjorie made a pot of Irish breakfast.

You don't need to explain about your wife, Peter, said the old woman, pouring him a cup. We know already. We'll spare you that.

News travels fast, he murmured, stung.

Small town, mate, said Don. Don't we know all about that.

Well, said Dyson, doing his best to recover. That pretty much explains why I'm back.

There was a long, hesitant silence. From the loungeroom up the hall came the antic noise of a cartoon. Dyson wondered if that huge ruined sofa was still there in front of the TV. A life-time ago, on the same cracked upholstery, he felt the hot weight of a girl's breasts in his hands for the first time, and it was odd to think of Ricky and Sky up there.

Sky, he said. She's Fay's?

They nodded.

Staying with you for a while?

Oh, said Marjorie with a tired smile. We've had Sky on and off for years. Most of her life, I spose.

Ah, said Dyson.

Well, said the old man. Like you, Fay's had her troubles.

She doesn't live in town?

No. She's been all over.

In trying to mask his relief, Dyson scalded his mouth with tea.

We thought of suing for permanent custody for the child's sake, said the old man. But it's a dead loss. Welfare and the courts – it's all about the rights of the mother no matter what.

Anyway, said Marjorie with a forced cheeriness that made it plain she'd cut Don off before he got into his stride. It's worked out well just going along the way we have, unofficially. Things are coming good in the end. Fay and you are in the same sort of boat in a way. You know, recovering. In fact it's amazing you're here, Peter, because Fay's due here any day. Maybe you two can catch up.

Well, said Dyson in alarm. To be honest I'm not—

It's been very hard for us, Peter, said the old lady. Life doesn't turn out how you plan it. And it's difficult when you're old, when you think that your job's done and you can rest a little. You're not prepared for dealing with the kinds of things we've had to deal with, to live through.

Stinking, filthy bloody drugs—

Don.

She's abandoned a child, said the old man. She's stolen anything we've ever had. We've spent all our savings on treatments and debts and she's brought thugs and crims into our home and frightened the tripe out of her mother. She's put us through a living hell.

But, said Marjorie emphatically, we have our precious Sky. And we're past the worst and we forgive and forget. Don't we, Don?

Yes, said the old man subsiding, contrite, in his chair.

And we're grateful for small mercies.

Dyson drank his tea. His mouth felt scoured now. A junkie, he thought. You couldn't honestly be surprised. It would explain the rash of calls a couple of years ago, the breathless messages on the machine.

We always loved you, Peter, said Marjorie.

Loved you as our own, said Don. Gawd, we even thought you'd be family in the end.

She needs safe friends, said Marjorie. Clean friends. She's putting her life back together.

And we need a break, son. Now and then. Just a blessed rest.

You're a good person, Peter. Say you'll think about it. Say you'll come and see her.

Dyson felt the heat of the stove in his bones. He looked at their ravaged faces. And rain peppered the window.

Dyson had no desire to see Fay Keenan. When she called that time he did not respond to her messages. He bore her no ill will but he did fear the force of her personality. The intervening years had not diminished his memory of the time, almost the entirety of his high school life, that he'd spent in her thrall. They began as fumbling fourteen-year-olds when he was her father's most promising player and she was the flashy captain of the girls' hockey team. They were a major item, a school scandal, infamous for their declarations of eternal love and the heroics of their lust. By the age of sixteen the love was gone but the lust lived on in a kind of mutual self-loathing. Their relationship had boiled down to a futile addiction, a form of entertainment for their classmates who saw them as a bad show which refused to go off the air.

Dyson's mother disliked Fay but the Keenans took to him. To the Keenans Fay and him were just two talented kids taking life by the throat. What they didn't seem to see was how strange and pathological the whole affair became. How these kids isolated themselves in their passion until they became friendless and obsessed. They didn't see them destroying each other. As a boy Dyson relished the warmth of the Keenan home and although the Catholic business mystified him, he recognized them as people of virtue and kindness, even forgiveness. By comparison his own mother seemed dry and inflexible. She looked down on the Keenans because Don worked for the railways. Dyson came to love them and in later years, when it was all over, he wondered if the whole grisly thing had lasted so long because he liked to be around the Keenans as much as their daughter. But that was just sentimental. What kept Fay and him together was sex. It was a habit only catastrophe could break.

Right from the outset there was something mesmerizing about Fay Keenan. She had a cockiness, an impulsive brio that was exciting. Dyson was never a courageous boy. Even in football he was talented but weak-willed. The coach's daughter had real guts. She was so pretty, so lithe, with a wicked laugh under all that blonde hair. Fay was smart, too. At school she coasted shamelessly. Her parents were convinced that she was destined for medicine or the law. She could really talk up a storm. Yet in the end Dyson hardly heard anything she said; he settled for the curve of her neck, the heat of her mouth, the spill of her hair across his body, and even when all they had to say to one another was carping ugliness, he was too well-fed, too passive, too lazy to break it off and move on. For the last two years of school they were miserable. They had their disaster and Fay failed her exams. They were just another small-town story. And in the way of such stories they met years later, stoned at a Christmas barbecue in the city, and screwed in a potting shed from which they staggered full of regret and recrimination.

It was so tawdry that it should have been comical, but Dyson could only see the damage they'd done each other.

A week after his dinner with the Keenans, Dyson took Ricky and a boy from his class out to Jacky's Bridge to fish for bream after school. The boys were new friends and still shy with one another and right from the start it was clear that the fishing idea was a dud. He didn't know what it was. Maybe they were too young or fresh to each other for the stillness required, but within ten minutes they were restless standing out there on the bank so he packed the gear and led them up to the bridge itself.

This is boring, said the other boy, Jared.

Yeah, said Ricky faintly, treading a line between solidarity and mutiny.

Well, you'll think differently in a minute, said Dyson. Here, climb up between these big posts. See these little flat bits? Lie there. Here, I'll show you.

Dyson crawled up beneath the supports of the wooden bridge and lay on his back in the moist gravel so he could look up at the sky slatted through the timbers. Sceptically, the boys joined him. He sensed that he was about to make a fool of himself and shame Ricky by association but he didn't have a better idea to entertain them with. He was also suddenly mindful that this was something he'd discovered with Fay. There was such a long list of local things he couldn't dissociate from her; she was there at every turn.

Dad? murmured Ricky, embarrassed.

Stay down. I can hear something coming.

The boys fidgeted beside him. Jared smelled of Plasticine or something else slightly musty. He was, very distinctly, a stranger, someone else's child.

Just then a semi broached the bend and Dyson began to laugh in anticipation. Within seconds the truck was on the bridge and the piles and sleepers roared. Spikes spat and rattled and the dirt beneath them shook. Dyson began to yell. It startled the boys a second until his voice was swallowed up by the great, hot shadow that passed overhead.

Hey, said Jared quietly in the aftermath. Cool.

For another half hour they lay there waiting, giggling, yelling and laughing themselves to the point of hiccups.

As she took delivery of her muddy son, Jared's mother seemed brazenly curious about Dyson. He stood blushing on her verandah as she sized him up. It seemed that word was out on him. He wondered if it was his apparent availability or his wife's suicide that interested her. Either way he didn't linger.

It was almost dark when they got home. The harbour lights were on, the jetties pretty in a way that they could never be in daylight. Dyson was only halfway out of the car before he saw a shadow on the verandah and then the glow of a cigarette. He knew it would be her. Ricky pressed against him as they mounted the steps.

Just me, said Fay.

Her face was little more than a white dab in the gloom.

Fay, he murmured.

Didn't mean to startle anybody.

That's okay.

First ciggie I've ever smoked on your mum's verandah, that's for sure.

Dyson found the lock and opened the house. He hesitated a moment before switching on the porchlight and when he did Fay seemed to cringe beneath it. Her face was pale, her hair without lustre.

It's getting chilly, he said. You'd better come in.

I can't stay.

No. Fair enough.

Dyson tried to understand what he was feeling. It was so strange to see her again. She blew smoke from the side of her mouth, the way she always had, and tossed the butt out into the yard.

This is your little boy.

Ricky, said Dyson.

Your dad and me, Fay said with an attempt at brightness. We went to school together.

Ricky licked his lips. Dyson ushered him inside toward the bathroom and stood in the doorway.

Mum told me about your wife.

Oh, he asked, startled. She did?

I'm sorry to hear it.

Well.

And she told you about me, I imagine.

A bit. She didn't elaborate. I met Sky.

Isn't she great?

Yeah. She looks like you.

So Mum didn't give you the gory details.

No.

God bless her.

Well, he said. She's a trouper.

Dyson tried to look past Fay to the harbour lights and the navy sky still tinted by the vanished sun, but even thin and wan as she was in the unflattering light, she had a compelling presence. The cargo pants and jumper hung off her and her lips were chapped. She seemed wrung out, chastened, even. Yet she took up all the available space out there on the verandah.

For some reason I wanted to tell you myself, she said looking him straight in the face, her arms folded across her breasts. Once I found out you were home I had to explain myself. We go back so far, you and me. I didn't want you finding out from someone else.

Sure, he said uncertainly.

Funny, you know. I've had to give up worrying about what people think anymore. Burnt all the bridges. But with you . . . it's different.

It shouldn't be. Fay, we don't even know each other. I don't mean to be . . . but we were kids.

And here you are.

Dyson folded his arms.

I was in rehab, Pete. I'm six months clean.

That's good. That's great.

I fucked up. Been fuckin up for years.

You don't have to talk about this, Dyson said, hearing water purl into the bath up the hallway.

But I want to. Maybe you don't wanna hear it.

I've got Ricky to get through the bath, he said. The hot water.

Yeah.

Maybe you'd better come in?

No. It's alright.

Can . . . can I do anything for you?

Like, why am I here? she said with a wry smile, eyes glittering.

It's just that I'm not that steady yet, myself. You know? I don't know what I can offer you.

I need a friend, that's all.

Dyson sighed, torn.

I know it'll be hard to trust me.

Fay.

I'm supposed to seek out good people. But it's alright. I understand. I'll see you.

Chilled and miserable, he let her walk down into the dark while behind him water pounded into the bath. He hadn't even let her tell him what it was that she was addicted to; he didn't even offer her that kindness. But how could he tell her that he wasn't as uncomplicatedly good as she imagined? How could he be honest with her and say that he was afraid of her and afraid of his own reactions, frightened of lapsing into old habits? Self-preservation – did it ever feel anything but ugly?

He pushed the door to and switched off the porchlight.

In the morning, bleary and unrested, he came upon Fay outside the school gate. He supposed that for a while at least such meetings would be inevitable. And then one day she'd be gone again. The sky hung low and dark. There was a bitter wind from the south. Fay wore a huge stretched jumper that looked like one of Don's and she hugged herself as she turned to him.

Haven't done that for a while, she murmured.

Bring her to school?

I think she was embarrassed.

Ah.

Hurts, she said fishing out a fag. But I spose I deserve it.

Dyson walked uphill, careful not to hurry, and she fell into step beside him.

Sorry about last night.

Well, he murmured. Me too.

Out over the sea a storm brewed. The air in its path felt pure and steely. Dyson couldn't help feel that Fay's cigarette was an offence against such clarity. In even thinking it he was, he knew, his mother's son, but that did not make it less true.

How's your folks? he asked.

Good. But I don't know how long I can live with them. They want me to stay a while but nobody's naming dates. I'm kind of on probation with Sky. And with them, I spose. They won't give her up easily. Not that I blame them. They've been good to me. Dad used to drive three hundred miles every fortnight to visit me in rehab. They've been great, you know, but I think I'll go mad if I stay too long.

Where would you go? he asked.

Oh, I'll stay in town. Rent somewhere close so they can all see each other. Sky needs them now. She knows I'm a fuck-up so she'll need reassurance. I have fantasies about a little house on one of those old dairy farms out along the coast. Something clear and clean, somewhere I can start again from scratch. You know what I mean?

Yeah, he said. I do.

But there's nowhere you can really *do* that. Everywhere you go there'll be some link. A bit of history. Anyway, I'm broke. Need a job but still feel a bit too ginger to cope with the stress.

I understand.

But in the meantime I'm going nuts. Jesus, I thought rehab was tough. I've got Mum watching me like a hawk and Sky expecting me to piss off at any moment. And the old man desperately trying not to spew out all his resentment and scare me off.

I spose it'll take time.

She sniffed angrily. Yeah. Time.

They came to his street and paused a moment.

You ever see any of the old crew? she said.

No, he murmured. To be honest I can hardly remember anybody else.

Scary.

He shrugged.

Well, she said. I'll leave you alone. Don't worry.

Dyson arranged his mouth to speak but found nothing to say.

Looks like I'm still trouble, she murmured. For you at least.

Did he imagine it or was there really a tiny twist of satisfaction to Fay's mouth as she said this, a thread of pride in knowing that she had a lingering influence over him?

He mumbled goodbye and walked home in the same turmoil that he'd stewed in all night. How could you help someone like Fay? How could you trust her? If it wasn't the drugs it was the old thrill of the power that she wielded. He just wasn't strong or confident enough to battle it right now. Wasn't his first responsibility to Ricky, to his own sanity? He had his own problems to deal with. Yet he felt like such a bloodless bastard and so disloyal to Don and Marjorie after all their years of kindness. He'd all but grown up in their home and here he was refusing to help their daughter. And that poor, wary little girl. How could he live with himself?

Rain fell all day. He sat inside with a fire burning, the household chores mounting up around him. It was the kind of day you could feel descending upon you, when you drag everything out and hash it over once again despite yourself. When you looked back at Sophie and the pregnancy, wondering what signs you missed. The precious time it cost after the birth before you realized something was badly wrong, before you finally spoke, acted, asked. And the dozens of times when you didn't hear, when you reacted clumsily, said and did the wrong thing. The drowning weight of it.

There were times, even while she was alive, when Dyson questioned his attraction to Sophie. They met in his early years of teaching. She was a physiotherapist with dark, short hair and green eyes. Any stranger could take a look at Ricky and see what Dyson had seen in his mother. They shared the same smooth, olive skin and vanilla scent. Sophie exuded a serious-ness of purpose that some people thought solemn. He loved her calm trust and the simple delight that lit up her face. Once, even before she got sick and everything began to seem forced and provisional, he allowed himself the bitter possibility that he may have fallen in love with Sophie from sheer relief that she wasn't Fay Keenan. Because when they met he was still raw. And there Sophie was, pretty, considered, dependable, a sanctuary from the narcissistic and mercurial. He did love her. But it gnawed at him then, as now, that he might have loved the safety of her above all else. Maybe she knew it all along. It was a nasty thought, because if she did then he could not truly console himself with the doctors' talk of chemical imbalance and postnatal depression. She would have had plenty to be miserable about, and he would have to wear some blame for her misery and maybe even her death. Even the weak are cruel in their way. You couldn't cling to victimhood all your life.

The fire was so bright in the hearth that even at the brink of despair he found himself finally and mercifully anaesthetized before it. As he sat there into the afternoon it sucked the air from the room and danced before him like a thought just out of reach.

He woke to a banging at the door and when he staggered up from the couch Fay was at the window. He opened the door. Ricky stood looking up at him with frank curiosity.

Rick. Hell. I fell asleep.

So we see, said Fay wryly.

Damn. But thanks for bringing him, Fay.

I know the way, said Ricky.

Yes, mate. Course you do.

Dad, said the boy holding up a sheet of butcher's paper. Look at my picture.

Dyson took the crumpled painting and held it away from him to see it. Jacky's Bridge! he said.

Here's me. Here's you.

Of course. And what about Jared?

Aw, I forgot him.

Dyson smiled. He looked up and saw Fay smiling too. Then he noticed Sky standing out on the steps in the drizzling rain.

You're all wet, he said. You better come in. Hey Rick, let's get some towels.

The fire was almost out but the house was still warm. Dyson towelled his son dry and watched Sky submit to the care of her mother. It was painful, the selfconsciousness of it. Outside the rain intensified, the day darkened.

I can't believe I slept through, he said.

Things happen, said Fay.

I'll drive you home.

No, it's okay.

It's pouring.

Fay shook her head.

You'll get drenched.

There were tears in Fay's eyes. Dyson stood there confounded.

The kids wandered over to the kitchen window to see water spill from the iron tank outside.

He's got a cubbyhouse, said Sky over her shoulder in a tone of accusation.

My Dad made it, said Ricky.

Dyson removed the booster seat so Fay could sit in the front of the car beside him. He made sure the kids were buckled up before he eased them all out into the deluge.

I had a blue with Dad, said Fay. He wanted to drive us, I wanted to walk. Well, I'd rather drive but I've lost my licence. Stupid, stupid.

Spose you just want some independence.

Life in a cleft stick, eh.

Dyson drove them out toward the beach where little weatherboard cottages seemed to cower under the downpour.

God, this rain.

Thought you hated winter, she said. What a joke, coming back here, then.

Over the tin roofs the sea was steely-smooth and the Norfolk Island pines rose like a stockade against the south.

That painting, Fay said. That was our bridge, right?

He nodded. They coasted in to the Keenans' place.

I won't tell them, she murmured.

Tell them what?

That you slept through.

Thanks for collecting him for me.

Can't have them thinking you left a child in the rain.

Bye, Fay.

Already Marjorie was on the porch unfurling an umbrella in preparation for their rescue. He could imagine old Don out there trolling the streets for them right now. He honked the horn as he pulled away.

On Saturday morning Dyson drove out along the coast with a pair of binoculars to show Ricky the humpbacks coursing their way towards the tropics, and for a while they stood on a head-land as a whale and her calf lolled in the clear, sunlit water at their feet. The boy was enchanted. Vapour and spray rose around them. The crash of tails whacking the surface res-onated in their own skin and hair. They hooted like sportsfans until the show was over. Heading homeward, with Ricky still euphoric, Dyson thought about the whaling station, now a museum, on the outskirts of town. He figured he'd let that keep a while. For now the boy was alight with wonder. Why dash that excitement with cold, nasty history right at the outset?

As they came back into town Ricky spotted the football oval and rose in his seat.

Dad, can we kick the footy?

The sun was out, there was a ball in the back of the car. Dyson wheeled them in to park beside the other cars around the boundary. A junior game was in recess so they dashed out to the western goal square and punted the ball up and back between the posts. While Ricky capered solemnly around the turf, Dyson took in the twelve-year-olds in their team huddles on the flank. Nothing had changed in thirty years – the coach's harangue, the half-sucked orange quarters on the grass, the fat and hungover parents nursing their breakfast meatpie and fag.

Dad, watch this! Frank Leaper snaps on goal!

Ricky hooked the ball across his shoulder. The kick fell short but Dyson ushered it across the line.

A car horn blared.

Through! cried Ricky.

Six points, Dyson said.

The horn went again: shave-and-a-haircut-ten-cents. Dyson looked over. Don Keenan waved from the wheel of his ancient Holden.

Out in the centre the umpire blew his whistle for the resumption of play and the teams straggled back out onto the park. Ricky whined and baulked at having to vacate the goal-square but Dyson herded him back to the sidelines. They drew up beside the old man's car.

Got a bit of a kick on him, said Don Keenan.

How are you, Don?

The old man shrugged. What doesn't kill you makes you older. Know anythin about addiction?

A few things, I spose, said Dyson leaning against the old HT as two boys flew for the bouncedown. The ball shied out to a solitary kid who was so stunned to have possession of it that he stood motionless until run down by the pack.

Thanks for takin an interest in Fay. It means a lot to us.

Dyson said nothing.

We're just about at our wits' end, said Don. No parent should have to see the things I've seen.

She's trying, said Dyson.

You got that right.

The ball soared, spiralling into the sun.

But we love her, said Don. You understand that, don't you?

Dyson said he did.

Late Sunday night, when Ricky was long abed and the fire all but out, there was a gentle knock at the door.

I'm sorry, Fay murmured. I just had to.

He let her in and with her came the night chill. They sat by the hearth but he didn't stoke the fire for fear of encouraging Fay to linger. She sat down in a quilted jacket, jeans and hiking boots and fingered the book he'd been reading. As she leant in toward the remains of the fire her hair crowded her face.

Everything alright?

She shook her head.

He sighed. Want a cuppa?

Yeah, she said. Coffee.

He went into the kitchen to fill the kettle. When he returned Fay was putting wood on the fire.

I should have been at a meeting tonight, she said. I've skipped two in a row.

So don't miss the next one.

There's no one I can turn to, Pete. You're it.

Your parents know you're here?

Yeah. They're freaking. When . . . when I get agitated and restless like this they think I'm gonna go out and score.

And are you?

I'm here aren't I? Shit, they're still searching my room and I'm thirty years old, for Chrissake. Least if I'm here they'll relax. God, they're ecstatic. You're the Golden Boy. Dad even drove me, she said with a girlish laugh.

He drove you here?

So fucking sad.

Dyson lowered himself into a chair and felt a new weight of fatigue on him.

Tell me about your wife, she said.

What kind of state are you in, Fay?

Frazzled, she said. Teetering. So tell me about her.

Dyson shook his head. Fay whistled through her teeth.

What do you want from me? he asked.

Respect, she said. No. Adoration. Shit, Pete, I just want a safe place to be. Someone trustworthy. I can trust you, can't I?

Fay pulled her knees up to her chin and in that single movement, with her hair down her arms and her eyes tilted up at him, she became an eerie ghost of her teenage self. Dyson got up and went back to the kitchen to make her coffee. He stood, shaken, at the stove. He turned a teaspoon over and over in his hand so that the light caught it.

You didn't answer me, Fay said in the doorway.

I don't know the answer.

Can't trust yourself, you mean.

Jesus, Fay, what is it that you really want?

I dunno, she said arching against the doorframe. Just now? Comfort, I spose. A few of the edges taken off. This fucking town – I shouldn't have come back.

So why did you?

I want my kid.

Dyson felt hemmed in now. He was revolted by her. He couldn't help it. All that restless will, the cruelty of it made him sick.

What are you thinking? she asked. Your face went black. What're you thinking about me?

Nothing, Fay.

I used to be a prize once. I was a trophy and you had me.

Let's go and sit by the fire, he said. Here's your coffee.

You're uncomfortable.

Yes.

I came here for comfort and you're uncomfortable, she said, her face flushed.

I don't think there's any comfort I can give you.

The simple pleasures, she said, lifting the mug to her mouth.

Maybe you should go.

You don't understand what I've been through!

And I'm rapidly losing interest in finding out.

You don't know what's been taken from me, what I've given up. It's inhuman. No one should have to go through what I've been through.

The blood was in her face now. Her eyes glittered. She was beautiful again.

Fay—

Jesus, I'm aching. I need love.

Your family—

I need more!

You'll meet good people, he said. It's a slow road.

I can't wait. Can't you see, I can't wait.

Think of Sky.

Don't do that to me, she said. Look down your nose, turn me away, lecture me. I really thought you were a friend.

I am, he murmured, and as he did so he knew it was a lie.

She dragged her hair back off her face and wiped her eyes. You can't even spare me a hug?

Dyson felt such a shit. He sighed and looked at her, relenting. Sensing it, she smiled.

Let's go to bed, Pete.

He froze even as he reached for her. Fay, you really should go.

What harm can it do?

Fay—

I can't drink, can't drive, can't live in my own place, can't do Mr Speed. Jesus, I can't upset Mum and Dad. A mercy fuck isn't against the law, Pete, it's not a blow against the Higher Power. Hello, my name's Fay Keenan and I'm desperate—

Stop it.

You used to beg me.

Please keep your voice down.

I can't believe you!

Well you'd better believe it.

It's so humiliating, she said beginning to weep. I'm coming apart here and you're just . . . just watching?

Fay, you'll wake Ricky.

I don't give a shit.

Just calm down.

She wiped her face with the sleeve of her baggy jumper. A glistening trail of snot and tears lay on the wool and Dyson stared at it while his mind raced.

You won't even hold me, will you?

No, he murmured. I'm sorry, but I can't.

I don't think we were ever friends.

You're probably right, he said. We were obsessed, caught up in something. Too young. We were children. We did damage.

Fay gulped at her coffee. She looked at him carefully as though taking his measure. She was beautiful. Any man would want her. She'd taste of coffee and cigarettes and tears and her hair would fall around you like a curtain.

You have no idea how my parents adore you, said Fay. I could have hated you for being in town when I came home. My big moment. Nothing I've done in the past six months to put my life right could impress them the way you did by simply arriving unchanged of old. And you know what? Stolen thunder and all, I was glad. Happy for them, happy for me. We really thought you'd be there for us.

I appreciate that, he said. But I don't think they expect me to sleep with you.

They don't know how cold and dead inside you really are.

That's probably true, he admitted, exhausted now.

You know they never did find out about our little secret. God knows, every other shitty thing I ever did somehow got back to them, but they never even suspected that. Two days shy of seventeen. And your fuckin mother paid for it.

Oh, Fay.

You know how my parents are. You know what it'd do to them. It'd crush them. Break their hearts.

Don't.

And you, the tin god. They could blame you for everything that's ever happened to me, everything I've put em through.

Dyson went cold. He held on to the bench and stared at her. God, how thoroughly she saw through him. He never really knew if Fay regretted the abortion they'd obtained all those years ago, but she gauged him well enough to sense how it ate at him. And she knew where his real vanity lay, what it would cost him to be reviled by her parents. When Fay took off to leave them in the lurch again, how could he live here in town with them, meeting them at the school gate every morning? What would he be to them, then, the killer of their unborn grandchild?

Pete, if I leave this house and go down to the trawlers and score tonight, what're you gonna tell them? That you turned me away? Ruined my recovery like you ruined me before?

Did I, though? he murmured. Ruin you. Is that how it was?

She laughed and put the mug on the bench.

There was a thud from the livingroom and Fay turned, startled.

Ricky? she called.

Dyson slipped past her and saw a log fallen out onto the hearth. A plume of smoke rose in the room and he kicked the smouldering wood back into the grate. He leant on the mantle to get control of himself.

Fay stood in the middle of the room waving smoke away. Her manic mood had broken.

So that's a no, then?

It's a no, Fay. Regardless.

It's blackmail, she said. I know.

It's vicious.

You think I'd do it? she asked, smiling. You think I'd tell them?

No, he whispered prayerfully. Because you love them. I think you love your daughter. You've come too far, Fay. Too much self-respect.

Dyson wondered if it might be true, whether she had any pity in her at all.

Well, said Fay. I spose we'll see, won't we?

Yes, Dyson said turning back to the smouldering log in the grate. I guess we will.

He kept his back to her.

The door shut so quietly that he had to turn around to see that she was gone.

On Her Knees

I WAS SIXTEEN when the old man shot through. A year later we moved back to the city where my mother cleaned houses to pay off his debts and keep us afloat and get me through university. She wouldn't let me get a part-time job to pay my way. The study, she said, was too important. Cleaning was a come-down from her previous job, eighteen years before, as a receptionist in a doctor's surgery, but it was all she could get. She told me there was more honour in scrubbing other people's floors than in having strangers scrub your own. But I wasn't convinced. The only thing worse than knowing she knelt every day in someone else's grotty shower recess was having to help her do it. Some days, between lectures, I did go with her. I hated it. There were many other times when I could have gone and didn't. I stayed home and stewed with guilt. She never said a word.

My mother had a kind of stiff-necked working class pride. After the old man bolted she became a stickler for order. She believed in hygiene, insisted upon rigour. She was discreet and deadly honest, and those lofty standards, that very rigidity, set her apart. Carol Lang went through a house like a dose of salts. She earned a reputation in the riverside suburbs where, in time, she became the domestic benchmark. She probably cleaned the houses of some of my wealthy classmates without any of us being the wiser.

She was proud of her good name and the way people bragged about her and passed her around like a hot tip, but I resented how quickly they took her for granted. I'd seen their patronizing notes on floral paper, their attempts to chip her rate down. The householders who thought most highly of themselves were invariably the worst payers and the biggest slobs. It was as though having someone pick up after them had either encouraged them to be careless or made them increasingly determined to extort more work for their money. Through it all, my mother maintained her dignity *and* her hourly rate. She left jobs, she did not lose them.

In twenty years she was only ever sacked the once, and that was over a pair of missing earrings. She came home with a week's notice and wept under the lemon tree where she thought I wouldn't hear. I tried to convince her never to return but she wouldn't hear a word of it. We argued. It was awful, and it didn't let up all week. Since the old man's disappearance we'd never raised our voices at each other. It was as though we kept the peace at all costs for fear of driving each other away. And now we couldn't stop bickering.

The morning she was to return we were still at it. Then, even while I took a shower, she stood in the bathroom doorway to lecture me on the subject of personal pride. It was as though

I was not a twenty-year-old law student but a little boy who needed his neck scrubbed.

I don't care what you say, I yelled. It's outrageous and I'm not coming.

I never asked you, she said. When did I ever ask you to come?

I groaned. There was nothing I could say to that. And I knew it was a four-hour job, two if I helped out. Given what the householder had accused her of, it would be the toughest four hours she'd ever put in. But I was convinced that it was a mistake for her to go back. It was unfair, ludicrous, impossible, and while she packed the Corolla in the driveway I told her so. She came back for the mop and bucket. I stood on the verandah with my arms folded. But she must have known I'd go. She knew before I did, and not even the chassis-bending slam I gave the door could wipe the look of vindication from her face as she reversed us out into the street.

The car reeked of bleach and rubber gloves. I sighed and cranked down the window. She drove with both ravaged hands on the wheel, her chin up at a silly, dignified angle. Her mask of composure belied a fear of driving, and the caution with which she navigated made me crazy, but I resolved to show a bit of grace.

What? she said, seeing something in my face.

Nothing, I said, trying not to sound sullen.

You're good to come with me.

Well. Figure you need the help.

Oh, it's not help, love. It's company.

I could have opened the door and got out there and then.

What? she asked.

I shook my head. I couldn't launch into it all again. She was worth twice what those silvertails paid her. She was more scrupulous, more honest, than any of them. She wouldn't even open a drawer unless it was to put a clean knife or fork into it. For her to be called a thief was beyond imagining.

I know it's not easy, she said.

It's demeaning, Mum! I blurted despite myself. Going back like this. The whole performance. It's demeaning.

To who?

Whom.

Well, excuse me, constable! she said with a tart laugh. To *whom* is it demeaning, then, Victor? You?

I looked out of the window, flushing for shame.

You men, she said brightly.

Actually, this is about a woman, Mum. What kind of person accuses you of thieving, gives you the sack and then asks you back for one week while she looks for somebody to replace you?

Well, it's her loss, said my mother, changing lanes with excruciating precision. She knows she won't find anybody better than me.

Not even as good as you. Not a chance.

Thank you.

Five-hundred-dollar earrings, Mum. She hasn't even gone to the police.

As far as we know.

In that postcode? Believe me, we'd know.

She must know I didn't steal them.

She just wants something, some advantage over you. There'll be a note there, you wait. She'll let it slide – this time – and later on, while you're all guilty and grateful, she'll chip you down on the rate. Back to a fiver an hour.

The Law, she said. It must make you suspicious. She's just made a stupid mistake. She's probably found them by now.

And not called?

These people, they never call. Silence, that's their idea of an apology. It's how they're brought up.

But she looked troubled for a few moments. Then her face cleared.

Oh well, she murmured. There's the waiting list. I can still fill a dance card in this business.

Sure, I said without any enthusiasm.

Anyway, we'll show her.

How's that?

We'll clean that flat within an inch of its life.

Oh yeah, I muttered. That'll put her back in her box. Go, Mum.

We pulled up in the leafy street beneath a block of Art Deco flats. You could smell the river. Even after three years at the university, whose lawns all but ran to the river's grassy banks, that constant, brothy presence stank of old money, of posh schools and yacht clubs. Sometimes it reeked of Law itself, of port and cigars, chesterfields, musty paper and the men who owned this city because of it. That smell kept me alert. It made me wary and determined.

Drive on up, Mum, I said. Use her car space.

I wouldn't give her the satisfaction.

I did not roll my eyes. I got out and hoisted the vacuum cleaner off the back seat. She grabbed a bucket full of rags and squeeze bottles along with the mop.

Don't you use her gear?

Not today.

Don't tell me. The principle, right?

She winked and I felt sick for her.

I followed her up the long garden steps. Veins stood out in her calves. Beneath her loose shorts her thighs were white and dimpled. She seemed so old. I balanced the Electrolux hose on my shoulder and stared at the tennis shoes that she scrubbed and bleached every week to keep them looking new. As if anyone but her gave a damn.

Up on the porch, she fished the key from her blouse. All the keys hung from a piece of string around her neck. The sound of them jangling onto her dressing table at night signalled the end of her day.

The apartment had a closed-up smell intensified by the pong of housebound cats. While Mum went through to the kitchen I stared a moment at the Klee reproductions, the dreadful cat photos in gold frames, and the Kokoschka poster which appeared to be new. I heard an envelope torn open and I came in as she held up the mauve paper, one hand on her heart.

What does it say?

Nothing, she said too quickly. She stuffed the note into her pocket and patted her hair. The envelope lay on the bench. There was money in it.

I opened the fridge, a huge American thing with two doors and an icemaker.

No snooping, she said. Not even today.

There were two kinds of white wine, tomato juice and jars of condiments. On one shelf was a stack of foil boxes, some kind of packaged food without labels. I closed the fridge and looked at the wine rack, a shoulder-high stack of bottles that, after her second week, my mother was requested to leave undisturbed, unrolled, unwiped and undusted.

Don't be a stickybeak, she murmured, pulling on gloves.

Today I just couldn't help myself. It wasn't only resentment. I was curious. What kind of person would do this? After years of faultless service there was no discussion, just the accusation and the brusque termination in three scrawled lines.

Cat tray, she said.

I went into the airless laundry where the litter tray lay beneath the steel trough. The stink was awful. I got down with a garbage bag and tried to breathe through my mouth but the dust from the grit rose onto my lips and tongue and I started to gag. I grunted a bit, swung the hair out of my eyes and got it done, twisting the bag shut. I was supposed to disinfect the tray and I'd never dared cut corners before, but I just tipped some litter in and left it at that.

From the bathroom came the sound of my mother's off-key singing. I paused at the doorway a moment where a stinging fog of ammonia spilled out into the hall. She stopped warbling as if conscious of my presence. She was bent over the tub, Ajax in hand, veins livid in her legs. As I walked on, the sound of her brush panted against the enamel.

I binned the cat bag and began damp-dusting. With every surface so crowded with *objets*, it was slow work. Every trinket, souvenir, ornament and figurine had to be wiped, lifted, dusted beneath and replaced precisely. Standing orders. Mum would inspect it like a sergeant-major at barracks inspection. We both agreed that nobody who cleaned their own place would bother keeping such junk. A week of doing for herself and this woman'd ditch the lot out with the cat litter.

It was a lonely apartment. We'd had a grim few years, Mum and I, but you wouldn't walk into our place and feel the same melancholy you picked up here. Another person might have found it tranquil, but to me it felt as stale as it smelled. I dusted the Andrew Wyeth reproduction and the steel and leather chairs. I brushed and wiped and waxed the long shelves of books and tried to imagine having strangers in our place looking in our fridge, touching our stuff, ripping hanks of our hair from the plughole. You'd have to imagine they were some kind of sleepwalker, that they were blind, incurious, too stupid to notice intimate things about your life. You'd have to not think about them, to will these intruders away. Or just be confident. Yes, I thought. That's what it takes to be blasé about strangers in your house – a kind of annihilating self-assurance.

The bookshelves in the livingroom were stocked with novels and popular psychology. There were big celebrity hardbacks as well as the usual stuff by Germaine Greer, Erica Jong, Betty Friedan. But I found both volumes of the Kinsey Report and boxed sets of erotica I took some minutes to thumb through, wondering how Mum had missed them.

In the study I flicked the duster across slabs of specialist material, academic stuff, lever-arch files and archive boxes. I found biographies of Paul Robeson, Leadbelly, Dorothy Day, Martin Luther King, each of them bristling with tabs of paper and pencilled notes. On the desk beside the typewriter was a pile of what I instantly recognized as student papers. The title of the topmost was *Throwing Off the Shackles: consciousness-raising and the delivery of change.* I turned the cover page and read a few paragraphs. It was all the safe, right-thinking stuff of the time but clumsily written. The comments in red biro were good-natured and forbearing.

I smoothed the paper back into place and dusted the pin-up board of snapshots above the desk. The photos were of people in heavy coats and hats with earflaps, of fir trees, snow, people with big, pink smiling faces and spectacles. Americans. The lantern-jawed woman who appeared in so many – it was her. She looked decent, happy, loved by friends and family. Even as I clawed through her desk drawers, finding nothing more remarkable than a tiny twist of hash in a bit of tinfoil,

I knew I wouldn't find anything that would satisfy me. Now I just wanted to get the job over with.

In the bedroom I worked in a frenzy. Every sill and architrave, each lamp and mirror got a grinding wipe. I Windexed the glass, waxed the girly dressing table. When it was done I went out for the vacuum, cranked it up and ploughed my way through the whole place. At one point, when the old girl glanced up from the kitchen floor, I averted my eyes.

The thought kept returning to me. Why would someone not report the theft of a pair of five-hundred-dollar earrings? Even to claim the insurance you'd have to report it. Perhaps it was my own uneasiness at having overstepped the boundaries, at having gone through somebody's stuff, which made me consider the chance that this woman might know about me, be aware that I'd helped here before. Could she have suspected me rather than Mum? Worse still, did she know who I was, that I was an undergraduate at her own campus? And then could it be possible that her failure to report a theft to the cops was an act of kindness towards my mother, an act of mercy toward me?

I vacuumed and raked feverishly. When I got to the bedroom, the cats who'd thus far evaded us leapt out from behind the curtains. They were sulking great Persians. I threw down the nozzle and chased them out of the room.

My mother was still in the kitchen.

Mum, I said. What did the note say?

Did you leave that machine going?

Was it about me? Does she suspect me?

You? Don't be stupid.

I haven't been here for months.

Turn that thing off.

No, I said feeling ridiculous. It doesn't matter, I'm going back.

Don't forget those curtains!

I gave the bedroom curtains a good going over. I could never understand how so much cat hair could accumulate in a week.

Mum came in while I was on my knees still vacuuming the flounces and folds of the patchwork quilt.

Windex? she said.

I pointed to the dressing table. She lingered. I turned the machine off.

What were you on about before?

Honestly, Mum, why didn't we just give the place a light go through? Or better, just take the dough and split.

Because it would look like an admission of guilt.

Shit.

Language.

But this won't convince her, Mum.

No, probably not.

You should report them missing yourself. Ask them to search our place. Force the issue. There's nothing that can come of it.

Except talk. Imagine the talk. I'd lose the rest of my jobs.

She was shining with sweat. Her hair had tightened into damp poodle curls. She had been so pretty once.

So you're stuffed either way.

Love, we grin and bear it.

I shook my head. I hit the button on the vac and blitzed the carpet beneath the bed. I could sense her still behind me, waiting to say something but I pretended to be absorbed in the work. Up at the head of the bed there was a nest of Red Tulip chocolate wrappers. They made a slurping noise as they were sucked into the machine. I only had half of them up when the ping of something hard racketing along the pipe made me turn my head.

Mum stepped on the button. The machine wound down to silence.

Money, probably, I murmured.

Let's open it up.

I cracked the hatch and felt around in the horrible gullet of the dustbag. From wads of lint and hair and dirt came an earring.

Five hundred dollars? she muttered. That's rich.

I didn't know anything about jewellery. I shrugged, gave it to her.

Look under there. The other one's bound to be close by.

I found it hard up against the skirting board.

She's left them on the pillow, she said. Forgotten about them. She's come in and swept them off as she got into bed. She hasn't even looked. That's all it was, just carelessness.

All this fake outrage. She couldn't be bothered going to the cops because they're cheap? Is that it?

I don't know.

It wasn't important.

It was important to me.

Well, you've cleared your name. That's something.

She shook her head with a furious smile.

Why not? I asked. Show her what we found, what she was too lazy to look for. Show her where they were.

All she has to say is that she made me guilty enough to give them back. That I just wanted to keep the job. To save my good name. Vic, that's all I've *got* – my good name. These people, they can say anything they like. You can't fight back.

I looked away at the floor. I heard her blow her nose. I was powerless to defend her. It was the lowest feeling.

I'll finish the kitchen, she said. Ten minutes.

I vacuumed the rest of the bedroom. The earrings lay on the bed. I looked at them. They were pretty enough but I was no judge. Perhaps their real value was sentimental. I snatched them up from the quilt and took them into the laundry. I chucked them into the cat tray. Let her find them there if she cared to look.

In the kitchen Mum was ready to go. The rags and bottles were in the bucket. She walked a towel across the floor and that was it.

What about the money? I said, looking at the scrubbed bench.

I'm worth more, she said.

You're not taking it?

No.

I smiled and shook my head.

You forgot the vacuum, she said.

Oh, yeah. Right.

I went back to the laundry, knelt at the catbox and picked out the earrings. I dusted them off on my sweaty shirt. In my palm they weighed nothing. I grabbed the Electrolux from the bedroom and made my way out again. In the kitchen I put the earrings beside the unstrung key and the thin envelope of money.

My mother stood silhouetted in the open doorway. It seemed that the very light of day was pouring out through her limbs. I had my breath back. I followed her into the hot afternoon.

Cockleshell

IT TAKES A WEEK OR MORE before Brakey admits it to himself –
he's watching her. The only reason he comes down here
amongst the peppermints at sundown is to see Agnes Larwood
light her kero lamp onshore, take up her gidgie and begin wading the shallows in search of cobbler. Some evenings she digs
for cockles if the tide is low enough, and he has seen her scoop-
ing crabs over on the flats, but mostly she's out here with the
gidgie looking for cobbler to spear.

He lurks back in the gloom of the trees, the last of the sun
in the hills behind him, while she moves slowly through the
water with the lantern held away from her, out to the side and
slightly ahead. Orange light glows on her calves. She wears a
tank top and boardshorts. Her tennis shoes look huge and
white underwater. She travels so cautiously that the water

folds away from her shins in silence. Behind her, as darkness falls, the lights of town show up across the broad harbour and her silhouette becomes more golden and less flat in the light of her lamp. Now and then she goes all still and he observes the barely perceptible drawing back of her arm, the spear almost invisible in her hand. Suddenly the water erupts at her feet and a second later the sound of the splash carries to him. In the lampglow the writhing catfish comes up skewered shiny-black and she slops to shore to kill it and pull the venomous spines from its head with pliers. She slips the fish into the bag slung across her shoulder, looks up a moment so that her face is illuminated and her eyes seem to be looking straight into his, before straightening and turning back to the water, lamp in hand.

Same as every other night Brakey stops following when the peppermint grove peters into a tangle of teatrees and bamboo. To keep a parallel course with her through that lot would be a noisy and perilous business in the dark, so he squats to watch her work her way from view, a silhouette for a time, then a bud of light and then she's gone behind the curve of the point. He feels a pang of loss. He just can't believe this is happening to him. He's known Agnes Larwood all his life and now he can't keep his eyes off her. It's as though he's turned into some sort of perv. He sat next to Agnes a whole year in primary school. She lives thirty yards away. They're on the same damn bus every morning and now he's noticing her. She's not beautiful, not like her older sister, Margaret, the one who ran away to the city with the bloke from the superworks. Maybe you could call Agnes pretty but what does that really mean? It doesn't explain the sudden hunger, this terrible fascination. A fortnight ago she was bog-ordinary. Agnes bloody Larwood. But tonight his blood is charging, it whacks in him like something trapped and it's been this way for a solid week.

He hunkers down in the dark to wait. Leaf litter from the peppermints smells medicinal. Way out across the water a car whines along the Angelus shore.

Agnes. Agnes? Agnes.

While she's gone he pictures her in his head. Thin arms and legs, brown from summer. Short hair, also brown. Or brownish. An even sort of face with, yes, regular teeth from the few recent memories of her smiling or even speaking. Somehow in his mind she still has her milk teeth, for that's when he recalls her most vividly when they were younger. Even. Regular. Brownish. Pretty. Ish.

In the old days, when they were kids, they played together off and on, the way you do when there are plenty of kids about and you find yourself falling in with someone for an hour or so. Cockleshell was bigger then and much more lively. With the meatworks and the whaling station still operating, the string of houses along the shore here was full. It seemed that there were kids everywhere and they ran in a loose mob, roaming the bush and the estuarine flats in search of entertainment. Their hamlet had its own sign out on the bay road back then. Cockle Shoal. But then as now people called the place Cockleshell and that's what Brakey knows it as.

He wonders how long he should wait. His mother gets anxious. All week she's been testy because he's come home long after dark. She spends most of her time feeling abandoned or preparing to be so and it's wearing him out. He crouches there a few more minutes, persecuted by midges and mosquitoes, and when there's no sign of Agnes coming back his way, he gives up and heads home. In the moonless dark, he feels his way with bare feet on the sand track and puts an arm out to fend off lurking branches. In a couple of minutes he sees the house lights, his place and hers. At this angle they're close enough to be a single glow but by the time he's clear of the peppermint grove they're distinct. Two weatherboard houses. Church music from the Larwood place, the smell of frying onions from his.

Inside his mother is silent at the stove. Her face is shut down. It's nothing new. The table's set. He washes his hands and, newly protected by his thoughts, settles himself into the silence she's prepared for him. He already knows what his mother thinks. To her, the world is a treacherous place. Nothing lasts. People cheat. They leave. They just up and go. Sooner or later they all bolt and you're left on your own, and the look of reproach she gives him now is but a variation on her whole demeanour, the assumption in every glance, every sigh, every mute chink of cutlery, is that he too will leave her high and dry, just as the old man did three years ago. He's fifteen and it's old news. He feels sorry for her, protective still, but he's had a gutful. He wants her to get over it but he senses that it's beyond her.

Don't worry about the dishes, she says when they finish eating.

It's orright.

I said *leave* them.

He shrugs and goes to his room. Through the louvres he can still hear the holy roller music from the Larwoods'. In the old days it was only ever screaming that you heard. The sound of breaking glass, the thud of feet on the floorboards. Eric Larwood, smashed out of his head, lurching from room to room. Some mornings Mrs Larwood hung the washing out with shaking hands, her bruises plain from Brakey's place. There were times when she came across the rough grass at night with a sobbing trail of kids in tow, and they bedded down in the lounge while Brakey's old man got his trousers on and went over to pacify the mad bugger.

The Larwoods were Poms. In the early days, when they were more migrants than locals, their whiny accent was stronger. Their house smelled of piss and fags and kero as though they never opened the windows, as if it was winter all year. It's been a long time since Brakey was inside that house. He wonders if the Larwood kids still wet the bed. He tries to imagine Agnes Larwood as a bedwetter. He doesn't even know the colour of her eyes; she's always looking down or sideways. Brownish, at a guess. He wonders if she still has that Larwood smell of cigarette smoke and bacon and kero. He can't recall the last time he was close enough to tell.

Old Eric was shop steward at the meatworks. Now the union's collapsed and the meatworks is gone, and he's nobody. He's quiet nowadays. It's been years since he's been on a rampage of the sort that anybody else can hear. Brakey's mother used to have a lot to say about the Larwoods but when Agnes's big sister Margaret took off at sixteen she did nothing more than sigh knowingly, as though this was merely confirmation of all her suspicions.

Brakey lies all evening on his bed. The TV murmurs through the wall. Church music wafts across the yard. He thinks of the two houses as becalmed, subdued, as though the life is mostly gone from them. He imagines the Larwoods sitting around in silence with only the strange chuckle of the kero heater between them when the music gives out.

He neglects his homework and falls asleep reading about Spartacus and six thousand crucifixions.

At the bus stop next morning, in the shade of the red flowering gum, he feels her looking at him. She's a few feet away, separate from her little brothers and the snooty little private schoolers from round the yacht club, and she looks up scowling from her book again to drill him with her gaze. Brown. Her eyes are brown. He looks away as the bus creaks in off the bay road and the small crowd stirs. They climb aboard.

Brakey, she says so close behind him that he grunts in startled surprise. Brakey, what're you doing?

What? I'm on the bus.

This week. At night. Why're you following me around?

He half turns to her. She smells milky. Her teeth are grown-up teeth. There's sun in the short spikes of her hair.

It's bugging me, she says.

He licks his lips, considers denying it. Even plans to ignore her now that, across the aisle, a couple of heads have turned their way.

Sorry, he croaks.

Did you do your maths?

Nah.

Bugger. Thought you might—

Agnes doesn't finish because the next stop is up and Brakey's mate Slater is getting on. She sits back – he feels her retract – as Slater slouches down the aisle. Slater is a sex maniac. He blew up his mother's vacuum cleaner in the kind of experiment that a sane person would never have thought of. Half the school still calls him the Electrolux Man. He knows all kinds of stuff about porn but girls are a total mystery to him. Slater is fun sometimes but he is not a bloke to confide in. Agnes Larwood will have to be a secret. At school she's not a complete tragic, but she's not exactly popular either. Brakey knows he'll have to be careful.

School happens in a kind of fog. He doesn't really take anything in, not even the fact that Agnes sits two rows from him in maths. Nor does he see anything unusual in the cops turning

118

up during English and taking Brad Benson out and not returning him to class.

It was that man from the bank, says his mother. He jumped off
at the Big Hole. Everyone's talking about it.

Brad Benson's dad?

Found his car and his shoes. Still looking for the body.

Hell, he says, standing there on the verandah with the
orange juice sweating in his hand. Cicadas chip away at the
warm afternoon air.

They all run away in the end, says his mother, going inside
and letting the screen door slap to.

Hot with sudden anger, Brakey throws the juice, glass and
all, out onto the unmowed grass and slopes off. One day, he
thinks. One day I'll be one of em, Mum, and you'll be happy.

He walks aimlessly up the bay and after the best part of two
hours he finds himself, hot and dry-mouthed, heading back
past the yacht club with the sun low on the hills behind him,
his outbound footprints heading at him all the way along the
shore. He sees that the marks from his heels are deep and the
big toe of his left foot drags a gouge at every step. A few small
boats are out. He sees old Percy the commercial netter in his
long dory, head down over his oars. Some kids are sailing out
past the flats but there's not much breeze. He hears clunks and
shouts and laughter across the water. On the sand at his feet,
left by the outgoing tide, blowfish and jellies glisten in death.
He kicks them aside spitefully. He's tired now but wild still and
pent up.

In the lee of the yacht club, where the bush gives way to the
posh new housing estate, he comes upon Agnes Larwood as
she sits on the sand to pull on her old tennis shoes.

You're early, he says.

So are you.

With his bare foot Brakey nudges the gidgie lying in the sand beside her. It's little more than a broomstick with a five-pronged head. The barbs are rusty but the points are sharp enough.

Hear about Mr Benson?

He nods.

Terrible, eh.

Yeah.

Poor Brad.

I don't like him, says Brakey.

Me neither, but it's still awful.

Yes, he murmurs, suddenly ashamed of himself.

He watches her tie the laces of her old Dunlop Volleys.

What did you used to call them again? he says. In the old days.

These? Plimsolls.

That's it. Plimsolls.

You all laughed.

Yeah.

We were fresh off the boat, I spose, she says, pulling the hessian bag to her and slipping the cotton strap over her bare shoulder. The rank odour of it rises between them.

Real Poms, he murmurs.

Agnes gets to her feet. She brushes the sand from her shorts. The light is dirty now; it's much later than he's realized.

Mind if I . . . come along?

She shrugs. You've got no shoes.

I'll be right. You've got a lamp.

Suit yourself.

For a long time they wade the clear, sandy flats without speaking. Eventually she lets him hold the little kero lamp so that he
doesn't feel so useless. It means he needn't trail along behind
her for fear of stepping on anything or spoiling her shots.
There are a few crabs about but no cobbler until they work
their way back to the seagrass alongside the boatpens. Now he
wishes fervently that he had shoes. The seagrass is dark brown,
almost black in the lamplight, and the whiskery little catfish
are hard to detect against it. As Agnes spears three in quick
succession, and he watches while she pulls the poisonous
spines off them with the pliers, he wonders how many more
they're walking past without seeing at all.

Ugly buggers aren't they? he murmurs.

I spose.

Any time he tries to make even the quietest conversation he
finds himself slipping against the glassy intensity of her concentration. His stomach is growling now. The light southerly
freshens a little. The ripples on the surface make it harder to see
fish on the weedy bottom. Rigging pings against masts above
them and mooring lines begin to groan. The slop of water
against a hundred hulls makes him think of people eating. Back
at the clubhouse there's music. The smoke of a barbecue streams
from one of the sleek brick houses of the new subdivision.

The seagrass feels both slippery and gritty underfoot and
between his toes. Brakey thinks of all those times Agnes and
her family sought refuge at his place in the middle of the night.
He supposes it's why Agnes and he haven't really spoken for
years. It must be kind of embarrassing for her. He walks close
to her. He can hear her breathing now. Moths plop against the
light in his hand. It surprises him that the Larwoods are so
broke that Agnes has to spear fish every night to keep them
going. He doesn't know how much the dole is and can't recall

Mrs Larwood ever going out to work. Old Eric hardly leaves the house these days, as far as Brakey can tell, but when you do see him sitting out on an old kitchen chair under the flame tree, he looks like a man beaten beyond saving. Brakey wants to ask her so many things. He wants to eat something too, or at least run his hand through the stubble of Agnes's hair.

Then there's a sudden shock up his leg. He lurches sideways. The hot glass of the lamp kisses his bare thigh for a moment and he yelps shamefully and staggers shoreward without even waiting for Agnes. The pain is like having a rusty nail driven into the ball of his foot. He flings himself down on the damp sand and draws the light close so he can examine the puncture and the swelling white flesh around it. He's heard of old men having heart attacks and ladies having pethidine injections to beat the pain but he just wants to shit all of a sudden and have the luxury of writhing about for a while and swearing his head off. Agnes slops in out of the dark. On the jetty above them someone laughs and he's filled with sudden hatred for all these poncy new bastards overtaking Cockleshell day by day.

It was only a matter of time, says Agnes. You okay?

I'm bloody wonderful, he spits.

He gets up, flailing a moment to keep his balance.

Hot water, they reckon, says Agnes.

I'll stick it in me tea then, he says. See ya later.

Brakey hobbles off in steaming humiliation, half hoping Agnes will come after him. But she doesn't.

When he finally stumps up onto the verandah his mother comes out with a tea-towel in her hand.

Your dinner's cold.

Good!

He goes straight to the table, lifts the plate covering from his meal and bolts the food in a hot frenzy that feels as ridiculous as it looks.

Are you on drugs? his mother asks with uncharacteristic timidity.

Not yet, he says.

She steps aside as he heads for the bathroom.

Sitting on the edge of the tub to examine his throbbing foot, he wonders what his mother might make of him and Agnes Larwood as a pair. The Brakeys have always had an air of gentle superiority about the Larwoods. Ten-pound Poms and not just English but the kind with that awful accent. And the old man, Eric. In his day he was a professional rabble-rouser, a drunk, a basher. The Larwoods were always shabby. Since the old man abandoned them, Brakey and his mother have done it hard. The house is beginning to shed paint and timber around them. There's never enough money. They're pretty shabby themselves but he doubts that his mother will see herself yet on a level with the Larwoods.

He scans the shelves for something that might relieve the pain. Amidst the powders and unguents he finds some balm which looks promising for a moment until he realizes that it's the stuff his mother applies to her cracked feet every summer's evening. Examining the tube, he's appalled and excited to discover that the ointment's active constituent is urea. He knows what that is. Piss! His mother bastes her heels in piss every night and he's anxious about her feelings about Agnes Larwood?

He sits in the bath with the shower pelting his head from on high. His foot hurts like buggery but he's not going to say a word.

Long before morning, he wakes from a dream in which the body of Mr Benson from the bank washes in from the Big Hole. Somehow it's found its way around the granite bluffs and headlands to the harbour entrance and come all the way in to Cockleshell on some unholy tide. Brakey's there in the shallows with Agnes beside him. Her face shines with sunlight. Together they roll the banker over in his beige suit and the swollen face that confronts them is his father's.

Brakey lies awake until morning, remembering the week in the city last winter with the old man and his girlfriend, a handsome woman not much older than him. It was a trial, an attempt at beginning to close the gap somehow, to reacquaint themselves. But the week was a misery. What can you ever do to get past the feeling that your father's chosen somebody else ahead of you? The only thing worse than that week was the aftermath when his mother pumped him and primed him for details and he remained sullen and mute. He'll never do it again.

By evening Brakey's limp is gone and the confusion of the school day has left with it. He's waiting amongst the peppermints when Agnes comes along the shore, and when she stoops to light her lamp in the twilight, he strides out so abruptly in his ancient Adidas that she gives a startled cry.

You're a lunatic, she says when he reaches her.

I know.

Mind if I come along?

I have a choice then?

Course.

Least you've got shoes tonight.

They wade for an hour while Brakey tries to ask questions and she stalks the shallows too preoccupied to answer. She doesn't speak to him about anything besides the angle at which he's holding the lamp. Finally they're back ashore, tipping water from their shoes, with six cobbler in the bag. The water smells soupy tonight and the air is thick with mosquitoes. Brakey looks at the lamplight on Agnes's thin arms.

Remember that old canoe someone had here when we were kids? he asks.

She smiles and laces her shoes again.

I wonder what happened to it, he says. We used to pile into it, five or six of us. And I remember the time you caught that big mullet with your bare hands. You stood up holding it like it was some kinda trophy. We couldn't believe it.

Agnes stands up. She gathers her bag and gidgie.

That mullet didn't know what hit it, Brakey says, unable to stop talking now. He feels the words come up out of him like a sort of panic. He blathers on about how that mullet must have been a foot long and what a natural she was when it came to hunting fish. He keeps talking even after she sets off down the narrow beach leaving him to fumble at his laces and scramble in her wake. Everything he says shames him and confirms the awful fact that he doesn't know a thing about her after the age of eleven. In his childhood memories she's everywhere, but after a certain point it's almost as if she'd moved away. He doesn't know what she thinks now, what she likes, who her friends are. Nothing. Worse, he doesn't understand why he suddenly needs to know everything about her.

By the time he's caught up with her she's past his place and hers. He doesn't say a thing until they're beyond the music teacher's house.

Where're we goin? he asks.

I'm going to the Beasley sisters', she murmurs. You better wait down on the beach. You'll give em a fright.

Oh. Okay.

Or you can just go home.

I'll wait, okay?

If you like.

Brakey waits in the warm darkness. He hears a long, sad note in the distance. A cow? A seabird, maybe. He cocks his head and catches it again – a saxophone. Water laps against the shore and some seabird calls across the estuary. He scuffs the white sand underfoot to make sparks and he's so absorbed by the little flashes of static electricity that he doesn't realize Agnes has returned until she touches his shoulder in the dark and he gives out a yelp of fright.

Sorry, she says. Didn't mean to scare you.

You didn't, he lies.

They head back up the beach in an awkward silence. Brakey smells the kero fumes of her extinguished lamp. He's still tingling from her touch. He wants to reach across the dark gap between them and feel her skin. But he speaks instead.

Do the Beasley sisters pay orright? he blurts.

Agnes says nothing.

I don't even know what cobbler's worth, he says with his heart halfway up his neck.

Agnes kicks a few sparks up.

It's gotta be worth more'n mullet, eh.

Jesus, Brakey.

Not that there's anything wrong with mullet, he rambles, but she cuts him off.

Look, spare me the pity, willya, she says angrily.

Brakey stops in his tracks, stammering.

Listen! she hisses so close to his face that he can feel the heat of her breath on him. I don't sell the fish, orright? For your information, we don't need the money that bad. I'm not

126

out here every night feedin the family, if it's any of your business.

Okay, he murmurs.

Call it a hobby, she says. Stickin fish, it's a stupid bloody hobby.

Brakey wonders if she'll cry. He panics a little at the thought, but she doesn't cry. Agnes just sighs. A dog begins to bark a long way down the bay.

I don't even like it, she says after a moment.

But you're good at it.

Oh, Brakey, you're thick.

He stands there. The lights of the yacht club are visible through the trees. The sandspit out the front of their houses glows white. They walk a little way until the shadows of the old net posts loom up on the grass.

You're gonna ask anyway, she says. So I'll tell you. I do it to get away. Simple as that. These days, it's like the house is dead inside, like everything's gone, like even the air is dead.

I thought . . . I thought things were better over there.

The drinking, you mean. You know the story of the drinking? Mum's miracle? Her church and her, they prayed. Every day for six months they were on a prayer chain. And then, one day, he just packs it in, he gives it away. Hallelujah.

Well, that *is* pretty amazing, says Brakey, thinking to himself that anything that stopped Eric Larwood drinking had to be a miracle.

Yeah, maybe. But it's weird, you know. There's nothing left. It's like there's nothing left of him at all. And Mum's too blind to see it. You can see this puzzled look on her face sometimes, like she can't quite figure out how come everything isn't alright now. She's had her miracle – everything should be sweet. And I can't stand it.

Brakey sits on the remains of the old net rack whose smooth, silvery wood gives a little beneath him.

He doesn't bash her anymore, and there's no screaming and smashing and all the rest of it. You know what I mean. I don't have to tell *you* what it was like. But there's nothing left. The works, the union, Margaret, and now the drink. He's like a ghost. I mean, that doesn't bother me, you know, I like him like that. He's harmless. But *she* wants more. For Mum it was always the drink. Blame the booze for everything. It was never him. Well, now she's got him and she's miserable.

You miss Margaret?

Not anymore, she says. Margaret was Dad's favourite. He loved her more than Mum, not that Mum saw it. I don't blame her for going. But it's better without her. Except it's like a cemetery in there.

You ever think of taking off? Brakey asks. When you finish school, I mean.

Agnes is still standing. The prongs of her gidgie catch the light from somewhere far off.

My brothers, she says. I can't leave them. I'd never leave them.

Brakey longs to reach up and take her hand. He's almost sick with feeling. And then he just does it. He leans out and grabs her arm and feels for her hand and Agnes drops the gidgie in surprise and clouts him one before shaking him off. She steps back and finds the spear in the grass.

Sorry, he mumbles.

Doesn't matter, she says.

Shit.

I'll see you later, Brakey.

He's too flattened even to say goodnight. He sits there for a while. A shag or something flies past over the water unseen but for the way it blots out clusters of harbour lights a mile away.

He thinks about Agnes and her hot breath in his face. Did he ever long for his father the way he does for her? He can't remember if it hurt this much.

Walking home through the last of the peppermints, he brushes hair from his eyes and as he does he smells fish on his fingers, and much later that night, in the last long hour that he lies awake in bed, he sniffs his hand now and then, full of regret, sensing that the smell of fish will be all that he'll ever have of Agnes Larwood and that it would have been better to have nothing of her at all.

He wakes to screams from next door. It's like the old days. His room is swarming with weird lights. The splash of breaking glass. Somebody's thumping on the door, rattling the boards of the verandah. Brakey reels out of bed and sees the hot pink glow through the curtain. The Larwood place is on fire.

He pulls on some shorts and collides with his mother in the hallway. Before she can even get up off the floor, he's opening the door to the Larwood boys in their pyjamas. Their faces shine with light and tears. Behind them, down on the steps, Agnes stands with her back to him to watch her mother, a motionless silhouette, before the flames.

Back inside, Brakey's mother is dialling the phone in the dark. Reports like pistol shots sound off from the blazing house. The little boys flinch at the sound. Every wall is crawling with flame now. Brakey can't believe how fast it's going up.

He won't come out, says one of Agnes's brothers. Brakey, he won't come out.

Brakey hesitates a moment before threading his way through the boys and past Agnes on the steps. The grass is wet and cold underfoot. He runs a zigzag through the strangely illuminated obstacles between the houses until he's abreast with Mrs Larwood, who appears to be talking to herself. He's already past her before it registers on him that she's praying. Already, even as he runs, his cheeks are scorching. He doesn't know how she can stand the heat. He backs off a little and skirts around the rear to see if there's a way in, but as he crosses beneath the clothesline there's a terrible metallic shriek and a shock that puts him asprawl in the grass. The gas bottles. He lies there a while, his face stinging, the hairs on his arms electric with heat and light, and a second explosion slaps over him. Even the ground is hot now. He feels crisp lawn digging into his shirtless torso. Weatherboards warp and fall into the yard. He sees the garden hose slough off the tap, melting against the laundry wall, and knows there's nothing he can do for Mr Larwood.

When he gets back around the other side, Agnes's mother has retreated some distance in her nightie. Her hair is mad with light and her face is calm but she resists his efforts to get her to come across the yard with him to join the others.

Over at his place, Agnes stands on the verandah in her jeans and shirt and boots. The boys crowd against her, tripping over the bags at her feet, while behind them in the unlit house, Brakey's mother moves from door to window like a flickering memory.

Brakey has the rest of his life to remember Agnes Larwood and the hunger he had for her those weeks the year he turned fifteen. He'll live to see Cockleshell disappear altogether and the luxury estate, Spinnaker Waters, take its place. Until she dies, his poor lonely mother will punctuate all talk of human affairs with the tart summation that *they all leave you in the end.* Yet he often wonders about Eric Larwood, the man who wouldn't leave. They dragged the charred shell of him out on a vinyl sheet. Agnes and her family bedded down one last time at Brakey's place but nobody slept. Next day the Welfare people came and they were never seen in town again.

Brakey never gets to be much good with women. For the rest of his life he's awkward around them, aware of his propensity to blurt out the wrong thing at just the right moment, never quite certain of the point at which he's allowed to make contact. He has learnt not to declare himself. Never again does he reach out uninvited to touch someone lovely. He shudders at the memory of himself at fifteen. What a lurker he must have been, what a creep!

He lives in the city now with a job and a few friends. Everyone, he's discovered, winds up in the city eventually. Even Agnes Larwood. She's a surgeon – he's seen her listed in the phone book. He has no desire to meet her, in fact he dreads the idea for both their sakes. Because part of him still loves her and he couldn't bear the humiliation. And because her life would unravel as soon as they met.

He fears that one day he'll be standing at a crosswalk on St George's Terrace and there, across the road, in the waiting crowd, she'll be, even and regular and brownish, but older, striding toward him at the change of the light, and he'll step straight up to her, despite himself, and blurt out the question that's been waiting in him half his life since that night in Cockleshell, the question she should be spared at all costs. He just knows he'll say: Agnes, tell me, of all the shabby Larwoods spilling sleepy and dishevelled from the burning house that night, why was it that you were the exception? With all the shaking and screaming and tears, how was it you seemed dressed and ready to go, calm at the sight of the body on the sheet next morning, and so serene when the Welfare came and took you off? It's Brakey – remember me?

The Turning

RAELENE COULDN'T STAND being in the caravan another bloody minute. After last night, the girls'd hardly look at her. They just sat out in the annexe on their beanbags watching 'Sesame Street' so loud it took the enamel off your teeth. She was crook as a dog and her face hurt. She gobbed a couple more Panadol and started bagging dirty clothes, half of which stank of craybait and bloke sweat and Christ-knows-what. Then she humped the whole lot over to the laundry block, wincing in the light.

The park was almost empty. There were a few tent sites with surfers on them, but apart from those and a few old farts with Winnebagos and pop-ups, it was just the permanents now, the skeleton crew.

Fresh-mown grass felt good beneath her feet and over the green smell of it you could almost taste the sea. It was actually a brilliant autumn day. Sunshine felt pure and silky on her skin; it took her mind off the chipped tooth and her throbbing lip.

In the laundry a woman she didn't know was pulling clothes from one of those skanky beat-up washers and Raelene sighed. She was sick of conversations with people passing through. Nothing you said to each other mattered a damn because you'd never see them again.

Raelene dumped her stuff on the bench and the other woman looked up. She had long tanned legs and her blonde hair was pulled back in a silver scrunchy. She was good-looking. No, bugger it, she was better than that, she was beautiful.

Boy, said the stranger brightly. That must have hurt.

Raelene put a hand to her mouth. A twinge of shame went through her.

Took me weeks to work up the courage to have my ears done, said the woman, patting the flat brown of her belly. Isn't it worse there? Didn't it sting like blazes?

Raelene stared a moment before she understood. She touched the stud in her navel and smiled the best she could. She was suffused with gratitude, a warm rush of feeling that nearly made her bawl.

It was nothin, she murmured. Easier'n gettin a tat.

You've got a tattoo as well? I'm such a coward.

Raelene turned around. The tat was in the small of her back, just up from her bumcrack.

Handle With Care, said the woman, reading.

Raelene felt stupid then. She knew what a fuckin irony it was. She blushed for shame.

By the look of her, the look that said leafy suburb, Country Road, briefcase hubby, this woman'd wrinkle her little nose for sure, but she didn't smirk, didn't turn a hair.

My name's Sherry, she said.

Raelene could have hugged her. Sherry. She was no stuck-up bitch. She was a real surprise, out of the ordinary. The whole hour they stood there at the machines or pegging up clothes on the listing hoists outside, Sherry never once mentioned Raelene's face. Her laundry was all button-down shirts and silk boxers and delicate bras and cottons while Rae's looked bleached and butchered by comparison – tracky dacks, Yakka shirts, kids' pants with holes and paint stains. Rubbish. But Sherry didn't seem to notice. She asked how long they'd lived here and what they did in the off-season and how old the girls were, as if she gave a bugger. She asked about Max's boat and who his skipper was, and whether there was anywhere in White Point you could buy fresh asparagus. Then she talked about her husband Dan and his new job at the depot. He was the local manager of live export. He dealt with the Japs, mostly. They'd bought a house here. They had a good feeling. They were renting a van while they had the place painted. There was something squeaky clean about Sherry. She was all wrong for White Point and wrong for Raelene but you couldn't help but like her, love her even. She was too bloody good-looking, for one thing, too beautiful to be believed. But she had something special. She listened. She gave a fuck. There was kindness in her. Straightaway she was a friend.

That month, while Sherry and Dan rented the twenty-eight-footer beside the windmill, Raelene saw her new friend almost every day and when she didn't she missed her. Some mornings they walked over the dune to play on the beach with the girls or lie with them in the warm shallows of the lagoon. Sherry told the kids stories or helped them build sandcastles. She wrote their names for them, did things Rae was often too slack to bother with. While Raelene worked on her tan out of the wind, Sherry plaited the girls' hair and read to them. Rae lay there listening, laughing, basking in the company as much as the sun. She hadn't had such a friend since school and even then her friends were backstabbing bitches.

Sherry changed the mood of the van park. You could feel the atmosphere shift around her and it wasn't just that every man within coo-ee wanted to get into her pants. It was something deep. Some extra life to her.

Sherry's bloke Dan worked office hours which is why he and Max never met that month. When Raelene finally met him his face lit up with recognition. Sherry, he said, never stopped talking about her. He had short, dark hair and a square jaw like a swarthy Ken doll. That was it. The two of them. They *were* a bit Barbie and Ken. He was very handsome but a bit too well-groomed for Rae's taste. Max was a slob but at least he didn't have girly-smooth hands. In fact they were a different species. Dan was funny but polite. He was attentive without staring at your tits the whole time. He was comfortable with himself. Maybe, thought Rae, being the boss does that to you.

Max got up at three or four or five to go fishing. He spent afternoons down the pub or over at the clump of vans everybody called the Cesspit. He'd heard of Dan because his boat fished for the company and he knew about Sherry because nobody could stop talking about her. But he never asked about either of them. He wanted to know where his thermos was and what was for dinner and when the fuck his luck would change.

He'd always been Raelene's kind of bloke, the sort of man her sisters always had, the kind their mother flirted with, blowing smoke and wisecracks from the side of her mouth. Rae didn't go men who dressed fancy or slapped on aftershave. She was a bit suss about TV men who talked about their feelings all the time and men who cried gave her the screaming creeps. Right from the start Max was a bloke who didn't muck around. He never pretended to be what he wasn't. The night they met, at a twenty-first, he stared at her like a hungry man, like she was food, and it made her feel powerful. All night she had tingles knowing he wanted her. During the speeches she led him behind the pool shed and with his cold belt buckle flapping against her thigh and his hands strong beneath her she knew she had what she wanted. She couldn't keep him a secret more than a few days. He was twenty and loaded with cash from fishing and he bought them both tickets to Bali where they got trashed for a week and screwed themselves silly. When she brought him home her mother made a fool of herself and her sisters were jealous. Raelene didn't hold it against them – it was only natural.

But Max was getting a gut now. After years of slinging craypots his back was stuffed. There was no way he'd be able to hold her up against a pool shed anymore. His teeth weren't great and under his new beard his mouth was turning down at the sides like a man disappointed. Raelene couldn't pin down when it was that Max turned sour. Maybe when the girls came along. Or when he saw deckhands younger than him getting jobs as skippers. He said he wasn't the brown-nosing sort, that you had to know the right people and there was some truth in that, but Rae knew that Max pissed people off. In the pub they called him Aggro Max. He often came home bloody and sore, especially after a live game on the big screen. His brother Frank was a footballer and you'd think he'd be proud but he wasn't. Just the sight of Frank loping out onto the ground made him scowl and the slightest fumble turned Max into a maniac. At first people thought it was funny to hear him call his brother a fairy, a retard, a waste of skin, but Frank was a star, a local, and White Pointers loved him.

Raelene imagined that she still loved Max. When they made love the whole van rocked. Whatever kind of bastard he was, he still needed her. After all these years he had that hungry look, staring at her arse and thighs when she got dressed, and the feeling that gave her was something she couldn't explain, not even to Sherry.

Sherry wasn't the nosy type, yet she was a good listener and now and then, lulled by the sun and the lapping water, Rae let on a little about Max and her. There was something neat about Sherry, something prim, so she tried to shock her with talk about Max and her in bed. Sherry surprised her by laughing and countering with stories of her own, what Dan liked, what she let him do. Sex is a blessing, she said. She was unshockable. Even when Raelene told her about Max's temper Sherry seemed more thoughtful than disgusted. Rae held back a lot of details but Sherry'd seen her face. She knew.

Love conquers all, said Sherry.

I dunno, she said doubtfully. Sometimes I don't think so.

You just need a little faith to see you through, Rae. You're a good wife, a good mother. Everything happens for a purpose, you know. You'll be alright, I just know it.

Talk like that heartened Raelene. She came away feeling good about herself and she stood in front of the narrow mirror and saw that she was still pretty. Smoking had left pucker lines around her mouth but her tummy was flat and her skin was clear and tanned. She was the same dress size she'd always been. She was no Sherry, though the boys from the Cesspit still paid her close attention whenever she walked by, and compared to some other women in town, like the girls in the Tuesday night darts team, she was a deadset trophy.

Raelene never did convince Sherry to come along to darts night and in a way she was glad because it meant that she didn't have to share her with the others. Rae didn't give a bugger about darts. Tuesdays were just a night out in a town where there was nothing else to do. Her teammates were rough old boilers in tracky dacks and stretchknit tops. They were good for a laugh once a week but they weren't really friends. They were proof that the further you let yourself go, the better you needed to be at darts. Rae was just making up the numbers. It was fun to imagine Sherry there, even if it was better that she didn't come.

When Sherry's place was ready and the removal truck had come and gone, Raelene spent three days helping her move in properly. The house was a big, brick joint, the sort that a middling kind of owner-skipper would build. Sherry and Dan had nice things – a glass table, white leather couches and a kingsize bed. While she and Sherry chatted and worked from room to room, the girls played in bubblewrap. They chased Sherry's cat and climbed in and out of boxes. They begged Sherry to tell them more of her stories, and she obliged them as she could. The girls always wanted David and Goliath or Jonah and the Whale. Sherry held them spellbound.

When Raelene got home from the third day the caravan was a mess and so was Max. He'd kicked the mirror out and there was blood all over the floor. The whole time she was washing and dressing his cut foot he pissed and moaned about coming back to an empty home and having to heat up his own lunch again and when Rae laughed at him for being so bloody stupid he clouted her in front of the kids. When he was gone, limping off toward the Cesspit, she settled the girls down, cooked them spaghetti on toast and bathed them in the sink before bed.

She was asleep when Max came home. She woke with his finger in her. He stank of beer and bait and sweat and, tired as she was, she opened up to him out of sadness. She could have shrugged him off but she couldn't be bothered. At least he was gentle and with his hands on her breasts and his belly against hers there was no harm in it and even a shadow of original feeling, a faint and momentary comfort that didn't claim her attention long. She lapsed back towards sleep and in that softened, dreamy state she felt like a kid again, lying in the back of a station wagon on a night drive home, the roar of the surf from the other side of the dune like the roadnoise in the wheel-arches, and the light flashing on Max's head as he rocked in her so like the blink of streetlights falling by. Raelene surrendered to the feeling. She floated warm and safe in something familiar, almost asleep again until she surfaced with a jolt and a cry and realized that she was coming despite herself and the sensation was like the mild shocks you sometimes got from the badly earthed taps in the shower block, and when the spasms passed and Max continued to labour away on his own behalf, there was such a wash of relief that she lay back immune, vaguely hearing but not taking in anything he said through his clenched teeth as sleep consumed her.

When she woke it was five o'clock and Max was gone. She stretched, luxuriating in the sudden spaciousness of the bed, and slept on until old man Harrison's mower came by at ten.

Sherry came by at noon and said nothing about the pancake foundation on her face. Rae knew she looked like a bad job from the panel beater. You could see it in the girls' faces. Sherry just hugged her and helped her pick up around the van before Max's boat got in.

In the afternoon, while Max ate his steak and eggs in weatherbeaten silence, still in his singlet and shorts and seaboots, Rae wondered about Sherry, what it was, apart from looks, that she had. It was a bit of a mystery.

On darts night Raelene left an hour early to drop by Sherry's on the way home. When Sherry came to the door she seemed alarmed. She held Rae by the shoulders and inspected her face, and it was only when she satisfied herself that there was nothing wrong that she relaxed and asked her in. Dan got up from the couch and offered her coffee, went and made it himself. For an hour or so Rae regaled them with tales of the darts girls. She stank of beer, she knew, and she smoked her Benson & Hedges and they gave her a saucer as an ashtray and were too decent to wave the smoke away. She wondered if it was money that made them different. But plenty of fishermen made loads more than Dan; it couldn't be that. She went home happy but puzzled.

Raelene made a habit of dropping by on darts night. Dan and Sherry were usually still up, watching TV. Some nights she was weaving a bit when she arrived but they didn't seem to mind. There were times when she knew she was pestering them, when she really was a pain in the arse, and once or twice, when she was completely pissed, she felt herself trying to provoke them like a bloody teenage daughter, but they remained unfailingly polite and courteous. Deep down Rae sensed that she wanted something from them. She just didn't know what it was.

One Tuesday she came by late. It was after eleven and the lights were out. When Dan came to the door he was only in his boxers. He looked startled, embarrassed. He said her name so loudly that Sherry appeared in the hall behind him with her lipstick awry and her hair all rumpled.

You've been at it! she yelled.

Would you like to come in, Rae? asked Dan.

Don't think so, said Raelene. It wouldn't be fair.

Sherry began to laugh. She tossed her gorgeous hair and stood there in her lace teddy a second before clapping a hand on Dan's shoulder and drawing him back from the door, smiling all the while at Rae and wiggling her fingers goodbye. For Raelene there was nothing for it but to pull the door to and walk back out into the quiet street laughing. But by the time she got home she felt desolate. She wanted what they had, that special something, and when she looked down at the outline of Max snoring in her bed she bawled quietly and the effort to keep silent hurt worse than a beating.

When Sherry didn't come over for a couple of days Raelene felt frantic. The first real cold front of the season came through and rain drove in off the sea. The swell spewed mounds of stinking kelp and seagrass onto the beach and all the boats stayed in, shaking and lurching at their moorings like chained dogs. Max was around the whole time, scratching his beard, eating and farting and sulking, and the girls got on Rae's wick, whingeing about going outside and needing the toilet, while all day every day the rain pissed down.

Why can't we have a bloody house? she screamed over the TV and the wind and the squalling girls. With a toilet, for fucksake, so we don't have to walk a hundred yards to have a shit! I mean, how bloody hard is it?

Max didn't even answer.

She trudged across puddles with the girls and bowed before

the rain. While each of them sat in a cubicle swinging their legs she tried to light a little joint she'd been saving but the bastard of a thing was too damp to catch so she ate it instead and five minutes later puked it back up.

Raelene couldn't stop thinking about Sherry and Dan. She was hooked now. Maybe even in love with them. The weird thing was that she felt no envy, not the hot green bilious envy you'd expect when you saw their stuff and their doll-like looks and what they had going between them. When she was with them they didn't make her feel low, they didn't rub her nose in the mess she was. They lifted her up somehow. They were kind of straight and maybe they wouldn't last long in White Point but she felt different with them.

There came a Tuesday when Raelene blew off darts night altogether and just went straight to Dan and Sherry's. When they let her in, surprised to see her so early but not at all reluctant to greet her, she saw that beside the empty plates and glasses on the dining table there were books open. Not just books – they were Bibles.

Raelene began to laugh. She heard herself, she sounded like a bloody madwoman and she wished she was drunk.

No darts tonight? asked Dan, putting the kettle on. His black hair was just too fuckin perfect.

Cancelled, she lied.

Feel like some gnocchi, Rae? asked Sherry. There's plenty left.

No, said Raelene, unable to settle, to sit, to look them in the eye.

She knew things about them, what they did in bed, what labels they wore, the kind of towels they bought and the sort of fabric softener they used and even, having laid the paper in them herself, how their bloody bathroom drawers were set out, but she suddenly realized that she didn't know them at all. She blinked like an idiot and thought about it. All the stories Sherry told the girls. Rae'd thought of them, if she'd noticed them at all, as old-timey tales, adventure stories. But it was church stuff.

So it's this, she murmured.

This? said Sherry, sitting and crossing her lovely legs and raking her fingers through her hair.

This! said Rae. She slapped a hand down on one of the Bibles.

Oh. That! said Sherry with a laugh.

Raelene felt the ricepaper cling to her sweaty fingers. She had to shake the thing free and she left the pages badly crumpled. Shit, she mumbled. Sorry.

It's fine, said Dan, shrugging.

I wondered what it was.

The Bible, said Sherry.

I know what the bloody thing is, she said, catching herself. I mean, I wondered what made you different, what it was you had. It's religion, isn't it?

Well, faith, yeah, said Dan with a nervous smile. That and plenty of Vitamin C.

Dan, said Sherry in the mildest scolding tone.

Raelene began to cry; she couldn't help herself, she didn't know why she was doing it. Sherry led her to the couch and held her. She smelt of garlic and tomato and Givenchy and Rae felt her patting her hair and stroking her neck while she howled. She was aware of Dan still in the room, of Sherry's body firm and cool against hers. It was like a trap, as though they'd been expecting this, and now was the moment they'd fall on her and drag off her blouse and reef up her skirt and hold her down for each other, whispering weird shit at her like on the movies and the sick thing was that she was ready for it. She wanted them both, wanted to *be* them. For a moment she didn't care if they killed her, even, as long as it was over quickly.

But nothing happened. Nothing more than Dan bringing her a cup of tea and Sherry reaching for a box of Kleenex. In the end, out of a kind of dismay, she stopped blubbering.

You look so tired, said Sherry.

Tired of my fuckin life, said Raelene, chewing her lips.

Well, what about Max? How about the girls?

I'm a shit mother, you know that.

You two wanna go for a walk? asked Dan.

There's nowhere.

The beach? The dunes?

I'm bloody stuck. I'm fucked.

The moon's out, said Dan.

I can take a hint, Dan. I'm goin, orright?

Don't be silly, said Sherry.

But Rae was on her feet now and her blood was up. She shook Sherry off and waved her arms at whatever it was that Dan was saying and launched out into the yard and the street where there was no one, only a salty wind.

Because it was still early, and she'd been bawling till her eyes felt lumpy and swollen as balls of sago, she could hardly waltz into the pub or just give up and slink home with Max still awake. So she went to the beach anyway, walked out along the great white sandspit that bordered the lagoon. Dan was right, the moon was up. It washed everything ghostly-bright. The air had a real winter sting to it. She was way under-dressed. Breaking waves flashed on the reef, flickered like her thoughts.

She *was* tired, yet it wasn't ordinary fatigue. It was a deeper exhaustion. She was sick of herself, appalled at what she'd been thinking only minutes ago, ashamed of what she was, a mother who didn't much care. Maybe someone like her didn't deserve better than Max. She didn't love him at all. But she was too scared to leave him, and not just because she was afraid of what he'd do to her or the girls if she did. No, she was really more frightened of being alone. The girls'd never be enough for her. She needed a bloke, she hadn't been without one since she was thirteen years old and now it was just unthinkable. The only way she'd leave Max was in the protection of another man. She needed a rescuer. She couldn't go alone. And in a town like this the available men were fat-gutted skippers whose wives had already left them or the adolescent deckies in the Cesspit across the van park. There was nobody. And now she'd have to endure it without even the comfort of friends.

When she got home, shivering and heartsick, Max was out to it and the girls needed extra blankets. She sat between their bunks and felt the contours of their bodies under her hands. She felt so low it almost hurt to breathe. She wondered if one day she'd ever work up the guts to top herself.

Late next morning Sherry dropped by but Rae saw her coming and retreated with the girls into the van. While the other woman knocked and called, Rae lay under the table with her hands over the girls' mouths. When Sherry was gone Rae went into a cleaning frenzy, scrubbing and scouring until her hands burned. The girls looked on bewildered. She roasted a chicken for Max's lunch and wore her sluttiest little dress, despite the weather.

The sun came out next day and Sherry found her making

Play-Doh with the girls. She seemed uncomfortable, anxious, and several times tried to shift their stilted conversation away from the good weather or the comings and goings of people in the park but Rae cut her off. For half an hour or so they just played with the kids and said nothing at all.

Raelene watched Sherry closely, saw the attention she lavished on the girls, how she always had her hands on them. She wondered if Sherry and Dan were able to have kids. Maybe they couldn't. Maybe that's why she befriended her, to get hold of her girls. They weren't your ordinary people, that's for sure. Maybe they were from some kind of cult that preyed on people like her. But then she caught herself. Jesus, she was sounding nuts now. Only yesterday she was crawling around in her own caravan, lying on the floor, hiding from her own best friend.

Sherry didn't come by the next day, nor the days afterwards. Raelene felt herself sinking. Her recent efforts to please Max fell away. She bought a fifty-cent Bible at the junkshop next to the bakery and spent the rest of the week reading in fits and bursts that made her head ache and caused her to grind her teeth in frustration. She found a couple of stories the girls liked but they were buried under whole avalanches of stuff so boring, so impossible, you could scream. The whole business made her wild.

On Tuesday she gave darts the flick again and went over to Dan and Sherry's. They seemed surprised and relieved to see her and they'd barely let her in the doorway before she launched into them about religion, about how she didn't believe a word of it and how sick of bloody hypocrites she was. She gave it to them about the Pope and George W. Bush and the priests who abused children and it just didn't help matters that they kept nodding and agreeing. She ran out of puff. Dan put the kettle on.

You never have any booze in this house, said Raelene, laughing to mask her awful embarrassment.

That's . . . there's a reason for that, said Sherry, smoothing down her skirt.

Because you're churchy, right?

Actually, said Dan, it's because I'm an alcoholic.

Oh. Jesus. Sorry.

Dan smiled, folded his arms.

White Point's a kind of second chance for Dan, said Sherry. For us.

That's why you don't work, Sherry?

Sherry shrugged.

And that's why the religious stuff?

Partly, said Dan. Booze leaves a pretty big hole.

A higher power? That kinda thing?

More or less.

We're kind of finding our way, said Sherry.

Shit. Raelene began to laugh again.

What?

I thought . . . I thought you were gonna kidnap me. It's so stupid.

Well, said Sherry, we had considered it.

Raelene fell into fits and Dan made the tea. They talked until midnight and Rae left restless, ashamed, full of yearning.

Raelene kept up the charade of heading off to darts night but she never actually went. In addition to spending every other morning with Sherry she put in a whole evening with Dan and her on Tuesdays. It was something to look forward to because what they talked about – argued about, most of the time – made her mind race. They prattled on about whether people were basically good or evil at heart. For a whole night they talked about souls and Dan confessed that he believed animals had them. Homosexuals were a troublesome topic. Raelene found herself arguing against their being consigned to Hell, even though she didn't much care for poofs, whereupon Sherry expressed doubts about Hell itself and Dan brought his Bible out and there they got bogged down.

Raelene warmed to the idea of Jesus and the business of forgiveness. The word *sacrifice* gave her goosebumps, reminding her of gory midday movies from childhood. She could see for herself what all this guff had done for Sherry and Dan; it was the thing that lit them up and she leaned toward it, even pined for it. If they'd been plain, homely people you'd have to dismiss everything they believed as weakness, as consolation, but they were beautiful. When someone as sexy as Sherry talked about becoming whole you had to take notice. Yet for all her yearning Raelene was not convinced of the details. She appreciated the sense of it – well, some of it – but she didn't *feel* anything.

Even so there was a time on one of those walks home along the stormy beach when there was no moon out and you could sense the heavy cloud but not see it racing inland and you only had the pale, vague strip of sand to navigate by. Rae found herself walking with her hands outstretched, overcome by the apprehension that she was about to stumble into something on the smooth, empty beach. She became breathless, panicky, and just as she'd started muttering aloud, talking herself down from this queer spin she was getting herself into, a patch of stars opened up low in the sky ahead of her and stopped her in her tracks. At first she thought of a shimmering bit of cloth, like a piece of the dress her mother once got from a bloke she almost married, but the image didn't last because she went on to thinking of candles and lamps and campfires and she felt woozy for a moment as if she was in the clouds herself and looking down through a gap to see the fires of a thousand desert camps. There were lights impossible to count and around them, in her mind's eye, people huddled, all of them searching like herself, afraid, wondering, looking into their fires, with the sky a blank over them. She didn't know why she thought of deserts and campfires except for the reading she'd been doing, all those name-strangled stories from the Old Testament that left her cold.

That night in bed, still rattled by the dizzy moment on the beach, while Max honked and farted beside her, she remembered a night from childhood. Other fires. A long, flat estuary and the shadows of trees and the smell of prawns cooking. Crabs on the boil. The smell of mud. Mosquitoes. The whole beach strung with lamps and campfires, so many families out there in the dark dragging nets through the water and laughing. And out of the darkness a man singing. A high, lovely voice. So slowly around it, like the tide rising, the sound of others joining in, men's voices, children, women, the whole night singing. But still at the core of it, that high sweet voice, her father's, faceless forever in the dark.

The cray season wound down into the last lean days of May. It hadn't been much of a season to begin with but now, with four weeks left and the water cold and the swell up most days, Max came in shitty. He was on two-day pulls; he should have been mellow but Rae could see he'd be looking for work in the off-season and the prospect made him nasty. He snarled at her, turned his nose up at her cooking and pissed his pay away at the pub. In the first week of June his brother quit football, just walked. It was a scandal. Max put a bloke through the window of the pub. There was talk of him pressing charges. He pushed Rae's face into the fridge door and her eye came up something awful.

While her shiner was still puffy Raelene drove Sherry to Perth with the girls for a day. The country was green again, the light soft and grey. The girls slept.

You know you should leave him, Rae, said Sherry. I have to say it. I couldn't live with myself if I didn't say it.

Raelene was shocked. She put a hand to her eye. She'd really bogged the make-up on but it hadn't fooled anybody. Having Sherry say this – it was like a betrayal. She'd never once judged Rae before.

I'm saying it as your friend, Rae. I mean it. We could get you somewhere today, someplace safe.

I've got no money.

I'll give you money.

You're *paying* me to leave him?

Rae.

What about love conquers all?

Nobody has to put up with—

And commitment? And forgiveness? All that stuff you talk, it's just talk then?

No, Rae.

Raelene suddenly felt like shit. It was worse than being hit. But she refused to give in and howl. She looked out at the road. This was her day in town.

In the city they trolled through boutiques and sat in cafés and let the kids arse about on escalators in department stores. They were careful with each other, subdued, but Raelene enjoyed herself. She came upon a shop that sold only religious stuff, books and crosses and statues of Mary. Sherry was amused by its gaudy window display but surprisingly reluctant to go inside.

A shop full of holy hardware, Rae. It's not really me.

I don't get you, said Rae. C'mon, it'll be fun.

I'll buy the girls an icecream, said Sherry.

Annoyed and bewildered, Raelene agreed to meet outside in ten minutes. She went in and checked out the books on prayer and the beads and the photos of the Pope in his bubble car. There was a whole table of statues, mostly Mary and the baby Jesus, and some with Christ holding his heart half out of his chest. Lying flat were several crucifixes with a suffering body on them. Always the crown of thorns, dabs of blood, a big, tanned, manly chest, a loincloth. Beside all these were snow-domes, the kind of thing you shook to make snow. They featured nativity scenes, mostly, but one in particular caught her eye. It was Christ walking on water. She knew the story. Yet it wasn't the setting that captivated her, nor was it the fact that the blizzard you created when you shook the little dome was not snow but a descending cloud of tiny white doves. She was seized by the look of him, his hair flying in the wind, the robe pulled back from his chest. He was all man.

She bought it and when she saw it Sherry gave a wry smile and just shook her head.

On the drive home they relaxed with one another again. Sherry talked about her old job as a legal secretary, told her how the drink had cost Dan the biggest job of his life, how humiliating it was, what it was like to see a man reduced to an incontinent, screaming mess.

And you didn't leave him, said Rae.

No, Sherry conceded. I never left him.

They drove in silence for a bit, the girls exhausted and dozing, the paddocks falling by, rolling green beneath a haze of rain.

The born-again business, asked Raelene. What's it like?

Sherry sighed thoughtfully. Well, she said, it's about getting into—

I don't mean what it's about, Rae interrupted. I mean, what it *feels* like.

Sherry glanced at her, confused.

The moment you suddenly got it, when it clicked, said Rae. You know, the change. When you turned, or whatever you call it.

Oh, murmured Sherry, that.

Yeah, said Raelene half laughing. That.

Well, it *was* a moment, actually.

Just curious how it felt.

Like a hot knife going into me, murmured Sherry sounding all foggy, a woman with her pillow voice on. Like . . . like I was butter and here was this knife opening me up. That's the best way I can describe it.

Raelene could only nod, saddened but somehow fortified in the knowledge, the confirmation this gave her, that she didn't believe. She'd come near, she was sure. From desperation, from outright need. Times when she and Sherry and Dan talked she felt tantalizingly close to some kind of breakthrough. True, she was often overwhelmed by emotion at their place, but that was, she now realized, just friendship, mere love. And once, walking home, there were the stars, that heady moment. That was the closest she felt. For a few days she'd thought she was only an arm's length, a breath away from copping something. But there was no piercing moment, no sudden unmistakable *feeling*.

You're happy, then? she asked. You and Dan?

Lucky, said Sherry. Grateful. Very happy.

Rae thought of them, doomed to drink orange juice and

endless cups of tea with awful secrets and lost careers behind them, childless and peculiar, stuck in a shitty little joint like White Point after what they'd done and where they'd been. Still happy. Unless they were fakers. But she doubted it. She'd watched them too long, too closely. She was, finally and indisputably, jealous.

By the end of that week there was no heat left in the June sun. Raelene dug the warm clothes from the bottom of the closet, all the sexless shrouding gear she hated, the girls' nylon dressing gowns, their winceyette pyjamas, the whole lot stinking of mothballs bad enough to make your eyes water. The sea was up so often Max hardly went and when he did the catch was never enough to cover fuel and bait; they were losing money. He was around all the time and with the rain thrashing the roof and walls day after day, the caravan felt like a 44-gallon drum they were all crammed into.

The few days Max went surfing he came home sated, almost content, but the rest of the time he was just simmering. Rae was glad when he had ropework to do at his skipper's shed, even relieved when he drifted over to the Cesspit to get wasted all day with the single blokes.

After her trip to the city Raelene didn't see as much of Sherry and Dan. She knew they were puzzled but she felt a distance between her and them, something she couldn't bridge. Only rarely did she drop by on a Tuesday night. More often she rugged up in her mothbally coat and walked the beach alone. She looked at stars when they were out but never felt any dizzy moments again. She thought about her father once or twice, wondered where he was. He was just a hole in her life now, no more than a shape, something she wanted but couldn't really remember. By her bed she kept the little cheap-arse snowdome of Jesus walking on the water. She liked the dinky birds and his rock star hair and how his chest looked, bared by the billowing robe. He had real pecs and a six-pack. Like a bodybuilder. He was ripped. After a few Bundy-and-Cokes she liked to think of him in his little dome and her in her little aluminium box, both of them trapped.

She was painting her toenails one afternoon, half watching the girls arrange their smelly cuttle collection on the old car seat they used as a sofa, when through the open flap of the annexe Raelene saw Max striding purposefully across the grass. Her skin tingled with alarm. She'd thought he was at the pub.

She got up to meet him, went out into the dull day, but he seized her by the arms and bullocked her back into the annexe. She felt the van slam into her back and head and he pinned her there.

Who is it? he hissed, bug-eyed with fury.

Who's what? she asked breathlessly.

Darts night. For fuckin weeks.

It's not what you think, Max, she said, conscious of the girls cowering nearby even if she couldn't see them with her head jammed back as it was.

Darts night. No, it's not what we thought at all, is it? he growled. Max's breath was rank with beer and smoke and his eyeballs were mulled up red as blood. So who is he, then?

Rae's arms throbbed where he gripped her. She thought of telling him the truth but it sounded so weak, so bloody awkward, and the bastard didn't deserve the truth, wasn't worth one honest piece of her.

Who the fuck is he? said Max, slamming her head against

the metal so hard she saw sparks rise between them, sparks and winged spots that floated and fell. She smiled at that. Thank Christ it's aluminium, she thought; be grateful there's a bit of give in it.

He roared then. He grabbed her hair and jabbed her back harder, once, twice, and the pain brought a sudden rage upon her.

He's bigger than you, Max, so be careful. You don't even know him but he owns you. He'll cut you to pieces, you fuckin coward. He'll come lookin, he'll suck the life out of you, he's every fuckin thing you aren't.

Max had both hands in her hair now. The girls were howling. She looked about for something to grab, to kill him with.

Tell me his name, you fuckin slut!

Raelene hit the van so hard it felt as though her eyeballs would spurt from their sockets. Her arms flailed above her as he slammed her back again and again. She felt the door edge, the hinge or something gouge her, couldn't get her hands to his stubbly face. She was powerless but for the smile that stung her mouth, sharp as a split lip. She had a name for him, her secret man. He was just the shape of a man but he was all man to her and any moment, when she got her breath back and her tongue steady, she'd spit that name in his face to see him explode. He'd go ballistic, do a complete fucking Rumpelstiltskin into the slab floor and she didn't care.

But the moment never came. Everything just stopped, like the power going off.

When she got back from the nursing post it was dark and the only sounds in the park were the spray of showers from the ablution block and the murmur of television from the sparse scattering of caravans. Raelene was glad she'd resisted old man Harrison's efforts to drive her home or anywhere else she wanted to go. She supposed she was grateful that he turned up when he did, put the girls in his car, carried her himself, got her seen to, but she grew weary of him threatening to go to the cops. All she could think of was the times she'd seen him fondling her undies as they hung on the line.

If Harrison kicked Max out now, evicted him from the park, she was homeless, the girls too. It was bad enough that the nurse was the sister of Max's boss. Raelene lied long and hard about the jagged gash and the great clumps of hair missing from the sides of her head. The older woman wasn't buying it, told her she was a fool, that she should be in hospital, should get away, get out while she still could. When she talked like that Rae felt lower than shit; you could feel the contempt in the woman's voice.

She sent Harrison back with the girls and let herself be stitched up in silence. When it was done she asked that the rest of her head be shaved while they were at it. The clippers were right there and her hair was such a mess already that she might as well start again from scratch. The older woman grumbled about being a nurse, not a hairdresser, but when Rae glanced at her she saw that the nurse was teary.

With her head so bruised, so tender, the buzzcut hurt more than the sutures, more than the bashing itself. Her hair fell in her lap, on the white lino floor, and she wept.

The short walk home did her good. The cold air stung but it cleared her thoughts. The sky was jammed with stars. By the time she got to the van she had her nerve back. She could face him. She could do absolutely anything.

She stepped into the annexe where the girls lay watching TV. Their beanbags were speckled with potato chips. The air was warm from the fan heater Harrison must have set up for them. She went on into the van and, as she expected, Max was gone. She sat on the bed, took up her little snowdome from the sidetable and shook it. A blizzard of doves. The girls appeared. They hung back in the doorway, afraid of her.

Mummy's had a haircut, she said. Everything's fine now.

She boiled them each an egg and cut fingers of toast to dip in the yolks, but neither would eat, so she filled the sink and bathed the girls and laid them in her bed and told them the story of Jonah and the Whale. As she curled between them, calming them, reciting the details of Jonah's deliverance even when she knew they were asleep, she could smell the horsey stink of Max in the pillow and was not afraid.

When the story was finished Rae pulled the concertina door to and cleaned up quietly. She couldn't face the shower block tonight. So she boiled the kettle and stripped to wash herself with a sink of hot water. The bruises were up on her arms already. She dragged on a tracksuit and looked at herself in what was left of the mirror. She looked like Joan of Arc, like a bloody nun. She refused to cry. She bared her chipped teeth. She looked fierce as hell.

She made herself a rum-and-Coke and sat out in the annexe to wait for Max. She watched TV with the sound off, was amazed at how fuckin pointless people were without their voices. Max's ute was outside. He wouldn't be far away.

By ten o'clock she'd had enough drinks and more than enough waiting. She pulled on a coat and boots and went across to the Cesspit. There were several rusty Land Cruisers and one-tonners parked around that nest of caravans. The vans themselves were set in a defensive formation like a bunch of circled wagons from a cowboy flick, and God alone knew what these scumbags were protecting themselves from. Their mothers, maybe, thought Rae, winding through junked bikes and pots and roobars and guyropes to the flap of the biggest annexe where the light of a TV flickered.

She lifted the flap and stepped into the vegetable fug of dope smoke. On mattresses and beanbags lay half a dozen deckies, none of them much older than twenty. Except Max. His head was back, his mouth open. Like the others, he was totally out to it. On the video screen two men had a woman on a shiny table, all three of them writhing pink under hard lights. Come on, bitch, said the one with a fistful of her red hair. The other slapped her arse muttering, yeah, yeah, yeah.

Somebody stirred on a beanbag, a boy holding a bong in his lap like it was a part of his own body, and he gazed at her openmouthed, squinting and blinking until Raelene stepped back through the flap into the pure night air.

Walking back she felt bruised and weary but fierce now and invulnerable. Like she'd climbed from some flaming wreckage an unlikely survivor. Spared.

As she undressed for bed she thought of calling Sherry. She wanted to tell her about this feeling, but it was late and she didn't want to return to the details of the rest of the day; it could wait. She was tired.

Just then the phone rang. She snatched it up.

Sherry?

Bob James, Rae.

Oh. Hullo, Bob.

You orright?

Fine, she said.

You sure?

Yeah, Bob. I'm sure.

Max there?

No, she murmured. You boys fishing tomorrow?

Yeah, said Bob. But, um, you better tell Max we don't need him.

A nurse isn't sposed to blab, said Rae.

Just tell him he's finished.

What about confidentiality?

Christ, girl, you got bigger things to worry about.

Why don't you mind your own fuckin business?

The boat is my business, Rae.

You're a bastard.

And you're a bigger bloody idiot than I thought you were, he said and hung up.

She put the girls into their own beds and thought about piling them into the ute and pissing off. But she was so tired. She lay on the bed to wait for Max. One look at her in the hard fluoro light, one clear glance at her now would strike him dead, she just knew it.

She tried to stay awake but the pillow drank her up.

She woke with him on top of her. He had her sore arms pinned and his pants were off. She struggled but the bruises made it hard. He grabbed her in the dark and slapped her. He shoved himself in her face, half smothered her until she got loose a moment and was halfway off the bed, her elbow snagged in the curtain, before he caught her and shoved her face down and hit the back of her head so hard she felt the gash open up. She didn't scream or cry out for fear of waking the girls; they'd seen enough already. She felt suddenly hot with love for them and said their names beneath her breath.

In the spill of light at the bedside she saw the little dome and her man upon the waves. She said his name, too, said it aloud with love enough to send a shudder through Max as he pushed her down. She knew she was safe from him now, not safe from tonight but gone from him altogether. He smelt of death already, of burning, of bile and acid. He was crying and she did not pity him. He was gone and it didn't matter when. Everything was new. In her dome it snowed birds as the van rocked, birds like stars. The moment Max speared into her and tore open her insides she was full of hot and certain feeling. She was free. She had already outlived him.

Sand

FRANK AND HIS OLDER BROTHER MAX walked behind the men
along the white beach at sunset. They walked for ages. The sun
boiled in the sea and the bare dunes turned pink. Tackle jingled and pattered on the rods over the men's shoulders. Frank
listened to the rhythmic clink of the lantern glass and fell into
step with it, singing under his breath: *hot cross buns, hot cross
buns*. Veins stood out in his father's legs. The men's footprints
were deep. They were like mouths with tongues of shadow
hanging out of them. *One-a-penny, two-a-penny, hot cross
buns*. It wasn't Easter but Frank couldn't get the song out of
his head.

Now and then Max darted ahead to walk amongst their
father's mates. He said things that made them laugh. He was
ten already and could make men laugh. He didn't miss their

mother. Frank knew he should shut up about her; it was only two weeks.

When they finally came to the rocks the men shoved pipes into the sand to stand their rods in and their father lit the gas lamp. The sun was gone but the sky was still light; it swirled yellow and green and blue like a bruise. When the tackle boxes opened he smelt whale oil and mulies. Frank watched his father tie on a gang of hooks whose curves flashed in the lamp-light. Around them the others muttered and smoked. They were just like ladies knitting, like his mother's friends. Max was down at the water's edge skimming shells out across the tops of waves that spilled across the shelf of reef.

Now that he was used to him, Frank loved his father. It took a few days every summer to like the sweet and sour smell of him again, to understand the dark cracks in his palms and the way he squinted behind the smoke of his fag. Frank watched him pick up a half-frozen mulie and stitch it up the hooks. Max came up and threw himself down on the sand between them.

Now you boys behave yourselves, he said getting up off his haunches. When the tide drops you can come out onto the reef with us, orright?

Can we play in the sandhills? Max asked.

Yeah, but don't go far. We might need someone to run the gaff out for us.

The other two men were wading out across the reef, the baits swinging in the last of the light, and before their father could join them they were casting into the gloom.

For a while Frank knelt in the warm sand to watch. You could see their heads and the curves of their rods against the sky. They were laughing. Moths came out of the dark to butt against the hot white glass of the lantern.

Max picked up the pack of matches that lay on the tackle box.

Let's go up the hills, he said, slipping the matches into the pocket of his shorts.

Orright.

They walked over to the steep foredune and clawed up it and on the other side the sandhills rolled on and on forever. Frank jogged behind his brother down into long gullies and for long stretches the sand was firm under foot. All the way Frank heard the matches rattle in Max's shorts. He breathed in time. He began to sing.

One-a-penny, two-a-penny—

Shut that up.

Sorry.

They ran until a wall of sand loomed and they kept at it until the slope made Frank feel they were running on the spot. In the end they clambered to the crest and straddled the knife edge of the dune so sand ran down the insides of their legs and spilled from the tips of their toes. If you listened hard enough you could hear the sand hiss as it slipped away. Max pulled out the matches and shook the box until it sounded like a rattler on a cowboy show.

What're you gunna do? said Frank warily. You had to be careful with Max. He had side teeth like a dog and a way of looking at you that you could feel in the dark.

You don't know what a blue flame is, do ya.

A what?

Watch this.

A match flared between them and Max lifted his legs and farted. Nothing happened until the flame scorched Max's fingers and he dropped it and left them in darkness.

That was it?

No, stupid.

Frank looked seaward. He couldn't see the beach or the grownups but the glow of the lamp was visible.

Max lit up again but nothing happened.

Here, he said, chucking the matches. Help me. Light one and hold it close.

Close?

To me bum, stupid.

When after several tries Frank got the match lit he saw that Max had slid his shorts off and was arched back with his bum off the sand.

Carn, hurry up!

Frank leant in and found himself peering at the dark squint of Max's bumhole. He began to tremble with pent up laughter.

Closer, stupid.

Frank took the flame right in but he wasn't very steady. He had the giggles now and something fizzed and Max recoiled with a howl.

You bastard!

Frank lurched to his feet. Max lunged at him and Frank spun away down the incline while his brother grabbed at his shorts. Frank could hear himself laughing as he went. Max was stronger and he could punch fast but Frank knew he could always outrun him. He spilled down into the hollow and found hard, flat sand as Max came roaring. The more he weaved and feinted the madder Max got. It was always like this, with him giggling nervously and Max bellowing behind. Frank knew how much Max hated him being faster. He could really duck and dart. At school lunchtimes the big boys always picked him for their footy team and they didn't care what Max said. Their mother called him Rabbit and she didn't care what Max said.

But the more he thought of Max behind him, boiling and spitting as he was now, the heavier Frank felt. He knew he could outrun him but the idea of Max got to his legs; the fear seeped into him and bogged him down until he just gave up and fell to his knees and waited for the flogging he knew would come. But when Max caught up he just sprawled out, panting.

I didn't mean it, said Frank. It was an accident.

His brother rolled over. A fat red moon emerged from behind the highest, farthest dune. Frank felt sand in his shorts. His undies sagged, full and bulky with it, the way they were the day he pooped his pants at school. He remembered the way he had to wide-leg it to the toilets. With all the kids laughing. And how he locked himself inside to wait for his mother. How Max came in and said he'd kill him if he didn't stop bawling and clean himself up. You're adopted, he said, they found you on the tip, in a kennel. The day went on forever and their mother never came.

Max, I didn't know how to do it.

Aw, shut up, said his brother.

It was an accident.

Orright, it was an accident. Let's dig.

Dig what? said Frank carefully. He was surprised at how fast Max was forgiving him and a little uneasy at how suddenly the moon had appeared.

A hole, dickhead. A tunnel. Like in the movies. An escape tunnel. We can come back to it, hide stuff.

Okay, said Frank, picturing it.

Over here, said Max. This bit's kind of wet and hard.

In the strange light of the moon they dug into the side of the bare white hill, just bored right in like dogs. They didn't speak. Frank was spurred on by the intensity of Max's work. He dragged away what Max scooped back between his legs and after a while all you could see was Max's feet sticking out of the side of the dune.

Funny, said Max, wriggling his way back out. It's quiet in there. You can't hear anythin.

Can I try?

Nah, you're too small.

Aw, Max! Please?

I dunno. Orright. Just a quick go. We gotta go deeper.

Frank wasted no time in case Max changed his mind. He wormed his way into the dark hole and was interested at how warm it was inside. There was an odd mineral smell but no sound, only his breathing. He lay there with his hand outstretched to touch the curved wall. Then he heard a hiss behind him. A bit of dry sand spilled against his feet from outside. There was a squeak and then more squeaks. It was Max walking around out there. He was climbing up the dune. No, he was stomping on it. Frank felt a thud overhead.

Max?

Frank got up on his elbows. There was another thud. A warm clod hit him in the back of the neck. Something fell in the dark ahead and a gust of air rose against his face. He scrambled backwards and was halfway out when it all came down on his head with a whoof and pinned him flat like the weight of a whole team piling in, going stacks-on-the-mill. All his breath rushed out and sand pressed warm into his eyes and ears and rammed against his tight-shut lips. Then his legs began to twitch; they flailed as though they didn't even belong to him. They writhed and churned in loose sand. His feet were free. His knees dug in so that his whole body could twist. Then he got an arm free and pushed up hard. The great heavy crust parted around his neck and he was out, on his feet, running blind and gulping in sobs of air and choking grit until he fell coughing, crying, alone on the sand.

Frank bawled until his eyes washed clear enough to see the

blurry moon. He saw the dunes all around him holding up the edges of the sky. Everything was white and woolly. Even his feet and arms were ghostly. He got up and ran. His feet chuffed in powdery sand. He was the only sound in the world.

He reached a crest and saw the dark plane of the sea flecked with moonlight. His chest hurt. It felt like he'd swallowed the earth but he didn't stop running.

When he saw the lantern he spilled down onto the beach, holding everything in. The men stood in the light with their rods and in their midst Max stood with a mulloway across his back, silver as a prince's cape, glistening from arm to arm, still wet and trembling. Their father turned with the gaff in his hand. The smile left his face. Frank wide-legged it towards them, apologizing all the way.

When an archer is shooting for nothing
He has all his skill
If he shoots for a brass buckle
He is already nervous
If he shoots for a prize of gold
He goes blind
Or sees two targets—
He is out of his mind!

His skill has not changed. But the prize
Divides him. He cares.
He thinks more of winning
Than of shooting—
And the need to win
Drains him of power.

Chuang Tzu

Family

AFTER THE SHIT FINALLY DIED DOWN Leaper chucked his board and wetsuit into the old HK and buggered off to White Point. It was four in the morning and he was still half pissed but there was no one out in the street, not even the dogged sportswriter who'd been camped outside in his Sigma since Sunday, so he went while he had the chance. He took it easy through the sleeping burbs and then as pony farms and market gardens gave way to the blankness of bush he began to relax a little. But the feeling only lasted a few minutes as fatigue overtook him and roos started appearing at the edge of the road so frequently and abruptly that he pulled over into a pine planta-tion, climbed into the back and slept in the jumble of stuff he'd tossed there in his haste.

He woke, shivering, barely two hours later. It was full

daylight and a winter mist hung in the trees. He climbed into the front. The image in the rear-view mirror startled him.

Jesus, he muttered. I thought you were dead.

The face scowling back at him was so closed, so drawn and bitter, that it might easily have been the old man's. Leaper felt flattened. He thought about driving back to the city but there was no food left in the house and the place was a stinking mire of bottles and pizza boxes. Back there the phone line was out of the wall and beneath a midden of dirty dishes and malarial sinkwater the mobile would be cactus by now. He couldn't bear to be there again. He'd left the TV on its back, wide-eyed and out of commission, like a kinghit wingman. Wherever you walked in the house there was a sinister crackle of newspaper underfoot, his season like a carpet, photos of him flying above the pack with the wind in his cheeks and his fingers splayed for the ball. Others of him with his hands on his hips, his head down, the coach in his face, all fingerpointing and gob spray, with the howling crowd at their backs, and in every room, though stained and wrinkled or even plain screwed up, there was that picture they printed and reprinted for days, with the back page headlines, the one of him walking, solitary, up the players' race with the game still in progress over his shoulder and the look of complete blankness on his face.

No, he wasn't going back to that. But this morning White Point didn't seem such a great idea either. What had he been thinking of? Family? Jesus, there was only Max, his brother, and a sister-in-law he'd never met, nieces he'd only heard about.

Leaper sat there a minute. He knew a surf would do him good. And right now, more or less sober for the first time in days, he couldn't think of anywhere else to go.

Two hours later he crested the ridge and looked down on the great train of dunes and the winter sea and the hamlet in the narrow margin between them. He was stiff and hungry but as he coasted through the main drag, low in his seat, he resisted the urge to pull in to the bakery or the servo for breakfast. Fibro houses and shopfronts rolled by. He stole a glance at the old baitshop that still bore his father's name and drove on down to the beach where the sand was white and hard-packed and the lagoon bristled with crayboats nodding and twisting at their moorings.

At the outer reefs that formed the anchorage, lines of white-water spilled landward with the rumbling, far-off noise of heavy traffic. Leaper drove around the beach to the wide spit of the point itself. A spray of terns rose in his path. He wound down the window to breathe in the salt smell. Even in the weak June light the glare off the sand was enough to make him wince.

There was nobody else parked on the point but out on the reef he could see the white flare of a board wake on a distant wave. When he pulled up he clawed the binoculars from the glovebox to watch the surfer carve lines across the smooth face until the swell hit the deep water of the channel where wave and rider subsided into the sea.

Leaper got out and stretched against the old station wagon. He was sore and lightheaded. The land breeze was cool at his back, and when he turned to put his face into it he saw the water tower from the caravan park rising bigheaded from behind the scrubby dune. It gave him a strange pang to see it again. He'd grown up in the shadows of its trestle legs. As boys, in that van park in the lee of the sandhills, the tower loomed over Max and him; its faded red tank was a bloodshot eye that never closed. From anywhere in town or from miles out at sea it was clearly visible, the home beacon. From what he could gather, Max still lived over there with his missus and kids on the same site and maybe even the same van the old man dragged up in the sixties. Perhaps he'd go over and visit. Maybe they'd put him up for a bit until he got himself sorted out. Before he got that far he needed to feel his muscles burn. He didn't want to run. He wanted the privacy of the sea.

He flipped up the rear window and dragged out his dusty board and laid it on the sand while he rooted around for the wetsuit. He didn't know if it was the cold or fatigue or simple nerves that caused him to shake so much but he had trouble getting the wetty on, and when he finally did he realized that he needed a piss, and because he was leery of sharks out on the reef and too cold to haul the suit off again, he just stood there and let go where he was. The hot flush down his legs brought an unexpected twinge of shame, a flash of the schoolyard that he buried in the business of waxing the board.

From where he knelt Leaper noticed that an osprey had built a nest on the water tower. It was new to him but the bird's guano-plastered wall of sticks was so well established that he suddenly sensed how long he'd been gone, just how many years stood between him and the boy he was when he learnt to play football on this very sandflat. Barefoot and bare-backed, he was the youngest of a feral mob of kids who roamed the town on their treddlies, haunted the jetty and played marathon games of footy with the sea and dunes as boundaries and only piled shirts for goalposts. Back then, the sandcrusted ball tore skin off his feet without him even feeling it. He ducked and weaved through the big kids and hung on the shoulders of grown men who laughed and said that he had springs in his feet. He was a natural. He had no idea that he was a freak. He only knew that Max hated it and he was late to the party on that front too. Leaper was so innocent that White Pointers thought he was dim, and looking back he wondered if maybe they were right.

With the board under his arm, Leaper jogged the few steps to the water and plunged in with a shout. For the first few moments he just put his head down and paddled to distract himself from the cold but after a few minutes he was comfortable enough to enjoy the dappled seagrass, the green sandy holes passing beneath him, the rhythm and repetition of the stroke, and the easy grace of his own body. There was something beautifully mindless in a long paddle or run or swim, a spaciousness he embroidered with whatever silly ditty came to mind to keep time. After the giddy relief from training, the muscles of his arms and back felt hungry for it again.

When he reached the inside reef he sat on his board a moment to find the passage through the limestone and coral. Whitewater pounded across the shelf and the gap was narrow. When he was through he began the business of duckdiving under broken waves until he reached the channel. There was a lot of water moving out here. He was five hundred yards from shore. The swell seemed to be picking up. He returned to the jittery feeling he had before he hit the water.

As he paddled, a lone surfer dropped down the face of a big, reeling right-hander with the kind of confidence that marked him out as a local. He jammed a turn hard up towards the falling lip and then seemed to hang in the wave's churning guts for a few seconds before a rush of trapped air spat him out. Leaper sat up in the channel to watch the rider come on in short, brutal signature turns until he slewed off the wave to settle in the quiet water beside him.

Thought I'd find you here, said Leaper with a grin he hadn't expected.

Well, I'll be fucked, said the other man without warmth.

How's it goin, Max?

Don't need a walkin frame yet.

So I see.

Long time since *that* board saw any saltwater.

Leaper nodded. A wetsuit did little to hide the fact that Max had stacked on some pudding, yet he still had his big deckie shoulders and his neck was like a straining-post. Max's hair was buzz-cut and he'd grown a biker beard that gave him a fearsome look and blurred his resemblance to the old man. Nobody would mistake Max for one of the friendly hippies who'd taught them to surf here in their early teens. His big brother looked savage and battleworn. There were pulpy scars on his eyebrows and a fresh dint in his forehead.

They sat there in the calm a few moments, turning their feet in the light-shafted water with the reef shadowy beneath them. Max regarded him with that sour, doubtful look of his.

So what's the story?

Leaper shrugged. I haven't been back for a while.

Christ, you haven't been anywhere for a while, from what I hear. The paper's full of it. They sack you?

I walked.

Fucksake.

Leaper smiled, but the skin felt tight on his face.

Frank Leaper. The White Point jack-in-the-box. A two-season wonder.

So it seems.

Jesus Christ.

Both brothers sensed the fresh set of waves that trundled in toward them. They swung around and paddled seaward in a response that was automatic. After the years they'd spent out here on the reef their sudden animation was instinctive; their bodies thought for them. Several big waves broke outside. They took them on the head, duckdiving with their boards to escape the worst of the impact. Leaper relished the sluicing concussion across his back; he loved the way the force of the water prised his eyelids apart and raked through his hair like a gale. He surfaced from each explosion of turbulence and paddled hard and fast, his limbs and ligaments lulled into some kind of boyhood recognition, until he reached the calm deep beyond the break and sat up blowing a little. He was light-headed and gripey with hunger but he felt unaccountably content, even at the prospect of dealing with Max.

His brother paddled past and sat some distance away. Leaper looked shoreward at the pink blob of the water tank above the dunes. He observed Max who fingered the water and stared out to sea. How would he talk to him, explain what had happened? And why should he bother; why did it matter? He'd spent his boyhood vainly trying to get Max's attention. He aped his older brother, adored him, followed him at school and on the beach, blind to the fact that Max was contempt-uous of him and had been from the moment he was born.

It was Max who introduced and fed the idea that his little brother was a bit simple. The fact that it wasn't true was obscured by Leaper's capacity to absorb and endure such meanness out of love, as though that's all it was, his cruelty, a mere test of brotherly love. He was, without doubt, naïve. Leaper instinctively believed the best of people, beginning with his family. In his mind Max was only ever joking. As a boy of eight, he really did think that their mother was only going on holiday when she brought them here to the old man one sum-mer, never to return. And he was almost twenty before he saw that, instead of hiding his feelings toward him, his father had no feelings at all.

Leaper wasn't so naïve anymore; he'd seen plenty in his two seasons of glory. But he didn't feel better or stronger for having been wised up. If anything he yearned for the unselfconscious part of him because, looking back, it was the only bit that felt authentic. This vigilant, grown-up version he'd been living was mostly an act. It was the reason he'd come unstuck this year in front of the whole country. He was certain of that; he'd had time enough to think about it. But what he thought might be achieved by talking to Max about it was a lot less clear. Even as he sat here he knew that his brother was part of the mess he'd made of himself – every minute in the water reminded him of something more that confirmed it – yet what did he expect from Max but the usual spitting disdain? You'd have to be a bit simple to persist with Max. And yet there were things to say. There was nothing to lose by saying them. Except maybe a few teeth and a bed for the night.

Another set bore down on the reef. This time they were ready. The brothers hustled and jockeyed for position and Leaper felt himself smiling with real pleasure at this instant reversion to form. He wasn't as strong as Max, but he was so much fitter that it should have been no contest except for the fact that he was out of practice. He pulled back and gave his brother the wave and Max launched into it with an expression that said it'd always been his. The old conviction.

Leaper sat in the spray with a bitter laugh. He watched Max's progress by the occasional flash of board or upflung arm that showed above the steady bending wave. Max still surfed with an angry intensity, a kind of misery Leaper saw in some footballers. It was the scrapping spirit of the bloke who played the percentages. No style, no natural flash, all power and no beauty. Max reminded him of the journeymen he'd played on, the ugly scramblers, disciplined triers. They were the ones who vented their frustration on the likes of him.

They weren't alike, him and Max. All their efforts were in opposite directions; it was what each of them needed to try for that caused the trouble. Trying. The very word was a provocation between them.

He hadn't missed Max. He stayed away from the old man's funeral; given the home-and-away schedule, he'd had excuses enough for not being there, but he didn't offer them.

Another wave reared from the deep. It seemed to stagger a moment as it confronted the shoaling reef, and a creaturely shiver ran along it as Leaper spun and paddled into his path. In a moment there was the old sense of being overtaken, of having been snatched up by something mighty, and he rose to his feet grinning. But before he'd even taken the drop and leant into his first turn, the wave was twisting on itself, hurling him out across the bubbling reef without the board underfoot. He hit the bottom hard and bounced across the coral reef in a welter of foam. When he surfaced, the board was tombstoning at the end of its leash and he could feel that he'd lost skin off his knees and elbows.

That was choice, said Max paddling by.

Stunned and winded, Leaper pulled himself onto the board and followed his brother back out to the break. He was surprised at the sudden flicker of anger that passed through him.

Some things are best left to the men, said Max when they sat up in the calm water outside.

Yeah, said Leaper. Whatever.

You never had the steel for it.

What? Football?

It's a man's game.

It's just a business, Max. You're so naïve.

Max glared at him, his beard streaming water, and Leaper felt his face flush with unholy pleasure.

You were soft, said Max with new feeling. You were a fuckin coward.

Leaper said nothing. He conceded that he was a lazy trainer and a lukewarm clubman, but he didn't shirk the hard stuff; it just never found him. He wasn't afraid of anything until the very end and even then, in the last awful, mid-season weeks, it was the very sudden and novel prospect of failure that scared him. The violence of the game didn't really register because Leaper had never been injured. There was all that talk of him being too thick to fear getting hurt – Max's old smear spreading beyond White Point – but it wasn't about being stupid because even when the rest of his game went to shit, when the ball felt like a sandbag and his legs like pot ballast, he still had a kind of spatial genius, his instinct for evasion.

So, what the fuck happened? Max asked, as if despite himself. There was an exasperation in his voice that surprised Leaper.

I couldn't do it anymore.

And what the bloody hell does that mean?

I don't really know.

That you *wouldn't* do it anymore. That's what it looked like.

Watching, were you?

Christ, you moron! You play for my team; of course I was watchin. Tearin my fuckin hair out. You just bloody stopped.

Leaper smiled. Max grasped at the water now, the tendons rigid in his neck.

I gotta live here, said Max. You're a bloody embarrassment.

But you hated it when I was good.

Fuck off.

Admit it.

Fuck off out of it.

Poor old Max.

You come here to blue with me? said Max with his pit-bull leer.

I dunno, said Leaper, noticing now that both his hands were bleeding.

You're a fuck-up.

Leaper could hardly deny it. Only a few months ago he was still the prodigy. But come March he was hot and cold – *enigmatic*, in the words of the commentators – and in April he'd become first a *disappointment* and then a *travesty*. There was no obvious source of trouble to point to, no knee reconstructions to endure, no contentious overpayments or distracting sex scandal. He was a mystery. His demise was as puzzling as his emergence. One week he kicked ten at a canter and the next he couldn't have earned a kick in a stampede. It just got worse. The crowd called him ordinary. The coach said he was rubbish. Players shunned him. Word was he wasn't trying and that was the biggest laugh of all.

Geez, Max, I thought you'd finally be happy. For once the whole world sees it your way. Vindicated, that's what you should be feeling.

You stupid little bastard. People dream of havin what you had. It makes em sick to see a spoilt prick like you walk away from what they couldn't have.

Just you, Max. Why don't you admit it? You're talkin about yourself.

You didn't try—

But that's what you don't get, mate. That's the whole problem.

You were more arse than class.

Fair enough. But I just played for fun, Max. I loved playing the game. Remember? Shit, *you* should remember. You hated my guts for it. Jesus, I was the only person you ever hated more than the old woman; it was like I was responsible for her pissing off as well as everything else. I was like some insect you had to squash.

You think you can take me? Max said, sculling closer. You reckon you can?

I dunno, mate. What's the point?

Won't or can't?

Aw, that again?

Why the fuck are you here?

I'm not sure. Maybe I wanted to say some things. There's nowhere to go.

You just walked off the fuckin ground. Up the race. In front of thirty-five thousand people and the TV. The country, you dumb cunt!

I couldn't play anymore. I told you. It was like the magic was gone.

Aw, and ya just dunno why.

Leaper washed the blood from the heel of one palm and looked at the cut a moment. It was nastier than he'd first thought.

Oh, I know why. It's no mystery to me, mate.

Fuck this, said Max, paddling for a wave after they'd let several roll through unridden.

Leaper turned and watched him go. For a long moment his brother's body was visible through the wall of water. The sound of all those tons of water falling was as huge as a stadium crowd. As he watched Max go, he wondered if he *could* take him now. Years of weight training had bulked him up; he was strong and quick and two years younger. And there'd be a certain satisfaction in dishing out a little of what Max had given him all through the years, the bullying bastard.

Leaper didn't catch any wave that came through. He was too churned up with thinking. Everything was arse-up again; it was just plain perverse. He'd had years to get past all this family shit and for a good while there he really had got beyond caring. He'd felt liberated. Those first two seasons he felt like an animal out of his cage. He played football unselfconsciously and lived the same way. Until news of the old man's death. The business of the funeral, and not going. It was about showing Max he didn't care. That was what poisoned him; it got into everything, this business of showing them. One ordinary game and then he wanted to show them he wasn't ordinary. Then he was showing the coach that he was trying. Jesus, it was all the showing and trying that ruined him. Because when he ran out onto the park not giving a shit, just excited to get a kick, to fly high and feel the mindless thwack of the ball against his chest, he was something inexplicable, something that delighted him as much as the fans. That's what left him when he played to prove every balding, wheezy lard-arse commentator wrong. The magic evaporated.

Wasn't that all he was doing here, hungry and tired and a bit chilled now at White Point – getting into Max's face, showing him he didn't care when it just wasn't true? Just having Max within arm's reach made him boil with memories. The time Max had tried to suffocate him in the dunes, bury him alive. The day at school when he shat himself and was locked in the dunnies while Max marshalled the laughing mob outside. Christ, if Max was shamed by last week's fiasco then why not enjoy his discomfort? But it felt poisonous. It took too much effort to keep it up. What he felt like was a cup of tea and about fifteen doughnuts in the warmth of Max's van. He wanted to see his girls. They were small, still; they'd smell of clean pyjamas and honey on toast.

Max paddled up beside him and cleared his nose horribly.

Won't surf either, eh? You're a case, Frank.

You still in the old man's van?

Took it to the tip.

Keep anything out of it?

Not much. What, did you want something from it?

No. Nothing. Hey, tell me about your missus.

Max scowled.

Raelene, that her name?

His brother nodded.

I was thinking of dropping over.

Don't, said Max.

It wasn't my fault I could play footy, Max. It wasn't my fault Mum did what she did. This is just stuff that happened to us.

You make me sick.

How come you're not working today? The cray season's not finished.

I got put off the boat.

Shit.

That's women for ya.

I really wanna meet her.

Don't come over.

Relax. I won't say a thing about you. Just had this urge to connect. You know?

Don't come. You can't come.

There was a strange note of urgency in Max's voice. Along with the fury there was a kind of pleading that Leaper couldn't believe.

Max?

Fuck off. Leave me alone.

Max paddled away a few yards as the dark lines of another set piled up in the distance. Leaper followed him out of habit, a reversion to old ways, until he caught himself and sat up. He was too tired for this, there was no point talking to him. Maybe he should just paddle in and go see Raelene despite him. But why bother? He didn't even understand the compulsion to meet her. Was it just to piss Max off or was he really curious about meeting the woman who'd married the bastard and was now family?

A surge of turbulence passed between Max and him, a sudden fattening of the water that caused Leaper to blink. His brother had his back to him, was still paddling away, when a bronze flash jerked him sideways on the board and drove him high in the water, spinning him round so that Leaper saw his open mouth within the streaming beard and the shark moiling beneath him. A second later he was all flailing arms that went under a moment until he surfaced in a pink smear.

Leaper didn't move. Max's teeth were tobacco-stained. His eyes were white. The straining cartilage of his nose was white. He sucked in a breath – it was as though he'd only just remembered how – and began to shudder before the whaler broke off and twisted away.

Leaper sat there.

Max groped for his board. It looked too short; it was half a board. Leaper saw the rest of it drift up the face of a wave that rose, tottered, and rolled past them unbroken.

You fuckin pansy! screamed Max. What're you waitin for?

Leaper hesitated.

Frank?

Leaper paddled into the spoiled water and took Max by the beard, tried to haul him onto his own board, but Max wouldn't be parted from the remains of his own, so Leaper towed him a way by whatever handful he could get of him, trying to get him into a stretch of clean water, but Max jerked and lashed so much that the sea churned with whorls and streamers of blood.

Frank?

Jesus, Max.

Leaper made himself get off his board and into the soup that Max was making.

Let go, he said. Max, let go of your board.

But Max wouldn't let go, couldn't let go. Leaper took his own board and wedged it beneath his brother. When he turned him shoreward he saw that one leg was too long and kicking out of sync, that below the knee it was hanging off him by a hank of neoprene. The wetsuit was slippery with blood.

Stop kicking! Stay still.

Leaper unstrapped his board leash and seized Max's thigh. While the rest of the leg went pendulous and heavy and half in the way, Leaper tied the thigh off as tight as the urethane cord would go.

Frank.

Just hold on, he said. I'll get you there.

Frank.

The shark's gone. We'll belly in across the reef.

Leaper held him by the buttocks and began to kick them shoreward. Max's head rose once, twice on his neck as if he was trying to look back.

I can do it, said Leaper. You'll be right now, you'll see. I'll show you.

Leaper saw Max's head ease down on the board. His brother's body shook beneath his own and he felt sick with triumph, with anger, from love. The water was thick as sand. Out past Max's head the tower showed through the spray of breaking waves. Swells overtook them. The tank was bleary, unblinking, above the dune.

Max trembled like a spiked snapper.

It was you, said Leaper.

Max said nothing.

You, he thought. When the grass went suddenly hard underfoot, and the ball forever out of reach, it was you lurking at the back of my mind. That's what fucked it, that's why I started to care. There you were, bro. Just the thought of you was a weight in my legs, and the more I cared the worse it was.

A bigger wave came upon them. Before Leaper could surrender to it he had to earn it. He kicked so hard he felt poison in his legs. But he got them the wave. Max's head was loose on his neck.

They bellied down the long, smooth face and beneath them the reef flickered all motley and dappled, weaves of current and colour and darting things that were buried with Max and him as a thundering cloud of whitewater overtook them. The blast of water ripped through Leaper's hair and pounded in his ears. The reef was all over him but he held fast to his brother, hugging him to the board, hanging on with all the strength left in his fingers, for as long as he could, and for longer than he should have.

Long, Clear View

YOU LIE AWAKE AND LISTEN to the rumble of talk through the fibro wall as it thins out into pent-up whispering. From the old man's sighs and your mother's patient murmur, you know that nothing's going right. The job, the town, the transfer, everything's off somehow. At school there are new boundaries you can't even see, lines between farmkids and townies, blackfellas and whites, boys and girls, gestures you just don't get. And they're all looking at you, the new copper's kid, as if you already know too much.

You pine for the city, the spill of suburbs you left behind and the way they absorb you, render you ordinary and invisible. But then you pull yourself up, knowing that longings like that are useless, as weak as wishing you'd never left primary school. You're not a baby. If you don't try to make a go of it then things will be worse for everybody. So you shut up and stop bawling. You go to school without whining and afterwards you walk alone to the beach or the harbour and try to keep an open mind.

But town is full of looks and nods and elbows in the ribs as though the place is too small to contain a surfeit of information. Locals have a way of talking across you, rather than to you. Adults raise their eyebrows and ruffle your hair with their teeth showing. You can feel their curiosity, their wariness, and it sets you on edge.

From the house at the crest of the hill you can see the whole town at a glance: the harbour, meatworks, cannery, grain silos and the twisted net of streets with their chimney-plumed houses. The longer you look out on it the more you sense it all staring right back at you.

It doesn't happen often but there are times when you have the house to yourself. That's when you go into your parents' room and take the rifle from the wardrobe. You just sit with it across your lap, there on the soft, wide bed.

The old Savage isn't much of a weapon, an old single-shot .22 with a battered stock and tarnished gunmetal, but you like the weight of it in your arms and the way its curves and contours feel shaped by many hands, much holding. It calms you down, that rifle. When you sight along the barrel the wood against your cheek is smooth. You narrow your vision to a piece of space the size of a fingernail and things and people enter and leave that little patch of light as you will them to.

You're not an idiot – you know all about firearms safety. Every time the old man is free he drives you out to some farm or other, and when you've filled the boot of the car with mallee roots for the kitchen stove, he brings the rifle out and you take turns knocking cans off a stump. The whole time he's drilling you about safety. You know about ricochets over water, about climbing through the fence with a loaded weapon. He's shown you grisly black and white photos of self-inflicted wounds, of gunshot corpses streaked with blood the colour of tar. Clear the breech. Check and check and check again. The safety catch is a fool's idea of safety. And you know from experience what a .22 hollowpoint does to a living creature. There's no such thing as a clean shot or an easy death. You've shot rabbits for the dog and killed foxes for farmers but you've got no more stomach for it than the old man.

Still, you love that rifle. But you take it seriously, and the gravity of a loaded, cocked weapon makes your hands tremble. You know it's old and ugly, yet you care about it the way you care for your dog, the kind of ravaged mongrel strangers will cross the street to avoid. You love it because it's yours.

You try to fit in but for weeks it's useless. You're nervous all day and at night you just lie there hearing more than you want to. Your little sister howls with colic across the hallway and even though you know she's stuffing her mouth with a pillow, you hear the old girl's muffled sobs through the wall. The mutt farts and groans outside your window. And at the change of shift there's the car in the drive and the creak of the stove door and the old man's shoes grinding on the kitchen lino. So, to keep yourself from being a baby, you think of that rifle in its naphthalene fog behind the coats in the wardrobe.

The old man keeps the breech-bolt hidden separately from the rifle. Without a firing mechanism the rifle is a dog without teeth. It's not even a weapon. Although you know where the bolt is stashed you don't go near it; you can't do anything stupid.

A few really bad days you sit at the window to watch people come and go. You can see anyone moving a mile away, so you track them in the sights as they make their way uphill. Like that wild-looking kid in the sheepskin jacket who's always around. Or the station wagons full of Aborigines on pension day. You contain them a little while. But you can't see trouble coming. You don't know what to look for.

And then, somehow, you forget to keep watch. You don't think of the rifle. You're overwhelmed by schoolwork, you sleep at night, and, without noticing, you become familiar. Although the town still seems temporary it feels normal for longer and longer stretches. You fall in love with an older girl. You learn to play basketball and even though you're rubbish at it you like the way the game takes you over. You play against blackfellas who whip you and then get you to walk them home to the hostel because they're afraid of the dark. You register the old man's sense of disappointment in Aborigines but that's a cop thing. You're in love with a girl who's out of reach. Just to pass her house you ride to the wharf where grain ships load and tuna boats disgorge icy bluefin. The wharfies and sailors and fishermen are scarred and broken-toothed and you ride past them, invisible.

On the wharf you find a battered foreign-language nudie magazine in which all the women's breasts are the size of pumpkins. You take it home and stash it in the cavity beneath the drawer in your desk. You consult it frequently, especially the swarthy centrefold who cradles her breasts like an armload of fruit. Eventually you notice how her eyes follow you. You try to concentrate on the dark splash of hair between her legs but she's looking back at you. One afternoon you ride down to the water and shove the rolled magazine through the planks of the whalers' jetty.

You watch the girl you love playing netball and wish you were visible again.

You blunder into the bathroom to find your mother with her breasts in her hands.

They're sore, she says. I'm weaning your sister.

Oh, you murmur. Right.

Afterwards, stroking the dog on the back step, you think of the twelve-year gap between you and the baby, wondering what it was that took the oldies so long.

When the old man gets a weekend off, he drives you all out to a salmon camp along the coast where you set up in an empty tin hut with a box of groceries and some sleeping bags. The autumn air is cool and salty, spiced with the tang of pepper-mint trees which spill down the dune to the empty beach. Together you catch herring from the stony headland and sit out by a bonfire telling jokes. Your mother is bright and girl-ish. Your father's quiet laugh makes you sleepy, and in the morning you mind your sister while the oldies walk the beach hand in hand. Before they return the baby has taken her first unaided steps and only you're there to see it.

The night you get back to town you wake to the scream of sirens. Lights crawl the wall and the phone rings in the hall-way. From the kitchen window you see the school in flames. The old man is out the door and you're left there in a fizz of excitement you're careful to conceal from your mother. In the morning you stand around on the oval with everybody else while the drizzle comes down and the gossip goes around about the kid recently expelled, the one who made bombs and filled condoms with bulls' blood and jacked up teachers' cars. You know who they mean – it's the dishevelled boy in the sheepskin jacket, the one you see everywhere – and kids are coming to you now, needling you for information because you're the copper's kid and you should know. Every time you shrug they take it as confirmation. And then it's in the local paper, the boy helping police with inquiries.

The rest of the week, with the old man on afternoon shift, you get home to find him sipping Nescafé with his baton and cuffs on the sink. He runs his thumbnail across the ribs of the draining board with a clouded look on his face. You want to ask but you know he'll tell you nothing and you respect him for it.

Demountable classrooms arrive at school. The wild boy is released without being charged. Somehow the old man seems mollified.

For the school social you gargle with Listerine, spray your hair with VO-5 and try to work up the guts to speak to the girl with the spoiled face, the one you haven't stopped thinking about for weeks. The music is awful. A bunch of blackfellas on special release from the prison farm play Status Quo and AC/DC like it's country and western and there's a strange current in the gym that saps your resolve. Kids are acting weird. Someone sets off a rotten egg bomb and an hour later, when the air has cleared, two ambulancemen and your own father burst in as news rolls in a swell across the dancefloor that there's a girl dead in the toilet. The lights come up. The band witters to a halt. As you file out with the others you see the old man emerge from the basement, cap askew, to search the crowd for you, and when he sees you his nod is curt and he's gone again. Out in the carpark detectives pull in. You recognize the swagger. Your basketball mates are gone already, so you head home.

Down on the corner at the unlit Esso station a match flares in a panel van as you pass. It's the wild boy, the one they call the bomber, slouched behind the wheel, just a shadow again behind a heat-ticking engine.

By morning someone else is dead. At breakfast, still in his tunic, smelling of sweat and smoke and Dettol, the old man tells about the boy found hanging in his own wardrobe. You don't know what to say. When he gets up from the table, leaving you and your mother blinking at each other, he empties his cup into the sink. On the way to the shower he stops a moment to run his fingers through your hair that's still tacky with spray, and you know quite suddenly and certainly that he's had the dead boy in his arms, that he's seen things he can't ever explain.

At school a kind of hysteria goes through the class. Girls weep ostentatiously outside the library and kids are pulled left and right from the classroom. A teacher takes you aside to quiz you about syringes at the gym but you just blink, speechless with confusion. You must know something, she says in exasperation. You of all people. But you don't know anything and there's something about her look that sets you against her.

You go back to lying awake at night, wondering what you do know, listening hard again at the wall for something to explain your disquiet. They talk in whispers in the other room. It's a kind of torture, like a dripping tap that you wish would stop, but you find yourself straining for it in anticipation. You know you're waiting so intently for trouble that you're making trouble happen.

The things you hear solve nothing; they're just nasty bits of information you could have done without, specks and splashes of dirt that puddle and pool in your head, things about the parents of kids you know, news of teachers, things you aren't meant to hear, stuff you shouldn't be listening to. Adulteries, bashings, robberies, a trawler fire, the boy hit by the school bus, and that kid's name over and over again, the one you still see now and then in his sheepskin coat and his Holden van. Not him. It's always him. The old man whispers it in the kitchen. Not him, I know it, I just feel it.

The old man looks blue around the gills. Your mother's face is closed. There's a creamy scum at the corners of his mouth. Their tea goes cold. Your mother peels potatoes almost vengefully.

You can't sleep at night. With the earpiece stuffed deep in your head you listen to the radio but all the chat is stupid and the music old enough to make a pensioner wince. When you read with a torch beneath the blankets the words slide and tremble on the page. Only a few weeks ago you were seized by fantasies of the girl with the strawberry birthmark and now you can summon neither face nor body at will. After school, weary and angry, you break mallee roots with a sledge and spike until your hair hangs in strings and your head hums.

Two kids drown. There's a rollover on the coast road. A girl has her stomach pumped. On the wharf a man is bashed until his nose comes away from his face. Then a rash of overdoses, of needles, of nighttime calls. There's no days off for the old man, no fun, no respite, no weekends away or drives out to farms to ping tins off tree stumps.

You never show up for basketball training so the team gives you the flick. When winter descends you ride to pass the short afternoons. Down in the harbour one day, wheelstanding and swooping along the wharf where the tuna boats are tied up and ice trucks parked askew, you come alongside a reeking boat when a bloke in a beanie steps out from behind a one-tonner and tells you to piss off right now if you know what's good for you, and as you wheel around in surprise, all but tipping yourself into the drink, you see a plain, dark car ease up. Rain begins to fall. Behind the water-streaked glass, four heads. You swerve and pedal away and like a cold runnel down the back of your collar, a chill of recognition leaks into you.

Out on a lonely beach some tourists find a boy with both legs broken. It's the bomber from school. After dinner the oldies go outside to talk. You watch them retreat from the rain into the woodshed. The dog capers about their shins. The old man hugs himself in his civvies, kicks the tin wall.

Walking home from school you have cars slide up beside you and hang at your elbow a while but you know well enough to keep tooling along as though you haven't noticed. Some people roll the window down to ask directions. A carload of girls throws a naked Barbie doll at your feet and squeals off. And there are some who idle beside you, obscured by flaring glass, who seem merely to watch.

At the coppers' picnic where the air is blue with barbecue smoke, the old man flips snags and chops alongside his workmates – pasty blokes in titty aprons and tracky dacks – but it's obvious he's not one of them. His smile is as mirthful as a baby's wind-grin. Dragonflies hang over the river. You watch the grownups in their floppy hats and floral frocks and hopeless Keyman jeans and notice every glance and guffaw and wiped mouth. The detectives are easy to pick. Around a ute piled with ice and beer, behind their wraparound sunglasses, they laugh like kings. You carry your sister through a knot of mouthy primary schoolers and see your mother stranded amongst the wives in the shade of the rivergums. She sees you too, winks, and pulls her hair back with a nervous yank.

You walk down by the river until your baby sister nestles into your shoulder and sleeps. You wonder what it'd be like to have a girl do that, a real girl like the one with the marked face, to sit by the river on a sunny winter day and doze warm-breathed on your neck.

At the end of every shift, after pulling into the drive, the old man sits in the car a while. You watch him chew antacids and flip his keychain. He's never home on time. Your mother doesn't mention it. You wish you knew what he was thinking, that someone'd say something.

And then comes the sudden transfer, a temporary posting a hundred miles away. When he tells you at dinner you push back your chair and barrel out into the yard, the crack of the screendoor like a gunshot in your wake. The dog bounds at you stupidly and you kick it down in tears. You stand in the woodshed and he finds you there.

You have to look after your mother, he says. I'll be back every two weeks. Just keep away from the wharf.

Why? you ask fiercely. Why?

I don't know, he says. Forget it. I just need you to be responsible. You're a good boy.

Before dark he's gone and your mother has left your dinner on the stove and gone to bed. You bathe your sister and put her down and eat your dinner cold and wipe out the high chair. In the night your mother cries quietly until the radio goes off the air.

A day later a constable comes by with a trusty from the prison farm. It's been teed up, he says. This bloke'll chop wood for you. Can't leave yez in the lurch. You see the skinny cop looking your mother up and down. She hasn't cried all day; it's as though the night's weeping has dried her out. She shrugs and shows the men to the woodshed.

There's something very close to a smirk on the young cop's face, as though he's emboldened by your father's absence, and you'd like to wipe it off with the axe handle.

As the cop is leaving, a truck pulls in and dumps two tons of mallee roots outside the fence and you and the prisoner look at each other a moment before your mother goes indoors and you cart the gnarled firewood by barrow and armload to the woodshed.

The trusty works unhurriedly. He's wiry. His arms are blue with tattoos. His sideburns curve down from a puffy slick of Elvis hair.

Is this a reward, you ask, or a punishment?

This, says the trusty, is Saturday.

You retreat to the back step to sit with the dog. Behind you, in the laundry, your mother wrestles with the twin-tub. All day you sit there keeping watch and the trusty ignores you.

Next day there's another one, an Aborigine. He's leery of the dog but works without pause all day, refusing even the tea and cake you're sent out with. That evening you beg your mother to make them stop sending trusties. You swear you'll do all the yardwork yourself – it's what the old man wanted – and besides, you tell her, you need the exercise. You don't say anything about the coppers coming to the house with their smug looks and hair-ruffling. You want to say more, to talk about the transfer and everything going awry around you but it's enough that she agrees, so you leave it at that and begin each day early by lighting the stove for breakfast and hot water, then feed the dog and split pine for tomorrow's kindling before you fill the box with a day's supply of slow-burning roots. School happens at a distance – you're there but barely present – and afterwards you come home to mind your sister or break roots until sparks fly and your muscles burn. You eat dinner without saying much for fear of saying everything and afterwards you stack records on the turntable – Tom Jones and Herb Alpert's Tijuana Brass – so your mother can listen while she irons.

Every night at dusk a paddy wagon cruises by. You stand, unwaving, at the kitchen window. You dry the dishes, jiggle your sister, do your homework and lie awake sore and heavy-lidded.

Some nights you're sure there's someone in the garden beneath your window. When you get up there's no one there. Other nights you just can't bear to look.

Nobody visits, but the patrol car rolls by at all hours.

You chop wood, you totter, you see spots, but when the old man calls you stand jangling and upright by the phone while your mother goes foggy and soft on the line so long that by the time she puts you on you're all wooden and formal and the old man sounds puzzled, even hurt, by the strange gap between you. But you have to clench your teeth so hard against sobs and silly laughter. You're only a second away from begging him to come home or take you with him.

Somebody steals your bike from the verandah but neither you nor your mother calls the police. Then one night there's a splash of glass out the front. You sit up in bed, startled as much by having found yourself asleep as by the sound itself, and you snatch up your torch, race through the house and throw open the door to see nothing more than a shattered beer bottle seething in a rime of bubbles on the path. When you flash the torchbeam around the yard and up and down the street, there's nothing. The town hunkers, half lit, in the valley below. As you head inside for the dustpan and broom your mother appears in the doorway. Stay inside, she says. Don't run out like that again.

But I had to see, you say.

Don't ever do it again. You hear me?

You look away and nod.

You're a good boy, she says.

And you *are* a good boy. You keep an eye out. You do your homework. You break two tons of mallee roots and your hands are leathery as a man's. The woodshed is full and the excess is piled against it like a drystone wall. In the afternoons your mother walks to the shops. You offer to go for her but she insists. Most times she takes the baby in the stroller and while she's gone you keep a look-out.

The rifle bolt lives in the old man's bedside drawer between the Bible and a book of knots and splices. You take it out to turn it over in your hands, and even though you love the slick action of it sliding down the breech, you resist the temptation to slip it in. That doesn't mean you can't nurse the rifle and hold the bolt in the palm of your hand. Without a bolt a rifle's not even a weapon.

From your parents' window you look out on the strange town. Down there people are quietly stealing, cheating, lying. They're starving their pets and flogging their kids and letting them hang in their wardrobes and burn in cars and choke to death in beachside toilets. And when legs are broken nothing happens, no charges are laid. It's as if things like this are suddenly ordinary. You can't believe how close you came to fitting in here. Everything you know and all the things you half know hang on you like the pressure of sleep.

You wait for your mother to appear in the street again, track her progress to the relative safety of the block and begin setting things back in their places before she reaches the gate.

You look so tired, she murmurs.

How many more weeks? you ask.

Four, she says. Four weeks.

You say nothing. But four weeks is impossible; you've already lost count and it feels like someone's just adding weeks now to see you suffer or else the old man's gone for good and no one's got the guts to tell you. But he'd never do that. You know he wouldn't.

Back from school one afternoon, you find the dog out by the woodshed, coughing, whining, turning in circles. Your mother leaves your sister with you while she walks it, drags it, carries it to the vet. You take the baby to your parents' room and bounce her on the bed for a while to calm your nerves. Without your old man's pillow the bed looks deformed. And your mother's gone so long.

You put your sister on the floor, let her totter around for a while. You take the rifle from the wardrobe, stand by the window and stay calm. But the baby goes from sucking on the corner of the bedspread to hauling on the curtains and you have to leap back from the window before anybody sees you.

The house is naked up here, a bare box in a square of lawn. The front fence is barely waist high. There's just not enough security, no protection. You open the bedside drawer and take out the bolt and slip it into the rifle. You check the breech, work the bolt and check twice more for safety, for piece of mind.

Finally your mother appears, hauling the dog up the hill.

Constipation, she says.

But you lie awake that night listening to the whimpering, writhing dog until you can't bear it any longer and go out to the laundry to lie down beside it. You think about the dressing table in the oldies' room with its barrettes and brushes and the single bottle of perfume which smells of the city, of frangipani and your old life. Across the table from your mother's things, in the shadow of those filmy curtains, is a conglomeration of cut-glass jars full of bits – silver uniform buttons, butterfly nuts, ballbearings, cloudy marbles, the spare keys to the hand-cuffs, some bitsy gemstones and a few bullets. There's a box of ammunition somewhere in the house but the only rounds you can locate are those three strays salted amongst all that crap. Trouble has found you and you're ready for it.

When your mother wakes you at dawn the dog is dead beside you. She goes straight to the phone but the vet doesn't answer. At the old man's new posting nobody picks up. Your mother is angry now but you're just tired. You dig a hole for the dog beside the shed where your two tons of wood stands like a wide, grey cairn. You declare that you're not going to school. She doesn't argue. She drinks coffee while you stoke the stove.

After an hour or so a paddy wagon pulls into the drive. Your mother goes out and you watch her talk to the smirking con-stable by the gate.

I have to go, she says coming in, straightening her hair with her fingers. I'm gonna sort this out. Your sister will be awake in a minute. Remember, Vic, you're responsible.

How long will you be? you ask.

Long as it takes, love.

When she climbs into the cop car and is swept out into the street, you lock all the doors and windows. You check the baby in her cot and get the rifle and slide the bolt into it. For a few moments you stand behind the sheer curtain in your mother's room and survey the town. There's a southerly blow-ing. Ragged lines of spume streak the harbour. Steam and greasy smoke pour from the cannery stacks and clouds mottle the pale fingers of the silos. A shift whistle. A ship's horn.

Townspeople make their way up and down the hill. They pedal and jog, steer their bawling trucks, their glossy cars and mud-spattered utes, easing by as though you're not even there. This window is an excellent vantage point. They don't know how ready, how alert you are.

You work the bolt in the breech. Check and check and check again. You cock the weapon and listen to the cold click of the firing pin when you pull the trigger.

Now your sister is awake.

You turn to the dressing table. You fish three shells from the cut-glass jars and stand each of them in its tarnished casing on the lacquered surface of the table. In the mirror your features are grave. There are great smudges beneath your eyes.

Your sister whacks and rattles in her cot across the hall. You load your rifle. In the gunsight you watch the strangers of your town take their dirty secrets from place to place. Beyond the glass their lips move but you can only hear your sister beginning to wail.

You can't leave the window. You're not sure what to look for but you know you have to be ready. From here you have a long, clear view. Responsibility is on you now, formless and implacable as gravity. You're just waiting for them to make a move. Let them. Yes, let them try.

The stock of the weapon warms your cheek, keeps you steady. You can't look at the bed for fear that you'll lie down and sleep. You can do this. You can hold out for as long as it takes to have everyone home safe, returned to themselves and how things used to be. You cock your weapon.

Reunion

IT WAS CHRISTMAS DAY AND HOT. There were only the three of us and lunch was sumptuous but without children it wasn't particularly festive.

Over coffee my mother-in-law, Carol, made an announcement.

They've asked us over to Ernie and Cleo's, she said.

What? said Vic, putting his cup down carefully.

Your grandmother will be there.

When did they invite you? I asked.

Us, Gail, said Carol. All of us. Cleo rang last night.

Our eyes locked for a moment in an odd, appraising stare.

Bloody hell, said Vic. That's a turn up.

So why don't we leave the dishes till later?

You're actually going? I asked.

I don't see why not, she said with a smile. You have to give people the benefit of the doubt.

I don't believe it, said Vic.

Will you come with me? Carol asked.

Vic and I glanced at one another and already he wore that round-shouldered look of apology. I shrugged. In the decades since Carol's husband had disappeared, his family had shunned her as though she were to blame. For her sake we couldn't refuse.

Just for an hour, said Vic.

Oh, said Carol with a laugh. An hour'll be time enough.

As we drove through the suburbs where new kites already hung from powerlines and shiny bikes lay askew on front lawns, nobody spoke much except Vic.

Things were never hostile between my mother-in-law and me, but they were often strangely cool. There was no battle of wills over her son, just a distance that couldn't be bridged, a civility that bewildered all of us and Vic in particular.

Everyone got enough air? he said, with a familiar panicky note of jauntiness in his voice. Hey, the streets are deserted.

It's the heat, said Carol from the back seat.

It's eerie, I murmured.

We're all just nervous, said Carol.

She was a substantial person, Carol Lang. I knew she'd endured a lot. Even in our earliest encounters, during the first tricky months of letting go, she'd been gracious and thoughtful. Yet there was something impenetrable about her. She resisted intimacy. Beneath the mildness there was a hard-won pride, a kind of dignity that was intimidating. If she'd ever had a life beyond motherhood she wasn't letting on to me, and the less of it she offered the less I came to enquire. In the company of this plain, quiet, grey-haired woman I became cautious, even defensive, conscious that I was not a mother, that I had no purchase. After five years, no headway.

You think they want us to eat? asked Vic.

No, said his mother. They made it clear we should come after lunch.

Just in time to do the dishes, he muttered.

Carol laughed and Vic laughed too. I'd never met Ernie and Cleo but I'd heard the stories. I had a headache just thinking about them.

Through a suburb of roundabouts and artful dead-ends, Vic brought us to the driveway of a house that seemed stranded somewhere between 'Gone with the Wind' and 'Miami Vice'. It had porticoes and pediments, but also pastels and palms. Rising from the cul-de-sac and the hectic styles of its neighbours, Ernie and Cleo's place stood high at the peak of a berm of rollout lawn. It was two storeys high and festooned with lights and decorations. In the drive were several cars.

Are you sure this is it, Mum?

This is the address they gave me.

I just don't recognize anything. The cars . . . nothing.

Well, you haven't seen them since you were at the uni.

He's obviously moved on from driving pig trucks, I murmured.

Or getting someone else to drive them for him, said Carol getting out.

Vic and I shuffled up to the door behind his mother and we stood fidgeting like children while chimes echoed through the house. We waited. Carol knocked. Her beige shoulderbag jiggled at her hip. Vic whistled a tune whose melody was beyond him. The only other sound was the general noise of people carousing in backyard pools.

We'll try round the back, said Carol. They might be in the pool.

We don't even know they've got a pool, Mum.

Vic, I said, what's the chances of a place like this not having a pool?

Imagine cleaning it, said Carol.

The pool? I said.

The house, Gail.

Yes.

Feeling conspicuous out there in full view of the neighbourhood, a whole street without evidence of people but for the slopping, screeching, laughing noise of poolside celebration, we hullo-ed the house a few minutes longer and then followed Carol through the open-doored garage into the yard beyond. Back there it was all coconut palms and aluminium wrought-iron and brick pavers. Not only was there a pool but also a cabana the size of a hangar.

The sliding doors at the rear of the house were ajar and Christmas music tinkled from within, but nobody came to Carol's calls. I noticed a tremor in her voice. She chewed her lip uncertainly and pivoted in her flat-soled shoes.

Try up at the pool? said Vic without enthusiasm.

Yes, said Carol.

What time did they say? I asked.

After lunch, said Carol firmly.

It's nearly four, I said.

I didn't want to seem too eager, she said.

It's quiet, said Vic.

Too damn quiet, I said, and with that Vic and I broke into nervous giggles. Carol stared us back into order.

We'll try that hut thing, she said.

It's a cabana, Mum.

Yes.

We stalked up the path with its bougainvillea and assorted water features and I felt a creeping hysteria. I was actually walking on tiptoe, throwing glances over my shoulder, shaking with silent, mortified laughter.

Yoo-hoo! said Carol at the pool gate.

Oh my God, muttered Vic. Get me out of here.

Once we were inside the pool fence it took quite a few moments to realize that the deep shade of the cabana was empty. The pool was strewn with bobbing toys. On the cold barbecue were a few wizened chops and prawns.

It's the *Marie Celeste*, I said.

It's rude, said Carol. That's what it is.

She turned, tottered a moment with eyes big as baubles, and a ball shot from beneath her as she went sidelong into the pool. I caught the bag but not her arm. When she surfaced her frock billowed beneath her arms and I couldn't help laughing.

Hell, said Vic, sensing trouble.

Oh my sainted aunt! cried Carol.

Not in this family, he said.

And then we were all useless with laughter. It was like something had possessed us. Vic lurched around the pool holding his knees and I laughed till my throat hurt.

Well, it's lovely in, said Carol.

Which is when I jumped. I still had her bag in my hand. The water was cool and stupidly chemical and I floated a moment with a spritz of trespass bubbling through my limbs.

At the edge of the pool Vic was only moments from joining us – he already had his arms behind him like wings – when a dark look travelled across his face.

Hey, he murmured. You reckon this is even the right house?

It better be, I said.

Oh, God, he said. Stay there, I'm gonna check.

Stay *here*? said Carol, still laughing. I don't think so.

We clambered out and followed Vic. There were towels at the cabana but we didn't stop to use them, just slopped back down the winding path with a new, feverish urgency.

Vic hesitated at the back door. He almost hailed the house as his mother had earlier, but then he looked at Carol and me and the puddle we were making on the pavers beneath the pergola, and eased the slider aside and let himself in. Carol and I looked at one another. I handed her the beige bag. She'd lost a shoe and her hair was flat. Her big sensible undies were showing through the cotton dress plastered to her.

We'll be a sight, she said.

But will we look too eager?

Bloody hell, said Vic emerging from the house. Let's get out of here!

What's wrong, love?

It's not them.

Oh gawd, I don't believe it.

My shoe. I've left my—

Bugger it, Mum, I'll lose my job.

We bolted back through the garage and piled into the Camry. As Vic hurtled us backwards down the drive I saw our footprints and drips on the concrete.

Oh, dear, said Carol.

Wrong house, Mum.

But I wrote it down. Seventy-eight Quay Largo.

Vic had hardly got the vehicle into forward gear when we saw the spill of Christmas partiers on the driveway of number seventy-five.

Oh my good God, said Carol.

It's Ernie, said Vic.

We can't stay now, said Carol. We can't possibly! Drive!

I felt myself sliding low in the seat.

Go, said Carol. Drive!

We shot forward. Vic mashed the gears. A spray of faces flashed by the window. Vic grappled the Camry round the corner and out of sight.

Carol and I were half dry when we got home. Vic went straight to the fridge and opened a bottle of champagne.

Here's to not being struck off, he said holding up his glass.

Oh, don't be melodramatic, I said. It was a simple mistake.

Maybe I wrote down seventy-five and read the five as an eight, said Carol. My writing's not good and my eyes are worse.

It doesn't matter, Carol. For what it's worth, I enjoyed it.

Give me a glass of that, said Carol. Vic, where's your manners?

But you don't drink, Mum.

You don't think I have an excuse, this once?

Pour your mother a drink, I said.

Yes, I've lost a shoe over all this.

Carol gulped the wine and refilled the glass herself.

They were at Ernie's, she said. The people, the neighbours, they were over the road at Ernie's.

Another coupla minutes they'd have sprung us in their pool.

They'll find the shoe, I said, breaking into a giggle.

You think they saw us?

We were all over their driveway, said Vic. Oh man, what if they got the rego of the car?

Oh dear, said Carol with a titter.

I'm serious, Mum.

Well, excuse me, constable!

I was laughing again; I couldn't help it.

Some reunion, said Carol. Actually, it went well, considering.

Kerbside drive-by, I said. The best sort.

No time for arguments. Ideal.

You two, said Vic. Jesus!

Victor, she chided. Not at Christmas.

Let's open another bottle, I said.

Gail? said Vic.

No, I want to. This is the most fun I've ever had at Christmas. I'm serious.

Carol laid an indulgent hand on my arm and I just kept talking.

When we jumped in the pool I felt ten years old.

When *you* jumped in the pool. Mum fell.

I had this forbidden feeling, this naughty feeling.

Vic groaned.

Be quiet Vic, let her speak.

When I was little we went to church three times of a Sunday, I said. But at Christmas only once. It's a bit arse-about, don't you think? We weren't allowed to say Merry Christmas because it condoned drunkenness. It was Happy Christmas or the doghouse. Oh, I'm sorry Carol, I wasn't thinking.

Because Bob was an alcoholic? she asked. Look at me, I am tipsy. You're too careful.

Oh.

My mother was a drunk, too, she murmured.

Really?

I used to fish her out of the pub at twelve years of age.

Mum, said Vic. What about a cup of tea?

She used to smash windows with her high heels. I never

wear heels, but now I drink. I used to want to be a teacher, you know.

You would have been good, I said.

Kindergarten. Do I seem the type?

I never went to kindergarten, I said. My parents wouldn't send me.

What was *wrong* with them?

I don't know, I said. I never had birthday parties either.

Never? asked Vic.

Not once? asked Carol.

I asked my mum about it a couple of years ago. I thought I just might not be remembering. But she said she wasn't really into that sort of thing.

Bloody hell, said Vic. You never told me this.

We never did home reading. Other kids had their mum or dad check their spelling lists. Nothing. Sports days, they never came.

Was it work? asked Carol. Some religious thing?

No. Well, the church did soak up all their time and attention. But with us . . . I don't think they ever got interested.

Vic started stacking plates and running water. Carol and I kept talking while he worked around us. The more I said, the more agitated he got. He didn't care for my parents, but now I knew he'd never speak to them again, and I thought that was probably fair. They were vain, careless people and I'd forgiven them, but there was no reason for him to; he had no need. I knew that Carol had only just buried her mother the year before. Just the way she held my arm, I knew she understood.

Don't mind him, she murmured. He gets upset on my behalf, too.

I know.

Has to defend everybody.

That's him.

I'm in the same bloody room, *girls*!

He was a dear boy.

Yeah, right.

By the way, son, what did you see in that house that made you skedaddle?

A wall of photos, he said. No red hair, no freckles, no ugly cousins. I knew I had the wrong joint.

They're all married now, said Carol. All of them with kids, apparently.

Lovely, he muttered. More wobbegongs. My cousins all looked like carpet sharks.

Careful, I said. You share the same gene pool.

Don't even say the word *pool*, said Vic.

Strange, but they're nothing alike, Ernie and Bob.

Vic was silent at the mention of his father. He plunged his hands into the suds and washed.

Bob was everything Ernie wasn't, said Carol. But you could never tell their mother this. Bob cleaned up every mess his brother made. And when he needed help he got nothing. Just this howl of disappointment, disapproval.

I've heard some stories, I said, hoping to head Carol off somewhat. Vic was clenching his jaw now.

Ernie and Cleo were off again – on again. They were like a bad movie. She ran away to Kalgoorlie once. Took the kids and all. Bob gets dragooned into driving Ernie up there to save their marriage. It's his mother's idea; in fact, she comes along. They drive all day, seven hours to Kal and get there on sunset. Mrs Lang words Ernie up and sends him in, and Bob and her sit in the car for two hours.

While Ernie and Cleo were hashing it out? I asked.

Well, that wasn't what they were doing.

Mum—

Bob and his mother sat out in the car while Cleo and Ernie had an amorous two hours, punctuated by the usual barney – which meant they were off again – and then the three musketeers drove home all night so Bob could make the morning shift.

I was laughing again. I couldn't resist it.

Vic, she said, is his father's son.

Thanks, Mum.

And neither of us, Gail, is his grandmother.

Family, said Vic. It's not a word, it's a sentence.

Rubbish, said Carol. It's an adventure.

Don't give her any more to drink, said Vic.

But I did. I took her by the arm and we sat out under the grapevines where our clothes and hair dried awry and the sunset made the sky all Christmassy and we talked and laughed until we forgot the man between us and made some headway.

Commission

THE DAY AFTER HER DIAGNOSIS Mum sent me in search of the old man. She'd lain awake all night thinking and she told me she just wanted to see him again before she died. Although it was five in the morning she knew I'd be awake. I couldn't believe what she was asking me to do – it was such a longshot, so unlikely that it felt cruel – but in the circumstances I had neither the heart nor the presence of mind to turn her down. I got out a map of Western Australia and studied it over a breakfast I had to force down with several coffees. I left messages at the office, kissed my sleepy wife goodbye and drove out of the city with the rising sun in my eyes.

Almost twenty-seven years had passed since I'd seen my father. I didn't know where he was or what he was doing. The only piece of information Mum had armed me with was the name of a bush pub in the eastern goldfields. It was there on the map, Sam's Patch. The pub seemed to *be* the town. It was the last known address. As I drove I held the folded map to my face a moment and smelled the classrooms of my childhood.

I was too tired to be driving such distances that day but I fought to stay alert. At the outskirts of the city, the foothills and the forests still bore signs of the week's drought-breaking storms. Road crews were out and men took chainsaws to fallen trees. A couple of hours east, machines were seeding wheat paddocks. Water lay in culverts at the roadside and birds gathered to wash themselves, hardly stirring as I passed. I drove until farms gave way to red earth and salmon gums, until the sun was behind me and the towns were mostly ruins amidst the slag heaps of mines long abandoned. Even out here, in staticky waves, the radio spewed scandal from the police royal commission.

Up past Kalgoorlie I turned off the highway onto a thin bitumen road which wound between old mineheads and diggings until it petered out amongst the remains of a ghost town. All that was left was the Sam's Patch pub and before I reached it I pulled over and switched off the engine to think a minute. The hours on the road hadn't given me any ideas about what to say or how to act. I'd concentrated so hard on staying awake that I was nearly numb and I sat there with the motor ticking and the window wound down long enough to feel queasy again at the thought of what I'd agreed to do. If this was it, if the old man was really in there, what sort of state would he be in after all this time? I tried to think in purely practical terms; I couldn't afford to feel much now. I had to consider the logistical details of managing him, of cajoling and threatening and maintaining him for the time it took to deliver him as promised. The feelings

I'd deal with later. But I dreaded it. God, how I dreaded it. He'd never been violent; I wasn't afraid in that sense. It was the fear of going back to how things were. Drunks and junkies take everything out of you, all your patience, all your time and will. You soften and obscure and compensate and endure until they've eaten you alive and afterwards, when you think you're finally free of it for good, it's hard not to be angry at the prospect of dealing with the squalor again. There was no point in being furious at my mother for needing this, but I couldn't help myself.

I drove up and pulled in to the blue-metal apron in front of the pub. It was a fine old building with stone walls and brick quoins and wide verandahs, stained with red dust and hung with barrows and wagon wheels and paraphernalia of the goldrushes. When I got out and stood stiff in the sunshine a blue heeler stirred on the steps and behind it, in the shadows of the verandah, an old man put his hat on but did not rise from where he sat. I licked my lips, summoned what I could of my professional self, and strode over.

Before the dog reached me I could see that the man was not my father. His low growl turned the heeler in its tracks. I stumped up onto the verandah almost faint with relief.

I'm looking for Bob Lang, I said without preamble.

And who would you be, then? asked the old bloke. He had the ruined nose and watery eyes of a dedicated drinker. His hat was a tattered relic of the last world war.

I'm his son.

Honest Bob. And you're the son.

You know where he is?

The old cove nodded, his lips pursed. In the top pocket of

his overalls was a spectacles case which he fished out in order to survey me.

Must look more like yer mother, he muttered.

I shrugged. I felt awkward standing there in my pressed jeans and pullover. The old fella considered my brogues with interest.

You in strife?

No, I answered.

He's a good bloke is Bob.

I nodded at this to humour the old bugger and because I knew it to be true, but acknowledging it was painful.

The old bloke hauled himself up with a scrape of boots on the boards and opened the screen door. As he went in he flung the door back for my benefit and I followed him into a hall-like room that seemed to be emporium, public bar and community hall.

This your pub? I said taking it in.

Nup. Live out the back. Thommo's day orf.

At the bar he took up a blank pad and the stub of a pencil whose lead he licked before drawing me a map and a route out to a destination he labelled *BOB'S CAMP*.

Bob the Banker, he said tearing the page off and passing it to me. There he is.

And this is us here?

That's us.

I straightened up and looked at the rows of bottles behind the bar. It occurred to me that it might be useful to arrive with supplies. I felt the bloke watching me and I don't know whether it was his undisguised interest or the bitterness I felt at having even to contemplate such a thing after all my mother had been through, but I decided against taking any booze, and so great was my relief at the decision that as I folded up his helpful scrap

220

of paper I thought I saw a flicker of respect in the other man's gaze, the afterglow of which lasted all the way to the car.

I drove on up the thin black road awhile until I found the dirt turnoff indicated by the pencil map. The track was broad but muddy from the recent rains and when I turned into it the car felt sluggish and skittish by turns. I really had to concentrate to keep from sliding off into the scrub. Out here the earth was red, almost purple. Set against it, the flesh-coloured eucalypts and the grey-blue saltbush seemed so high-keyed they looked artificial. I had expected a desert vista, something rocky and open with distant horizons, but this woodland, with its quartzy mullock heaps and small trees, was almost claustrophobic. Mud clapped against the chassis and wheel arches. When I hit puddles, great red sheets of water sluiced the windscreen. Wrestling the wheel, I drove for half an hour until I came to a junction marked with a doorless fridge. It corresponded to my pencil map; I turned north. Five minutes later I turned off onto a slippery, rutted track that ended in a four-way fork. After some hesitation I took the most northerly trail and drove slowly through old diggings and the pale blocks of fallen walls. The car wallowed through shimmering puddles and the track narrowed until saltbush glissed against the doors.

I'd begun to sweat and curse and look for some way of turning back when I saw the dull tin roof and the rusted stub of a windmill amongst the salmon gums. A dog began to bark. I eased into the clearing where a jumble of makeshift buildings and car bodies was scattered, and the moment I saw the man striding from the trees beyond, I knew it was him. I stalled the car and did not start it again. I was dimly aware of the dog crashing against the door, pressing itself across the glass at my shoulder. It really was the old man. He was taller than I remembered and I was startled by the way he carried himself, the unexpected dignity of him. All my manly determination deserted me. I uttered a shameful little o! of surprise. It was all I could do to unstrap myself and lurch out of the vehicle so as not to be sitting when he arrived. The dog clambered at my legs, but at the old man's piercing whistle it desisted and ran to his side. For fear of looking fastidious I refrained from brushing the muddy pawprints from my jumper and jeans. I sat on the speckled hood of the car, folding and unfolding my arms. He came on through the waist-high saltbush, and when he reached me and the red dog sat as instructed, I saw that he was sober. I saw the wattles of his neck, the sun-lesions on his arms, the black filaments of work in his hands and the braces that held up his pants. He wore an ancient jungle hat, a faded work shirt and steel-capped boots more scarred than his long, melancholy face. His eyes were startled but clear.

Is it your mother?

Yes, I said.

What do you need?

She wants to see you.

He looked past me then and took a long breath. The dog whined and watched him.

You better come in. If you want to.

Will you come? I asked, angry at how sick with love I was at the very sight of him.

Of course, he murmured. If she asked.

She asked.

I have to . . . I need to organize myself.

How long will it take?

I have to think.

It's a long drive.

You'll need a cup of tea.

He turned toward the dwelling and I followed him. By the time I reached the cement slab of his verandah my brogues were ruined. He directed me to an armchair beneath the sagging tin roof where I kicked off the shoes. I felt strangely short of breath and when I followed him indoors I was unprepared for how strongly the shack smelled of him. It was not an unpleasant odour, that mix of shaving soap, leathery skin and sweat, but the sudden familiarity of it overwhelmed me. It was the scent of a lost time, how my father smelled before the funk of antacids and the peppermints that never quite hid the stink of booze. I nearly fell into the wooden chair he pulled out for me. While he stoked up the old Metters stove and set the blackened kettle on it I tried to compose myself.

The shack was a one-room bushpole construction with a corrugated iron roof and walls. In three walls were mismatched timber windows whose panes were scrubbed clean. At one end stood an iron bed and a rough bookshelf and at the other was the wood stove set back in its tin fireplace. Between them where I sat was a deal table and two chairs. Black billies and pots hung from a wall. A steel sink was set into a jarrah frame. The hand-poured cement floor was swept. There were photographs of my mother and me above the bed and one of him in uniform. I felt him watch as I took them in. Myself at fourteen, all teeth and hair and hope. And my mother in her thirties, smiling and confident.

And Kerry? I asked despite myself.

The old man pointed back to the doorway where, above the lintel, a faded shot of my dead sister hung like an icon. A chubby toddler in a red jumpsuit.

How long have you lived like this?

Sober? he said, misunderstanding me. Fifteen years.

Fifteen years, I said.

He clamped his jaw and looked down but there was an involuntary pride in his posture as I repeated his words.

I have to see to things. Before I go.

Okay.

It's too dangerous driving back in the dark, he said. There'll be roos all over the road. Can you wait till morning?

I had hoped to head back today, I said, realizing as I did so that if we left now we wouldn't reach the city until the early hours. After last night Mum would be in no fit state and the drive was probably beyond me.

You're welcome to stay here. But there's rooms back at the pub if you'd rather not.

I'll stay, I said after something of a pause.

The kettle boiled. He made tea and cut up some damper. We sat a while blowing steam – he from his tin mug and me from the china cup he'd given me. I tried the damper with the butter he brought in from the kero fridge and it was good.

You coming like this, he said. It's . . .

It's sudden, I said.

He nodded sadly as though that was not what he'd been about to say.

How do you live? I asked.

Don't need much out here. Get the pension. I look after things, hold things for people.

Bob the Banker, I said trying not to sound ironic.

Yeah.

What things?

Oh, money. Gold. Valuables.

What people?

There's a few blokes here and there still prospecting. Some of them just pretending these days. Often as not just drinking or going off their rockers and lying low. Old sandalwooders, fettlers, some strays and runaways. Don't trust each other. Don't trust emselves anymore. So they leave stuff with me.

They trust you, then.

Yes.

Why you?

The question affronted him but the old man seemed determined not to take offence.

Well, because I don't drink. Because . . . because I'm trustworthy.

Honest Bob, I murmured, ashamed at the bitterness in my voice. But it was hard to sit there and see him after so long, in the wake of such disappointment and creeping shame. I'd had years of boyhood bewilderment and then, once I was old enough to see it, a decade of fury at how my mother suffered. In the end there was only a closed-down resignation, the adult making-do that I'd grown into. And now I had to sit with him and hear him declare himself trustworthy.

Once upon a time it had been true. Honest Bob. He was straight as a die and what you saw was what you got. I believed in him. He was Godlike. His fall from grace was so slow as to be imperceptible, a long puzzling decline. Even during that time he was never rough or deliberately unkind. If he had been it would have been easier to shut off from him. He just disappeared by degrees before our eyes, subsiding into a secret disillusionment I never understood, hiding the drink from my mother who, when she discovered it, hid it from me in turn for fear I would lose respect for him. She turned herself inside out to protect him and then me. And at such cost. All for nothing. He ran away. Left us. I grew up in a hurry.

I was, my wife says, an old man at twenty-five. I felt

poisoned by lies. So many subtle tiny doses over the years that something in me gave out. I was no longer capable of forgiveness. If Gail, my wife, hadn't come along, I wonder what would have become of me. She has such a capacity to forgive. I doubt I could have reinvented myself by sheer force of will, though that would be my natural tendency. I have stumbled upon a good life. But my mother was too stubborn, too loyal, to move on. And now she was dying in that same state, fierce with hopeless love, and I was a breath away from screaming it all back in the old man's face.

He drank his tea and the afternoon light slanted across the table between us. After a time he cleared his throat.

I have to see some people, he murmured. Before I leave. In case there's any misunderstanding.

You want me to drive you?

Well, it would be quicker. It's too mucky for the pushbike.

Alright, then. We'll go now.

He brought me an old pair of Blundstones. They were soft with use and felt strange on my feet. The insoles were indented by his toes and sunk at the heel. We left the dog behind and slewed up muddy tracks for an hour or more, stopping well clear of humpies and dongas in the long shadows of diggings and ruins while the old man went in to consult people who were never more than silhouettes to my eye. Their dwellings were scraptin and ragwall. One bloke lived in an orange school bus that had sprouted lean-tos and outbuildings. While my father was in the bus with him I walked out through trenches and disused shafts to an abandoned hut. I was fed up waiting in the car, and the old place had caught my eye. On the dirt floor was a rusty bedstead. The hessian lining of the walls had come away to pool on the dirt. The single room was stacked with empty bottles and the tin fireplace was overflowing with ash that had set white and hard in the rain. On one bare pole a postcard was tacked. It featured a map of the state with the word SECEDE! super-imposed on it in faded yellow. A man's pants hung rotting on a chair. I'd been in some desolate rooms in my time but I never saw anything so melancholy.

We finished our rounds at dusk. I was completely lost and only my father's directions got us home.

You hear about the royal commission? I asked as I drove.

Someone said it was on.

All their names are in code.

The old man said nothing.

You're not curious?

It's a long time ago, he murmured. It's a shame to get this car dirty.

When we reached his place the dog came hurtling from the dark, sudden as memory.

The night was surprisingly cold. It took some time for the stove to warm the room to the point where it was comfort-able, but when it was we sat in the light of two hurricane lamps and ate the stew the old man ladled from a cast-iron pot.

This is good, I said.

Goat, he murmured.

You shoot them? I couldn't help but smile.

Now and then. What? he asked.

Nothing, I said. It's just like . . . I dunno . . . stepping back in time. Out here, I mean.

He shook his head, said nothing.

The smell of that wood, I said. What is it?

Desert pine.

Smells like cypress.

He nodded.

The Yanks have taken Baghdad.

I don't have an opinion on it.

Fair enough.

We ate in silence for a time. The dog sprawled before the stove swooning in the warmth.

I hear you're a lawyer now.

Yeah.

What kind?

Industrial relations.

On whose side?

The little bloke.

That's good, he said. That's good. Gotta look after the little bloke.

Well, that's the theory.

He pushed his plate away and sat back.

Your mother, he said. She's sick?

Yes.

He closed his eyes a moment and nodded and it struck me that he was disappointed, hurt even.

How sick?

She's dying.

He sighed and looked at his hands. He shook his head sadly. He looked at the dog.

Well. It . . . it hasn't been for nothing then.

What hasn't?

Sobering up. I couldn't have gone drunk.

I don't think she cares anymore, I said bitterly.

I wouldn't have. I wouldn't have gone drunk.

That's irrelevant.

I wouldn't have gone, he said with feeling. It's not irrelevant to me.

Jesus, you've been dry fifteen years anyway, it turns out.

Every day. Every day in readiness.

For what, seeing her?

Not seeing her. Facing her.

I sighed in exasperation.

Even another fifteen years would have been worth the wait.

It's not really about you, I said. I'm doing it for her.

I know that, he said hotly. But who's *she* doing it for?

I'm buggered if I know, I said in disgust, but even as I said it I realized what it was. This whole expedition. It was her way of bringing the two of us face to face.

Have you written to her?

Not since I've been straight.

Why not?

He shrugged. Shame, I spose. And I didn't want to get in her way.

She's still married to you!

So I believe.

I sighed. It's good that you're sober.

I'm proud of it, he murmured, with tears in his eyes. You won't understand. But it's all I have.

I sat there and hated myself, hated him too for making me the dour bastard I am, forged in shame and disappointment, consoled only by order. Childless. Resigned.

I'm sorry, he said, wiping his face. I wish I could undo it.

But you can't.

No.

So what the hell was it, Dad?

I lost my way, he said.

Yes, well, we're across that already. You lost your way and we all got lost with you. But you never said. You'd never tell us. It's like this cloud, this dark thing had found you and you wouldn't say what it was. The job. There was something you did.

No, he said. Is that what you think? You think I'm sitting here waiting to be named in the inquiry?

I've wondered, I said without pleasure. I'm sorry.

I saw things, he said miserably. Well, I half saw things. Things I didn't really understand at the time. Don't even really understand now. But it was the surprise of it, knowing that I was on the outside. It was like wheels within wheels and once I sniffed something crook I saw there was no one safe to tell. I was stuck, stranded.

Nobody at all?

For a while I thought I was going nuts, he murmured, his face turned from the murky lamplight. Didn't trust myself. Thought I was imagining it. But then there was this kid I remember. Smalltime petty crim. Had his legs broken out on Thunder Beach. You remember that place?

I nodded. I remembered the beach vividly and now I knew who he was talking about.

People said he got into a car with detectives, I said. That same afternoon.

That's it, said the old man. Two of the demons were down from the city.

What was it about?

Drugs, I spose. Never really understood it. Just that he'd fallen foul of em. And any question, any witness account died on the vine, didn't matter who it came to. Felt like, whatever was going on I was the only bloke not in on it. And the city blokes were in on it; it was bigger than that little town, that's for sure. So who do you talk to? Even if you've got the balls, who can you trust? It ate me alive. Ulcers, everything. I should have quit but I didn't even have the courage to do that. Would have saved us all a lot of pain. But it's all I ever wanted to do, you see, be a cop. And I hung on till there was nothing left of me, nothing left of any of us. Cowardice, it's a way of life. It's not natural, you learn it.

He got up and collected the plates and cutlery. He took a lamp from the table and hung it on the wall over the sink where he tipped in water from the kettle. With his back to me and his head down in the rising steam he looked like a figure from another time, a woodcutter from a fairytale, a stranger without a face, an idea as much as a man. I wanted to get up and help but I sat there behind him while the stove clucked and hissed and the dog snored.

I believed him. I couldn't help myself. What he said gave some shape to the misgivings of my youth, the sense that things were not alright around me. And I felt pity for him, for the trap he'd found his way into, but none of it changed what we'd lived through, my mother and I. It would take another lifetime to forgive him that. Even then I knew it might not be fair to blame him for her cancer but none of me was about to release him from it. From his very posture there at the sink, the quiet, cautious way he handled the pieces that he washed, you could see that he sensed it.

So you're not curious about the royal commission? I said at last.

They won't be losing much sleep, he said.

When he had wiped up and put the gear on the spartan shelves we went outside and stood at the edge of the verandah to see the hugeness of the sky and the blizzard of stars upon us. The cold night air had the cypress tang of woodsmoke.

So how did you get off the booze? I asked him.

Went to a meeting in Kal.

Just the one?

Only the one.

And what? I said with a dry little laugh.

It was looking at them, he murmured. The others. They disgusted me.

What, you didn't feel sympathy?

Any more than you're feeling now, you mean? No. It was like looking in the mirror and all their whining faces were mine. I'd had enough self-pity.

So?

I was living behind the pub then. The Golden Barrow. Had a donga out the back, called meself a yardman but basically I was an alcoholic sweeping floors for drinks. Came out here, walked it with the dog. And hid. Had a humpy way back off the track. Think I was tryin to work up the nerve to kill meself. Lots of shafts out here, no shortage of means. Spent months plotting and planning. Went mad, I spose. Nobody left alive anymore to tell those tales on me. And then I realized that I'd been six months without a drink. There was none to be had. Woke up one morning, it was winter, and the sun was on this fallen tree, this dead grey tree, and there was steam rising off the dead wood. And I felt . . . new. Had this feeling that the world was inviting me in . . . like, luring me towards something. Life, I dunno.

I didn't expect it to be beautiful here, I said for no reason other than not knowing what to say. The cold burned my face and, whenever I moved, the chill of my jeans branded my legs.

Just the sight of those bottle stacks outside the old blokes' huts used to make me thirsty. But it fades.

You read a lot, I see.

Yes. It's an education. But my eyes are going.

We'll get you some glasses, I said.

What time d'you want to leave?

Oh, first thing.

Fair enough.

He gave me his bed that night and unrolled a battered swag on the floor in front of the stove where he slept with the dog, each of them snoring quietly through cycles of synchronization, while I lay awake rattled by the smell of his body in the blankets about me and the strangeness of the hut with its animal sounds and sudden silences. I wondered how my mother would receive him, how she would react to the knowledge that he'd salvaged himself, and that she'd found him too late. And when she was gone, what then, what would I do about him? I lay there for hours on the narrow iron bunk like a frightened boy and late in the night I covered my face with the pillow which smelled of him and cried at the thought of my mother.

When I woke, the old man was sitting by the stove, shaved and dressed in the lamplight. It was early morning. His swag was rolled and on his knee was a battered cashbox which he held like a man entrusted.

Fog

LANG PULLED OVER BY THE CREEK. He parked in a wedge of sunlight between trees and switched off the ignition. He listened
to the soughing wind and the static surf of the two-way. The
van stank of sweat and puke and Pine-O-Cleen. He hoisted his
belt where the handcuffs snagged against the upholstery of the
seat. Burrowing in his tunic for an antacid, he looked out
across the sodden September paddocks. His mouth was chalky.
His guts felt like hell.

On the seat beside him lay the last court summons of the
day. Delivering them was work for a junior. It was another
slight, a message to pull his head in, and maybe even a way to
get him out of town for a while. At least it was time alone, a
bit of respite. If he spaced it right he'd be back for the change
of shift and home for tea. Ten minutes to himself, no harm in

that. Trouble was, there'd been a lot of ten-minute breaks lately and some of those had run to an hour or more. It wasn't like him. He didn't used to be this way.

Lang had only been in town a year. Ten months, to be exact. It was a plum posting, something to be excited about. A quiet country town on the coast. Pretty harbour, decent school, miles of white beaches. Compared to the strife-torn desert communities he could have faced, it was a gift. But within weeks of his arrival he began to feel uneasy. It wasn't the town. It was the blokes in the job. Conversations dried up as he came into the crib room. Glances were exchanged. He sensed that there were arrangements and alliances he wasn't privy to. He wondered if it was his reputation as a bit of a straight arrow. Within months he'd gone from being uneasy to feeling unsafe.

He eased the little flat bottle from between the seat springs, uncapped it in his lap and took a quick belt. It was cheap stuff. He didn't even like brandy. This was, he told himself, just a temporary thing.

A cow bellowed out of sight. Wattlebirds clacked in the trees around him. It was peaceful here and suddenly warm and for a moment he could believe that all this aggravation would pass, that the sleeplessness, the gut-burning anxiety, the creeping sense of paralysis would work themselves out. Maybe he'd put a few more bits of the puzzle together, find an ally. He just needed one honest copper to watch his back. But the flash of brandy-heat faded and he thought of Carol and the kids. They'd been through enough already. The bastards had got to them, made their point about laying off and staying clear. And that's what he'd do; there was no alternative. He'd keep his head down, bide his time, and in a year or so apply for a transfer.

The radio spluttered. There was a report of climbers lost out in the ranges. He listened to the two-way traffic as the beginnings of a search took shape. On another frequency the SES volunteers were chatting excitedly. One climber lost, another had raised the alarm. Lang dialled back to his own channel and wedged the bottle under the seat. He knew he wouldn't be home for dinner. He had the van turned around and was out on the highway before his call-sign came over the air.

It took half an hour to get out amongst the ranges and when he turned into the dirt carpark at the foot of the sheer bluff called The Dial, the sun was gone behind low, threatening cloud, and the vollies were already assembled, still studding their orange overalls in front of the trucks. Lang pulled on his plastic poncho. He stuffed the antacids and the brandy bottle into his tunic and made his way over to join the briefing. Macklin was talking. He and Lang were of the same rank, but Macklin had been here two years and he knew the geography. To that extent, at least, you could trust him.

Lang looked at the map taped to the side of the truck and pulled the hood up over his cap as a misting rain began to fall.

How's it looking? he asked Macklin as the vollies broke up into task groups.

Pretty straightforward, said Macklin, dragging on his own coat. Couple of hikers. The woman's over in the truck with the quack. She's totally hysterical. Far as we can tell, the bloke's fallen off the first tier. It's all thickets at the base there. He's set us a bit of a task.

Any chance of a chopper?

Nup.

I'll go with the western group.

That's the plan, Bob. Let's hope it's done by dark. I'm cold already.

Lang took a walkie-talkie from the truck and wished he had a decent pair of boots. He joined a chirpy bunch of volunteers as they set out down the long belly of the walk trail. The valley was thick with wandoo and marri and beneath the trees the scrub sprouted tiny darting birds and a blur of insects. The bush smelt tart, peppery. Everything looked blue in the late afternoon light.

After fifteen minutes the trail swept up towards the broad base of the bluff. There were no trees, just tight mallee heath and low boulders. The trail was good but the going was much tougher on the steep incline, and as the keen and the fit scrambled ahead of him and the wheezers lagged behind, Lang found space enough to consider the deep and tangled thickets beneath the peak. A bloke would take some finding up there; it was a nasty bit of country and there was plenty of it. He wondered how far you'd fall, whether you'd be swallowed, even cushioned, by all that teatree and banksia or if the tight-packed canopy might resist the impact and send you bouncing down the slope to burst like a bag of trash against the first big rock in your path.

He chewed an antacid. Every upward step tightened his hamstrings. Sweat soaked through his shirt and into his tunic and rain dripped from the peak of his cap and ran down his nose.

At a boulder the size of a beached whale, Lang rested a moment and looked back down to the carpark where two more police vehicles were pulling in. Young fellas, he thought, dragged in early for the evening shift. Beyond the little beige clearing of the carpark, the land stretched away blue in the distance. The surrounding peaks were headless in the mist. It was beautiful up here, and if it hadn't been for the hiss and squawk of the walkie-talkie, it would have been peaceful too.

At the foot of the bluff Lang bunched the searchers up the best he could on the steep, narrow trail. Above them The Dial rose in a series of granite extrusions whose peaks were obscured now by rainy mist. As Lang stood there waiting for stragglers and to-ing and fro-ing with Macklin on the air, the sky seemed to lower itself even further and the light grew dimmer. He broke the searchers up into pairs and told them to work ten yards apart across the ground immediately below the bluff and to meet back here in one hour. But with them all strung up and down the track in single file it was a case of Chinese whispers and he wasn't sure how clear he'd made himself. He was anxious about the poor light, the lack of time, the ambulance that still hadn't arrived.

Lang had a feeling about this bloke who'd fallen. He could picture him cannoning down, bouncing across the thicket below them, so while the vollies fanned out enthusiastically he picked his way back down the incline a distance and was just about to make a sweep when he was joined by a latecomer in a fancy parka. The girl was eighteen or so and obviously no SES volunteer.

She introduced herself but he didn't really hear the name because he'd already seen the camera slung from her neck. Just his luck, a journalist, and a cadet at that. She was trying to seem nonchalant but she couldn't disguise her excitement. He let himself be quizzed briefly, and with his job voice on he explained his hunch about the faller. He spelt the word trajectory without being asked and before she had much of a chance to get it all down in shorthand he plunged into the spiky thicket and got on with it.

From the outset the going was tough and it just got worse. Soon they were no longer walking but swimming through vegetation. Lang felt staked and whipped at every turn. His cheeks stung, he lost his footing. He tried hurling himself against snarls of foliage that resisted him. He began to worm his way through at an angle like a man in a stadium mob.

When the vegetation stood taller than him he navigated by the looming shadow of the bluff overhead. They'd long lost sight of other searchers and now there was no one within earshot. Lang grew anxious but he didn't want to unnerve the girl. She was green enough to press on trustingly. He knew he should turn back but he couldn't make himself. He was goaded on by the girl's presence. It wasn't about her being young and pretty. He didn't even think of her notebook and camera. It was about proving something. To her, to himself. That he was a policeman, someone you could trust. Head down, conscious of her panting behind him, he pressed on.

Eventually the thicket was too dense to move through unless they got down on all-fours and crawled. Lang was overheated. His mouth was scummy and he wished he'd brought water. He looked for something that might bear his weight if he climbed up to gauge their position. But no branch would hold him and he couldn't find a stone to climb. The girl watched him scramble to get his head above the canopy.

Give me a leg up, she said. See if that gets me high enough.

Lang got down on one knee and felt the damp litter soak through his trousers as the girl stepped up. She knocked his cap off in her struggle for balance and wound up gripping whiplike boughs above her. Her tennis shoes slid off his leg.

They each gave a sheepish laugh.

I could get up on your shoulders, she said.

It was an awkward prospect but he brushed off his trousers and squatted for her. She didn't weigh much but his back and thighs strained as he hoisted her up. He held her calves as delicately as he could and did his best to turn a slow circle for her.

He was conscious of her thighs against his ears. He told her to look for the track behind them, for orange overalls or any tell-tale movement, but she said she saw nothing, only bush. As he lowered her to the ground he lost his balance and they pitched over together. There was a nasty clunk as something spilled out onto the rocks and at first Lang thought of the brandy bottle. He was relieved to see that it was only the walkie-talkie. But his relief was only momentary. The radio looked okay but he couldn't raise Macklin or anyone else on it. There was only static. He sat back with his gut churning, and saw that the girl's face was cut. It wasn't much more than a scrape but she'd dabbed at it already and was looking, appalled, at the little smear of blood on her fingertips.

It's orright, he murmured. Rest a moment and we'll leg it back to the track. What'd you say your name was again, love?

Marie, she said.

Like Maori? he said. As opposed to Maree?

I spose. Yeah. Are we okay?

Well, we haven't found anybody. But we haven't lost ourselves, if that's what you mean. We'll have to shut down and try at first light.

This stuff, she said, tilting her head at the tangled mass of stems and branches, it's kind of claustrophobic.

Lang considered offering her his hanky to swab the blood but the state of it was enough to give him pause. She wiped the blood off on her corduroys.

Did you hear that?

A bird, he murmured.

Don't think so.

Lang listened. It was a sobbing sound.

That's a human, she said.

I doubt it.

Listen!

Lang wondered if it was the girl's insistence that changed things but the noise began to sound human. It was close by and downhill. He tried Macklin again and got nothing back. It was very late in the day. He figured they had less than an hour's light left.

We'll have a look, he said. We'll crawl down.

Here, she said, offering him a plastic water bottle.

She was a pretty kid, probably the daughter of a proud cow-cocky or clergyman. She had thick brown hair and an upturned nose and her eyes were bright with excitement. All her clothes seemed new, especially the parka. Even after all this exertion she smelled of Cool Charm. She had a generous mouth but right now, in such a situation, she didn't know quite how to arrange it. There was something of the school prefect about her which amused him. She was the sort of girl who was out of his league when he was a boy but who would not be beyond his son. Maybe Vic would bring home girls like Marie before long.

He drank a little water and thought of the brandy in his tunic. When she took the water bottle back she wiped the neck with the heel of her palm the way she must have learnt in the playground. Her hands were shaking.

You might get front page, he said.

She smiled gamely and drank.

On all-fours, pressed into the stony litter by the gnarled arches of scrub, Lang led her down the steep incline, pausing intermittently to listen for that noise. But now he heard nothing.

His pants were ruined and his uniform cap long gone when they came upon the climber upside down against a lichen-furred rock the size of a headstone. His legs were so far awry that Lang knew at once they were broken. He was already dragging the bloke down onto flatter ground before the girl had a chance to register the find. The climber and the girl cried out at more or less the same moment and Lang found himself laughing. As the girl crawled up beside him he pulled off his poncho and covered the bloke who seemed to have lost consciousness. She pulled the camera from its case and quickly took a photo. Lang was stunned by the flash. It altered his mood like a slap across the chops.

Is he alive? she said.

Yes, he muttered angrily. Shoot first, he thought, and ask questions – you'll go far, love.

Now what? she asked, a little chastened.

Lang felt the bloke's pulse but it was hard to distinguish from his own. He scrambled up the rock to get a view of the mountain and saw the long grey slope completely transformed by mist. Most of The Dial was gone now and the horizon seemed to begin a yard above the scrub. He let out a piercing coo-ee but it was like shouting into bedclothes. He couldn't even see the carpark now. He slid back down beside Marie and the injured hiker.

You want to stay with him or scuttle back out to the track? he asked. Even if it's dark when you find the trail it'll be easy enough to follow it back down to the others. Just leave something out, your bottle or your camera or something to mark the spot.

No, she said, looking suddenly horrified. No, no, I couldn't find it. Look, it's nearly dark – I couldn't find it.

Think of the story, he said, trying to sound kinder than he felt.

No, I can't.

He considered things a while, hoping the silence might give her the chance to find some courage and change her mind. But she avoided his gaze and said nothing.

Well, can you stay here while I go? he asked. We can't carry him. His legs are buggered and without a stretcher we'll be dragging him under the scrub by his arms. Marie, we've gotta get some other people up here.

Oh, please, I can't.

She began to cry. He felt a flush of anger.

Don't leave me here. Please.

Lang considered his handkerchief but was delivered once again when she fished out her own. He squatted beside the climber whose name he'd already forgotten and smoothed the twigs and grit from his blond beard. The fellow's fingernails were torn and he stank of sweat. Why couldn't you have stayed home today, sport? he thought. Why couldn't you have stuck to the track and let me be?

Marie, he asked as soft and warmly as he could. Can you do something for me? Can you yell?

Yes, said the girl, mopping at her eyes.

Get up on the rock and give it your best. Big loud voice.

Lang hunkered beside the bloke while the girl shrieked and squawked and coo-eed into the fog. He felt sick now and needy. He patted the bottle flat inside his tunic. He thought about the chances of taking a slug while the girl was occupied and more or less out of view. He eased the thing out and looked at it a moment. A rush of heat came to his face. The need, the shame, the awful fact of it glinting in the meagre light. God Almighty, what was he thinking? With a journalist an arm's-length away. In a community this small. It was five kinds of suicide he was courting, as if this whole search and rescue wasn't cock-up enough. Printed or whispered, news of Senior Constable Lang and his work-hour brandy on the mountain would be a fire nobody could put out.

The girl bellowed on and on, her voice breaking tearfully.

He turned the bottle in his hands. He thought of shoving the thing into the hiker's fancy jacket. But it went too much against the grain. It felt like planting evidence, like falsifying the record. He'd made a mess of things these past months but he'd not fallen that far. Even looking at the booze caused his throat to tighten. He flung it uphill so hard he saw stars.

What was that? said the girl. I heard something.

A rock, he murmured. I chucked a rock.

Oh.

You see anything?

No.

Give it a few more minutes.

Lang knew they were here for the night now but he felt better for ditching the brandy. He listened to the girl's voice burn and then break and when it was dark he called her down. They sat in silence for a while until he began to shiver.

Maybe you should put your coat back on, she murmured.

Best keep him warm, said Lang.

But you're wet.

Can't get any wetter then.

In the long quiet that ensued, rain dripped from foliage overhead and small creatures rustled unseen around them. A car horn sounded three times. Macklin was calling the stragglers in. Lang clicked the transmit button on the walkie-talkie. He tried spelling out his name in Morse but made a meal of it. He settled for a group of three clicks every few minutes.

The hurt climber began to mutter.

I have a banana, said the girl. You want half?

You have it, said Lang.

I can only eat half.

It'll keep you warm, he said.

I'm not cold, she said. Just . . . scared.

They'll find us. We might be here a while but they'll find us eventually.

This is my first week. I'm no good at this.

Well, he said kindly, you got the story.

Hell, I'm in the story now.

Yeah, we're both in it now.

What about him? Will he be alright?

I don't know. There's nothing we can do.

I can't bear it – we've found him but we can't help.

Exactly.

She noticed the resignation in his voice. She even seemed to bristle a little.

You sound like you're used to it, she said.

You never get used to it.

The climber began to murmur and whimper. Lang kept the man's head as still as he could.

I hate this, said the girl.

Lang levered himself upright and his leg burned with pins and needles. He scrambled up the small stone plinth to see what he could make out in the valley below. The fog was complete. He couldn't see any lights but for a moment he thought he heard the faint thrum of an engine, a generator maybe.

He got down. The cold was right in him now. The climber was motionless but breathing. Lang thought of the long, bitter night ahead of them.

I honestly thought I was tougher than this, said the girl.

You're doing fine, he said.

You start with these ideas about yourself.

Yep.

You wouldn't know.

Tell you a story, he said.

If you like.

Coupla months back I got called out to a prang. Farmkid was riding his trailbike behind the school bus. That awful twisty stretch through the karri forest. He's muckin around for the benefit of the girls at the back window. Fun and games, you know. Then suddenly he's at his place and just swerves away, pulls out from behind the bus into the path of a car coming the other way. I was pretty close when I got the call. Had twelve kids looking on while we waited for the ambulance. Just kneeling with him. Waiting.

I heard about this.

I tell you, it was a long time to wait. You're in uniform. People expect you to do something. But you can only wait. He was conscious, you know. I was talking to him. He knew why we were waiting. There wasn't a mark on him.

That's enough, she said. Don't tell me any more.

Died in my arms.

Stop.

And then I had to walk up the hill and tell his parents.

Lang let her blow her nose.

Got a boy like that myself, he said. He's a good kid.

Sorry. I thought I was tougher than this.

You'll be fine, he said. He felt all warm, like he'd just had a quick slug. He felt good.

The girl blew her nose. Lang caught his breath a little. Such talk made him lightheaded. It was hard to pull back. He had an urge to keep going, to explain himself, to blurt out everything he'd been stewing over all year; he could already taste the relief of it – Christ, he needed to, he was burning up with it – but even as he steeled himself and tried to think where to start, the girl began to cry. She lunged across the climber and grabbed him by the sleeve of his tunic and he saw just how close he'd come to total disaster.

She was too young, too rattled. You couldn't put your life into the hands of someone like this. Jesus, she was a kid, a cadet they'd sent out for a lost dog story. What the hell had he been thinking? And what, in the end, could he give her that would stack up? Hunches, irregularities, misgivings from a cop who wasn't a team player, an officer considered flaky and unreliable. They'd boil him alive.

You believe in God? she whispered.

Wish I didn't.

That's a strange thing to say.

Lang said nothing. A kind of cold anger sank through him at the thought that he'd almost gushed everything to this child. He wished he hadn't passed up half the banana, that he hadn't chucked the brandy when he so badly needed it now.

I said that's a strange thing to say, she said.

Why don't you try and sleep?

I can't.

We should keep warm, said Lang. Let's lie either side of him and pull my poncho over all of us.

If you like.

She seemed reluctant to let go his tunic, even more reluctant to lie beside the injured man. He could hear the talk in the crib room now: Lang cosied up on the hill with the fresh little chick from the paper.

Where's your camera? he asked before they arranged themselves.

Here, she said fishing in her jacket.

Leave it out, he said. I've got an idea.

He couldn't see her face in the dark but she seemed hesitant about handing over the camera. He sensed her loss of confidence in him and it stung. He tucked the thing as far into his tunic as he could and lay back with the hiker beneath the partial cover of his dripping poncho.

Before long the girl began to sob quietly. Beneath the poncho the cocktail of their sweat and breath and the odours of perfume and wet wool became more discomforting to Lang than the cold or the damp or the stones beneath his hip. He had neither the words nor the will to console her. In fact he came to dislike her as much as he did the stale-smelling man between them, the idiot who'd caused all this trouble.

No, he decided. He'd say nothing. It was what he was best at now. When you've lost your pride there's nothing left to say.

He lay there to wait it out. At the first break in the fog he'd take the camera up the rock and set the flash off at regular intervals. Eventually he'd guide the vollies up to where he was. It'd come out alright. They wouldn't freeze to death. The girl, Marie, would forget her blubbering fear because she'd get her rescue piece on the front page. She'd have her victim, her ordeal, her stoic hero. It'd be a great story, a triumph, and none of it would be true.

Boner McPharlin's Moll

To say that I went to school with Boner McPharlin is stretching things a bit because he was expelled halfway through my first year at high school. That would make it 1970, I suppose. I doubt that I saw him more than five times in his grotty hybrid uniform but I was awestruck when I did. We'd all heard about him back in primary school. The local bad boy, a legendary figure. And suddenly, there he was, fifteen and feral-looking, with grey eyes and dirty-blond hair past his shoulders. In his Levi's and thongs he had that truckin stride, like a skater's wade, swaying hip to hip with his elbows flung and his chest out. He had fuzz on his chin and an enigmatic smirk. His whole body gave off a current of sexy insouciance. To me, a girl barely thirteen, he was the embodiment of rebellion. I wanted that – yes, right from the first glance I wanted it. I wanted him. I wanted to be his.

I watched him swing by, right along the lower-school verandah with a bunch of boys in his wake – kids who seemed more enthralled by him than attached to him – and I must have been pretty obvious about it because my best friend, Erin, stood beside me with her hands on her hips and gave me a withering look.

No way, she said. Jackie, no way.

Erin and I went back forever. We were at a cruel age when we clung fiercely to girlhood yet yearned to be women, and everything excited and disgusted us in equal measure. Sophistication was out of reach yet we could no longer remember how to be children. So we faked it. Everything we did was imitation and play-acting. We lived in a state of barely suppressed panic.

I was only looking, I said.

Don't even look, said Erin.

But I did look. I was appalled and enchanted.

Boner McPharlin was the solitary rough boy that country towns produce, or perhaps require. The sullen, smouldering kid at the back of the class. The boy too brave or stupid to fear punishment, whose feats become folklore. When he strutted by that day I knew nothing about him, really. Only the legend. He was just a posture, an attitude, a type. He represented everything a girl like me was supposed to avoid. He posed some unspecified moral hazard. And I sensed from Erin that he was a peril to friendship as well, so I said nothing about him. I went on being thirteen – practised shaving my legs with the old man's bladeless razor, threw myself into netball, tore down my Johnny Farnham posters and put David Bowie in his place. I had a best friend – I shared secrets with her – yet they felt inconsequential once I saw Boner. Boner was my new secret and I did not share him.

I don't know what it was that finally got Boner expelled from school. He did set off pipe bombs in the nearby quarry. And there was, of course, the teacher's Volkswagen left on blocks in the staff carpark and the condoms full of pig blood that strafed the quadrangle in the lead-up to Easter, but there were plenty of atrocities he didn't commit, incidents he may have only inspired by example, yet he took the rap for all of it. With hindsight, when you consider what happened later in the seventies when drugs ripped through our town, Boner's hijinks seem rather innocent. But teachers were afraid of him. They despised his swagger, his silence. When he was hauled in he confessed nothing, denied nothing. He wore his smirk like a battlemask. And then one Monday he was gone.

The rest of us heard it all at a great remove. Everybody embellished the stories they were told and the less we saw of Boner the more we talked. Much later, when there was a fire at the school, he was taken in for questioning but never charged. I heard he went to the meatworks where his old man worked in the boning room. That was where the name came from, how it was passed from father to son. On Saturdays Boner lurked in the lee of the town hall or sometimes you'd see his mangy lumberjacket wending through cars parked around the boundary at the football.

At fourteen Erin and I began to be dogged by boys, ordinary farmboys whose fringes were plastered across their brows by built-up grease and a licked finger, and townies in Adidas and checked shirts whose hair didn't touch their collars. They were lumpy creatures whose voices squawked and their Brut 33 made your eyes water. We were more alert to their brothers who drove Monaros and Chargers. But we weren't even sure we were interested in boys. We were caught in a nasty dance in which we lured them only to send them packing.

The drive-in was the social hub of the town. My parents never went but they let me walk there with Erin and we sat in the rank old deckchairs beside the kiosk to watch *Airport* and *M*A*S*H* and *The Poseidon Adventure*. We wore Levi cords, Dr Scholls and 4711 ice cologne. Neither of us would admit it, but in our chaste luring and repelling of boys, Erin and I were locked in competition. There was a tacit score being kept and because she was so pretty, in an Ali McGraw kind of way, I was doomed to trail in her wake. I kept an eye out for Boner McPharlin and was always thrilled to see him truckin up toward the kiosk with a rolly paper on his lip. I kept my enthusiasm to myself, though there were times on the long walk home when I thought aloud about him. I was careful not to sound breathless. I did my best to be wry. I aped the new women teachers we had and adopted the cool, contemptuous tone they reserved for the discussion of males. I was ironic, tried to sound bemused, and while I waxed sociological, Erin lapsed into wary silence.

At about fourteen and a half Erin started letting a few boys through the net. Then they became a steady stream. Our friendship seemed to survive them. I tagged along as though I was required for distance, contrast and the passing of messages. She made it clear she wasn't easy. Nothing below the waist. Friendship rings were acceptable. No Italians. And she did not climb into vehicles.

I must have been fifteen when Boner McPharlin got his driver's licence. Suddenly he was everywhere. He wheeled around town in an HT van with spoked fats and a half-finished sprayjob in metallic blue. That kind of car was trouble. It was a sin-bin, a shaggin-wagon, a slut-hut, and as he did bog-laps

254

of the main drag – from the memorial roundabout to the railway tracks at the harbour's-edge – the rumble of his V-8 was menacing and hypnotic. Sometimes he cruised by the school, his arm down the door, stereo thumping.

Erin and I walked everywhere. Outside of school there was nothing else to do but traipse to the wharf or the beach or down the drab strip of shops where the unchanging window displays and familiar faces made me feel desperate.

I wish something would happen, I often said.

Things are happening all around us, said Erin.

I didn't mean photosynthesis, I muttered.

By the time anything's happened, it's over.

Well, I said. I look forward to having something to remember.

We were in the midst of one of these ritual discussions when Boner pulled up beside us. It was a Saturday morning. We stood outside the Wildflower Café. I had just bought a Led Zeppelin record. In the rack it had been slotted between Lanza and Liberace. Over at Reece's Fleeces people were buying ugg boots and sheepskin jackets. The passenger side window of Boner's van was down.

Jackie, said Erin.

Nothing wrong with saying hello, I said.

Even as I turned toward the mud-spattered car growling and gulping at the kerb, Erin was walking away. I saw the black flag of her hair as she disappeared into Chalky's hardware. Then I stepped over and leaned in. Boner's smirk was visible behind a haze of cigarette smoke. I felt a pulse in the roof of my mouth.

Ride? he said, just audible over the motor.

I shook my head but he wasn't even looking my way. He squinted into the distance like a stunted version of Clint Eastwood. Yet he must have felt something because he was already putting the car into gear and looking into his side mirror when I opened the door and slid in. He seemed completely unsurprised. He peeled out. Heads turned. I clutched the LP to my chest.

Boner and I drove a lap of town in silence. We idled past the pubs on the waterfront, the cannery, the meatworks, the silos. We passed grain ships on the wharf, the whalers on the town jetty and eased up by the convict-built churches on the ridge where the road wound down again toward the main beach.

I tried to seem cool, to make him be the one to break the silence, but he seemed disinclined to speak. The van was everything you'd expect, from the mattress and esky in the back to the empty Bacardi bottle rolling about my feet. Feathers and fish bones hung from the rear-view mirror. Between us on the bench seat was a nest of cassettes, tools, and packets of Drum tobacco. I knew I'd done something reckless by climbing in beside Boner McPharlin. I'd made something happen. What frightened me was that I didn't know what it was.

We didn't stay at the beach – didn't even pull into its infamous carpark – but wheeled around beneath the Norfolk Island pines and headed back to the main street of town. We slid into a space outside the Wildflower and a dozen faces lifted in the window. The big tricked-up Chevy motor idled away, drumming through the soles of my denim sneakers.

So, I said. How's things at the meatworks?

He shrugged and looked up the street. Erin stood in the door of the café, her hair ensnared by a rainbow of flystrips. Her face was clouded with rage. I wanted to prolong the moment with Boner but could think of nothing to say.

Well, I chirped. Thanks for the ride.

Boner said nothing. He eased in the clutch and scoped his mirror, so I got out and hesitated a moment before shoving the door to. Then he took off with a howl of rubber and I stood there hugging my record in the cold southern wind with a jury of my peers staring out upon me from the café.

In the doorway Erin did not step aside to let me in. She tucked her hair behind her ear and stared into my face.

I can't believe you.

Don't be wet, I said.

Jackie, what did you do?

I took a breath and was about to tell her just how little had happened when a jab of anger held me back. The crossly-folded arms, the solemn look – it wasn't concern but a fit of pique. I'd ignored her warnings. I'd let her walk away without giving chase. And now, worst of all, I'd upstaged her. The realization was like a slap. She was jealous. And this very public interrogation, the telegraphed expressions to everybody inside – it was all a performance. We weren't friends at all.

All I gave her was a sly smile.

Oh my God, she murmured with a barely-concealed thrill.

What? I asked.

You didn't!

I shrugged and smirked. The power of it was so delicious that I didn't yet understand what I'd done. With little more than a mute expression I'd just garnered myself a reputation. I was already Boner McPharlin's moll.

It was a small town. We were all bored out of our minds. I should have known better, should have admitted the unglamorous truth, but I didn't. I discovered how stubborn I could be. The stories at school were wild. I wasn't ashamed – I felt strong. I found a curious pleasure in notoriety. The rumour wasn't true but I owned it. For once it was about me. But it was lonely, too, lonelier for having to pretend to still be friends with Erin. To everybody else her protestations about my purity looked like misguided loyalty, friendship stretched to the point of martyrdom, though from the chill between us I knew otherwise, for the more she said in my defence the worse I looked, and the further my stocks fell the faster hers rose. By the end of that week I wanted the rumours to be true. Because if I was Boner's jailbait then at least I had somebody.

After school I stayed indoors. I went nowhere until the next Saturday when, in a mood of bleak resignation, I went walking alone. I was at the memorial roundabout when Boner saw me. He hesitated, then pulled over. I will never know why he did, whether it was boredom or an act of mercy.

He pushed the door open and I got in and through the sweep of the roundabout I had the weirdest sense of having been rescued. I didn't care what it took. I would do anything at all. I was his.

Within five minutes we were out of town altogether. We cruised down along the coast past peppermint thickets and spud farms to long white beaches and rocky coves where the water was so turquoise-clear that, cold or not, you had the urge to jump in fully clothed. Wind raked through our hair from the open windows. The tape deck trilled and boomed Jethro Tull. We didn't speak. I ached with happiness.

Boner drove in a kind of slouch with an arm on the doorsill and one hand on the wheel. The knob on the gearstick was an eightball. When his hand rested on it I saw his bitten nails and yellow calluses. He wore a flannel shirt and a battered sheepskin jacket. His Levi's were dark and stiff-looking. He wore Johnny Reb boots whose heels were ground off at angles.

The longer we drove the stranger his silence seemed to me. I couldn't admit to myself that I was becoming rattled. We drove for thirty miles while I clung to my youthful belief that I could handle anything that came my way. Slumped down like that, he looked small and not particularly athletic. I knew that while he had those boots on I could easily outrun him.

We drove all the rest of that day, a hundred and fifty miles or more, but no beach, no creek nor forest was enough to get him out from behind the wheel. Now and then, at a tiny rail siding or roadhouse, he slid me a fiver so I could buy pies and Coke.

At four he dropped me at the Esso station around the corner from my house. There were no parting speeches, no mutual understandings arrived at, no arrangements made. Boner left the motor running. He ran a hand through his hair. The ride was over. I got out; he pulled away. It was only after he'd gone that I wondered how he knew this would be the best place to drop me. I hadn't even told him where I lived. I didn't expect him to be discreet. It didn't fit the image of the wild boy. I was as irritated as I was flattered. It made me feel like a kid who needed looking after.

But that's how it continued. Boner collected me and dropped me at the Esso so regularly that there arose between me and the mechanics a knowing and unfriendly intimacy. They knew whose daughter I was, that I was only fifteen. Like everyone else who saw me riding around with Boner after school and on weekends, their fear and dislike of my father were enough to keep them quiet. Perhaps they felt a certain satisfaction.

My father was the council building inspector. It wasn't a job for a man who needed to be popular. Dour, punctilious and completely without tact, he seemed to have no use for people at all, except in their role as applicants, and then he was, without exception, unforgiving. For him, the building code was a branch of Calvinism perfected by the omission of divine mercy.

His life was a quest to reveal flaws, disguised contraventions, greed and human failure. Apart from dinner time and at the end-of-term delivery of school reports, he barely registered my presence. My mother was passive and serene. She liked to pat my hair when I went to bed. I always thought she was a bit simple until I discovered, quite late in the piece, that she was addicted to Valium.

My parents were lonely, they were insular and preoccupied, yet I still find it hard to believe that they knew nothing at all about Boner and me that year. If they weren't simply ignoring what I was up to then they truly didn't notice a thing about me.

I loved everything about Boner, his silence, his incuriosity, the way he evaded body contact, how he smelled of pine resin and tobacco smoke. I liked his sleepy-narrow eyes and his far-off stares. The bruises on his arms and neck intrigued me, they made me think of men and knives and cold carcasses, his mysterious world. Sometimes he'd vanish for days and I'd be left standing abject at the Esso until dark. And then he'd turn up again, arm down the door with nothing to say.

He never told me anything about himself, never asked about me. We drove to football games in other towns, to rodeos and tiny fairs. When there were reports of snow we travelled every road in the ranges to get a glimpse but never saw any. Out on the highway, on the lowland stretch, he opened the throttle and we hit the ton with the windows down and Pink Floyd wailing.

It's not that he said absolutely nothing, but he spoke infrequently and in monosyllables. By and large I was content to do all the talking. I told him the sad story of my parents. I filled him in on the army of bitches I went to school with and the things they said about us. Now and then I tried to engage him in hot conjecture – about whether David Bowie was really a poof or if Marc Bolan (who *had* to be a poof) was taller than he looked – but I never got far.

We drove out to the whaling station where the waters of the bay were lit with oily prisms and the air putrid with the steam of boiling blubber. I puked before I even saw anything. At the guardrail above the flensing deck, I tried to avoid splashing my granny sandals. Boner brought me a long, grimy bar towel to clean myself up with. He was grinning. He pointed out the threshing shadows in the water, the streaking fins, the eruptions on the surface.

Horrible, I said.

He shrugged and drove me back to town.

Although everyone at school assumed that Boner and I were doing the deed every time I climbed into his van, there was neither sex nor romance between us. Erin and the others could not imagine the peculiarity of our arrangement. There was, of course, some longing on my part. I yearned to kiss him, be held by him. After the reputation I'd earned it seemed only fair to have had that much, but Boner did not like to be touched. There was no holding of hands. If I cornered him, wheedling and vamping for a kiss, his head reared back on his neck until his Adam's apple looked fit to bust free.

The closest I ever got to him was when I pierced his ears. I campaigned for a week before he consented. It began with me pleading with him and ended up as a challenge to his manhood. One Sunday I climbed in with ice, Band-Aids, and a selection of needles from my mother's dusty sewing box. We parked out off the lowlands road where I straddled him on the seat and held his head steady. A few cars blew by with their horns trailing off into the distance. The paddocks were still. I pressed ice to Boner's earlobes and noticed that he'd come out in a sweat. He smelled of lanolin and smokes and that piney scent. When he closed his eyes, the lids trembled. I revelled in the luxury of holding him against the seat. I lingered over him with a bogus air of competence. Like a rider on a horse I simply imposed my will. At the moment I drove the needle through his lobe I clamped him between my thighs and pressed my lips to his clammy forehead. He was so tense, so completely shut down in anticipation of contact, that I doubt he felt a thing.

For a few weeks my riding with Boner brought me more glamour than disgrace. The new hippy teachers gave me credit for pushing social boundaries, for my sense of adventure and lack of snobbery. To them my little rebellion was refreshing, spirited, charming. They preferred it to my being the dutiful daughter of the council inspector. I knew what they thought of homes like ours with the red-painted paths and plaster swans. Their new smiles said it all. But when my experiment proved more than momentary their Aquarian indulgence withered. They despised boys like Boner as much as my parents would have, had they known him, and after a while my feisty rebellion seemed little more than slumming. Boner was no winsome Woodstock boy. He was a toughie from the abattoir. My young teachers' sisterly hugs gave way to stilted homilies. Free love was cool but a girl didn't want to spread her favours too thin, did she. I grimaced and smirked until they left me alone.

The gossip at school was brutal. In the talk, the passed notes, the toilet scrawl, I sucked Boner McPharlin, I sucked other boys, I sucked anybody. And more. At the drives Boner hired me out, car to car, Jackie Martin meatworker. Slack Jackie. The slander hurt but I bore it as the price of love. Because I did love him. And anyway, I thought, let them talk, the ignoramuses. Part of me enjoyed the status, the bitter satisfaction of being solitary but notable. I was, in this regard, my father's daughter.

I could bear the vile talk behind my back, but all the icy silence on the surface wore me down. I had enough remoteness at home. And Boner himself barely said a word. I craved some human contact. The only people who would speak to me were the opportunists and the outcasts, boys newly-emboldened to try their luck and hard-faced sluts with peroxided fringes who wanted to know how big Boner's bone was. The boys I sent packing but the rough chicks I was stuck with. They were a dim and desperate lot with which to spend a lunch hour.

At first they were as suspicious of me as they were curious. I was a cardigan-wearing interloper, a slumming dilettante. Their disbelief at Boner's having chosen *me* was assuaged in time by the incontrovertible fact of it, for there I was every afternoon cruising by in the van. I didn't challenge the legend. On the contrary, I nurtured it. By nods and winks at first and later with outright lies. I told them what they wanted to hear, what I read in *Cleo* and *Forum*, the stuff I knew nothing about. It seemed harmless enough. We were just girls, I thought, fakers, kids making ourselves up as we went along. But the things I was lying through my teeth about were the very things these girls were doing. That and much more. And they had the polaroids to prove it.

Only when I saw those photos did I begin to understand how stupid my playacting had been. One lunchtime five of us crammed into a smoky toilet stall, our earrings jangling with suppressed laughter. The little prints were square, felt gummy in my hands, and it took me several moments to register what I was looking at. God knows what I was expecting, which fantasy world I'd been living in, but I can still feel the horrible fake grin that I hid behind while my stomach rolled and my mind raced. So this was what being Slack Jackie really meant. Not just that kids thought you were doing things like this with Boner McPharlin; they believed you did them with anybody, everybody, two and three at a time, reducing yourself to this, a grimacing, pink blur, a trophy to be passed around in toilets and toolsheds all over town. All the gossip had been safely abstract but the polaroids were galvanizing. With all my nodding and winking I'd let these *creatures* believe that I was low enough to have mementoes like this myself, conquests that would bind us to one another. I'd never felt so young, so isolated, so ill. Those girls had already lived another life, moved in a different economy. They understood that they had something men and boys wanted. For them sex was not so much pleasure or even adventure but currency. And I was just a romantic schoolgirl. Maybe they suspected it all along.

I didn't go to pieces there in the fug of the cubicle but afterwards I subsided into a misery I couldn't disguise. I had always believed I could endure what people thought of me. If it wasn't true, I thought, how could it matter? But I'd gone from letting people think what they would to actually lying about myself. I'd fallen in with people whose view of life was more miserable and brutish than anything I'd ever imagined. It was as though I'd extinguished myself.

I went to class in a daze. The teacher took one look at me and sent me to the sick room.

Are you late with your period? asked the nurse.

I could only stare in horror.

You can imagine how the news travelled. I'm sure the nurse was discreet. The talk probably started the moment I left the class. Jackie went to the sick room. Jackie was sick at school. Jackie was bawling her eyes out. Jackie's got a bun in the oven.

It wasn't that I refused to answer the nurse's question. I was simply trying so hard not to cry that I couldn't speak. And saying nothing was no help at all.

During the final term of that year I went back to being a schoolyard solitary. I spent hours in the library to avoid scrutiny and to stave off panic, and the renewed study brought about a late rally in my marks. I heard the rumours about my 'condition' and did my best to ignore them. The only thing more surprising than my good marks was the new pleasure they gave me. It was all that kept me from despair.

I still felt a bubble of joy rise to my throat when Boner burbled up but it didn't always last out the ride. On weekends, as spring brought on the uncertain promise of the southern summer, I took to wearing a bikini beneath my clothes and I badgered Boner to let me out at the beaches we drove to. I couldn't sit in the car anymore. I wanted to bodysurf, to strike out beyond the breakers and lie back with the sun pressing pink on my eyelids. I wanted him there, too, to hold his hand in the water, for him to feel me splashing against him. But there wasn't a chance of it happening. He let me out but I had to swim alone. The beaches were mostly empty. There was nobody to see my flat belly. The water was cold and forceful and after swimming I lay sleepy-warm on a towel. The best Boner could do was to squat beside me in his Johnny Reb boots with a rolly cupped in his palm.

I began to demand more of Boner. Perhaps it was a renewed

confidence from good marks and maybe it was a symptom of a deeper bleakness, a sense of having nothing left to lose. Either way I peppered him with questions about himself, things I hadn't dared ask before. I wanted to know about his family, the details of his job, his honest opinions, where he wanted to be in ten year's time, and his only responses were shrugs and grins and puckerings and far-off looks. When I asked what he thought of me he murmured, You're Jackie. You're me navigator.

I didn't find it charming; I was irritated. Even though it dawned on me that Boner was lonely – lonelier than I'd ever been, lonely enough to hang out with a fifteen-year-old – I felt a gradual loss of sympathy. I could sense myself tiring of him, and I was guilty about it, but his silence began to seem idiotic and the aimless driving bored me. With no one else to speak to, I'd worn myself out prattling on at him. I'd told him so much, yearned so girlishly, and gotten so little in return.

The weather warmed up. The van was hot to ride in. The upholstery began to give off a stink of sweat and meat. I found shotgun shells in the glovebox. Boner wouldn't discuss their presence. I found that a whole day with him left me depleted. I missed being a girl on foot, I wanted the antic talk of other girls, even their silly, fragile confidences. Boner wouldn't speak. He couldn't converse. He couldn't leave the van. He wouldn't even swim.

I tried to find a kind way to tell him that it wasn't fun any-more but I didn't have the courage. One Saturday I simply didn't go to the Esso. On Sunday I helped my startled mother make Christmas puddings. The next week I stayed in and read *Papillon*. I watched 'Aunty Jack'. When I did venture out I avoided places where Boner might see me. It was only a few days before he found me. I heard him ease in beside me on the road home from school. I felt others watching. I leant in to the open window.

Ride, Jack? he murmured.

Nah, I said. Not anymore. But thanks.

He shrugged and dragged on his rolly. For a moment I thought he'd say something but he just chewed his lip. I knew I'd hurt him and it felt like a betrayal, yet I walked away without another word.

Every summer my parents took me to the city for a few weeks. I was always intimidated and selfconscious, certain that the three of us were instantly identifiable as bumpkins, though I loved the cinemas and shops, the liberating unfamiliarity of everybody and everything in my path. That year, after the usual excursions, we walked through the grounds of the university by the river's edge. The genteel buildings were surrounded by palms and lemon-scented gums and here and there, in cloisters or against limestone walls, were wedding parties and photographers and knots of overdressed and screaming children.

I sensed a sermon in the wings, a parable about application to schoolwork, but my father was silent. As we walked the verandahs he seemed to drink in every detail. There was a softness, a sadness to his expression that I'd never seen before. He rubbed his moustache, wiped his brow on the towelling hat he wore on these trips, and sauntered off alone.

What's with Dad? I asked. Did you guys have your wedding pictures taken here, or something?

My mother sat on a step in her boxy frock. Sweat had soaked through her polka dots to give her a strangely riddled look.

No, dear, she said. He wanted to be an architect, you know. Thirty years is a long time to have regrets.

I stood by her a while. Despite the languor of her tone I sensed that we'd come to the edge of something important together. I could feel the ghosts of their marriage hovering within reach, the story behind their terrible quiet almost at hand, and I hesitated, wanting and not wanting to hear more. But she snapped open her bag and pulled out her compact and the moment was gone, a flickering light gone out.

On the long hot drive home that summer I thought about the university and the palpable disappointment of my parents' lives. I wondered if the excursion to the campus had been an effort on their part to plant a few thoughts in my head. Consciously or not they'd shown me a means of escape.

In the new school year I more or less reinvented myself. Until that point, except for my connection with Boner, I had believed that I was average; in addition to being physically unremarkable I assumed I wasn't particularly smart either. The business with Boner was, I decided, an aberration, an episode. For the bulk of my school life I'd embraced the safety of the median. And now, effectively friendless, with the image of the university and its shady cloisters as a goad, I became a scowling bookworm, a girl so serious, so fixed upon a goal, as to be unapproachable. I never did return to the realm of girly confidences. Friends, had I found them, would have been a hindrance. In an academic sense I began to flourish. I saw myself surrounded by dolts. Contempt was addictive. In a few months I left everyone and everything else in my wake.

Of course no matter what I did my louche reputation endured. These things are set in stone. Baby booties and

condoms were folded into my textbooks. The story went that
Boner had dropped me for not having his child, that he was
out to get me somehow, that my summer trip to Perth had
involved a clinic. Last year's polaroid tarts were all gone now
to Woolworths and the cannery, there was nobody to share the
opprobrium with. Yet I felt it less. My new resolve and confidence made me haughty. I was fierce in a way that endeared
me to neither students nor staff. I was sarcastic and abrupt,
neither eager to please nor easy to best. I was reconciled to
being lonely. I saw myself in Rio, Bombay, New York; being
met at airports, ordering room service, solving problems on
the run. I'd already moved on from these people, this town. I
was enjoying myself. I imagined an entire life beyond being
Boner McPharlin's moll.

Boner was still around of course. He wasn't as easy to spot
because he drove an assortment of vehicles. Apart from the
van there was a white Valiant, a flatbed truck and a Land
Rover that looked like something out of *Born Free*. Our eyes
met, we waved, but nothing more. There was something un-
resolved between us that I didn't expect to deal with. Word
was that the meatworks had sacked him over some missing
cartons of beef. There were stories about him and his father
duffing cattle out east and butchering them with chainsaws in
valley bottoms. There was talk of stolen car parts, electrical
goods, two-day drives to the South Australian border, meetings on tuna boats. If these whispers were true – and I knew
enough by now to have my doubts – then the police were slow
in catching them. There were stories of Boner and other girls,
but I never saw any riding with him.

Town seemed uglier the year I turned sixteen. There was
something feverish in the air. At first I thought it was just me,
my new persona and the fresh perspective I had on things, but

even my father came home with talk of break-ins, hold-ups, bashings.

The first overdose didn't really register. I wasn't at the school social – I was no longer the dancing sort – so I didn't see the ambulancemen wheel the dead girl out of the toilets. I didn't believe the talk in the quad. I knew better than to listen to the bullshit that blew along the corridors, all the sudden talk about heroin. But that overdose was only the first of many. Smack became a fact of life in Angelus. The stuff was everywhere and nobody seemed able or inclined to do a thing about it.

It was winter when Boner McPharlin was found out at Thunder Beach with his legs broken and his face like an aubergine. They made me wait two days before I could see him. At the hospital there were plainclothes cops in the corridor and one in uniform outside the door. The scrawny constable let me in without a word. Boner was conscious by then, though out of his tree on morphine. He didn't speak. His eyes were swollen shut. I'm not even sure he knew who I was. With his legs full of bolts and pins he looked like a ruined bit of farm machinery.

I stayed for an hour, and when I left a detective fell into step beside me. He was tall with pale red hair. He offered me a lift. I told him no thanks, I was fine. He called me Jackie. I was still rocked by the sight of Boner. The cop came downstairs with me. He seemed friendly enough, though in the lobby he asked to see my arms. I rolled up my sleeves and he nodded and thanked me. He asked about Boner's enemies. I told him I didn't know of any. He said to leave it with him; it was all in hand. I plunged out into the rain.

I visited Boner every day after school but he wouldn't speak.

I was chatty for a while but after a day or so I took my home-work with me, a biology text or *The Catcher in the Rye*. For a few days there were cops on the ward or out in the carpark, but then they stopped coming. The nurses were kind. They slipped me cups of tea and hovered at my shoulder for a peek at what I was reading. When the swelling went down and his eyes opened properly, Boner watched me take notes and mark pages and suck my knuckles. Late in the week he began to writhe around and shake. The hardware in his legs rattled horribly.

Open the door, he croaked.

Boner, I said. Are you alright? You want me to call a nurse?

Open the door. Don't ever close the door.

I got up and pulled the door wide. There was a cop in the corridor, a constable I didn't recognize. He spun his cap in his hands. He was grey in the face. He tried to smile.

You okay, Boner? I said over my shoulder.

Gotta have it open.

I went back and sat by the bed. I caught myself reaching for his hand.

Least you can talk, I murmured. That's something.

Not me, he said.

You can talk to *me*, can't you?

He shook his battered head slowly, with care. I sucked at a switch of hair, watched him tremble.

What happened?

Don't remember, he whispered. Gone.

Talk to me, I said in a wheedling little voice. Why do you want the door open?

Can't read, you know. Not properly. Can't swim neither.

I sat there and licked my lips nervously. I was sixteen years old and all at sea. I didn't know how to respond. There were questions I was trying to find words for but before I could ask him anything he began to talk.

My mother, he murmured, my mother was like a picture, kinda, real pretty. Our place was all spuds, only spuds. She had big hands all hard and black from grubbin spuds. I remember. When I was little, when I was sick, when she rubbed me back, in bed, and her hands, you know, all rough and gentle like a cat's tongue, rough and gentle. Fuck. Spuds. Always bent down over spuds, arms in the muck, rain runnin off em, him and her. Sky like an army blanket.

She's . . . gone, your mum?

I come in and he's bent down over her, hands in her, blanket across her throat, eyes round, veins screamin in her neck and she sees me not a word sees me and I'm not sayin a word, just lookin at the sweat shine on his back and his hands in the muck and she's dead now anyway. Doesn't matter, doesn't matter, does it.

Boner gave off an acid stink. Sweat stood out on his forehead. I couldn't make out much of what he was saying.

Sharks know, he said, they know. You see em flash? Twist into whalemeat? Jesus, they saw away. It's in the blood, he had it, twistin all day into hot meat. And never sleep, not really.

Boner—

Sacked me for catchin bronzies off the meatworks jetty. Fuck, I didn't steal nothin, just drove one round on the forklift for a laugh, to put the shits up em. Live shark, still kickin! They went spastic, said I'm nuts, said I'm irresponsible, unreliable.

The bedrails jingled as he shook.

But I'm solid, he said. Solid as a brick shithouse. Unreliable be fucked. Why they keep callin me unreliable? I drive and drive. I don't say a word. They know, they know. Don't say a fuckin word. Don't leave me out, don't let me go, I'm solid. I'm solid!

He began to cry then. A nurse came in and said maybe I should go.

Boner never said so much again in one spate – not to me, anyway. I couldn't make head nor tail of it, assumed it was delayed shock or infection or all the painkillers they had him on. When I returned next day he was calmer but he seemed displeased to see me. He watched TV, was unresponsive, surly, and that's how he remained. I had study to keep up with. The TV ruined my concentration, so my visits grew fewer, until some weeks I hardly went at all. Then one day, after quite a gap, I arrived to find that he'd been discharged.

I didn't see him for weeks, months. The school year ground on and I sat my exams with a war-like determination. As spring became summer I kept an eye out for Boner in town. I half expected to hear him rumble up behind me at any moment, but there was no sign of him.

I was walking home from the library one afternoon when a van eased in to the kerb. I looked up and it wasn't him. It was a paddy wagon. A solitary cop. He beckoned me over. I hesitated but what could I do – I was a schoolgirl – I went.

You're young McPharlin's girlfriend, he said.

I recognized him. He was the nervous-looking constable from the hospital, the one who'd started hanging around after the others left. I'd seen him that winter in the local rag. He was a hero for a while, brought an injured climber down off a peak in the ranges. But he looked ill. His eyes were bloodshot, his skin was blotchy. There was a patch of stubble on his neck that he'd missed when shaving, and even from where I stood leaning into the window he smelt bad, a mixture of sweat and something syrupy. When I first saw him I felt safe but now I was afraid of him.

Just his friend, I murmured.

Not from what I've heard.

I pressed my lips together and felt the heat in my face. I didn't like him, didn't trust him.

How's his memory?

I don't know, I said. Not too good, I think.

If he remembers, said the cop. If he wants to remember, will you tell me?

I licked my lips and glanced up the street.

I haven't seen him, I said.

I go there and he just clams up. He doesn't need to be afraid of me, he said. Not me. Tell him to give me the names.

I stepped away from the car.

I only need the other two, Jackie, he called. Just the two from out of town.

I walked away, kept on going. I felt him watching me all the way up the street.

Next day I hitched a ride out along the lowlands road to Boner's place. I hadn't been before and he'd never spoken of it directly though I'd pieced details together over the years as to where it was. I rode over in a pig truck whose driver seemed more interested in my bare legs than the road ahead. Out amongst the swampy coastal paddocks I got him to set me down where a doorless fridge marked a driveway.

I know you, he said, grinding the truck back into gear.

I don't think so, I said climbing down.

I glanced up from the roadside and saw him sprawled across

the wheel, chewing the inside of his cheek as he looked at me.
The two-lane was empty. There wasn't a farmhouse or human
figure in sight. My heart began to jump. I did not walk away.
I remembered how vulnerable I felt the day before in town in
a street of passing cars and pedestrians while the cop watched
my progress all the way uphill. I didn't know what else to do
but stand there. He looked in his mirror a moment and I stood
there. He pulled away slowly and when he was a mile away I
set off down the track.

A peppermint thicket obscured the house from the road. It
was a weatherboard place set a long way back in the paddocks, surrounded by sheets of tin and lumber and ruined
machinery. I saw a rooster but no dogs. I knew I had the right
farm because I recognized the vehicles.

As I approached, an old man came out onto the sagging
verandah in a singlet. He stood on the top step and scowled
when I greeted him.

I was looking for Boner? I chirped.

Then you found him, he said, looking past me down the
drive.

Oh, I stammered. I meant your son?

His name's Gordon.

Um, is he home?

The old man jabbed a thumb sideways and went inside. I
looked at the junkyard of vehicles and noticed a muddy path
which took me uphill a way past open sheds stacked with spud
crates and drums. Back at the edge of the paddock, where
fences gave way to peppy scrub and dunes, there was a corrugated iron hut with a rough cement porch.

Boner was startled by my arrival at his open door. He got up
from his chair and limped to the threshold. Behind him the
single room was squalid and chaotic. There was an oxy set on

the strewn floor and tools on the single bed. He seemed anxious about letting me in. I stepped back so he could hobble out onto the porch. In his hands was a long piece of steel with a bronzed spike at one end.

What're you making? I said.

This, he said.

But what is it?

Shark-sticker.

You, you spear sharks?

He shrugged.

So how are you?

Orright.

Haven't seen you for ages, I said.

Boner turned the spear in his hands.

I hitched out, I said.

He was barefoot. It was the first time I'd seen him without his Johnny Rebs. He had hammer toes. Against the frayed hems of his jeans his feet were pasty white. We stood there a long while until he leant the spear against the tin wall.

Wanna go fishin?

I didn't know what to say. I lived in a harbour town all my life but I'd never had the slightest interest in fishing.

Okay, I said. Sure.

We drove out in the Valiant with two rods and a lard bucket full of tackle and bait. Boner had his boots on and a beanie pulled down over his ears. It took me a moment to see why he'd chosen the Valiant. He didn't say so but it was obvious that, for the moment, driving anything with a clutch was beyond him.

Out on Thunder Beach we cast for salmon and even caught a few. We stood a few yards apart with the waves clumping up and back into the deep swirling gutters in a quiet that didn't require talk. I watched and learnt and found to my surprise that I enjoyed the whole business. Nobody came by to disturb us. The white beach shimmered at our backs and the companionable silence between us lasted the whole drive back into town. I didn't tell him about the cop. Nor did I ask him again about who bashed him. I didn't want him to shut down again. I was content just to be there with him. It was as though we'd found new ground, a comfortable way of spending time together.

We saw each other off and on after that, mostly on weekends. These were always fishing trips; the aimless drives were behind us. We lit fires on the beach and fried whiting in a skillet. When his legs were good enough we'd climb around the headland at Massacre Point and float crab baits off the rocks for groper. If he got a big fish on, Boner capered about precariously in his slant-heeled boots, laughing like a troll. He never regained the truckin strut that caught my eye on the school verandah years before. Some days he could barely walk and there were times when he simply never showed up. I knew he was persecuted by headaches. His mood could swing wildly. But there were plenty of good times when I can picture him gimping along the beach with a bucket full of fish seeming almost blissful. No one was ever arrested over the beating. It didn't seem to bother him and he didn't want to talk about it.

I didn't notice what people said about us in those days. I wasn't even aware of the talk. I was absorbed in my own thoughts, caught up in the books I read, the plans I was making.

During the Christmas holiday in the city, I met a boy at the movies who walked me back the long way to the dreary motel my parents favoured, and kissed me there on the steps in the street. He came by the next morning and we took a bus to Scarborough Beach and when I got back that evening, sun-burnt and salt-streaked, my parents were in a total funk.

The boy's name was Charlie. He had shaggy blond surfer hair and puppy eyes and my father disliked him immediately. But I thought he was funny. Neither of us had cared much for *The Great Gatsby*. Charlie had a wicked line in Mia Farrow impersonations. He could get those eyes to widen and bulge and flap until he had me in stitches. In Kings Park I let him hold my breast in his hand and in the dark his smile was luminous.

The first time I saw Boner in the new year he was parked beside the steam cleaner at the Esso. The one-tonner's tray was dripping and he sat low in his seat, the bill of his cap down on his nose. I knew he'd seen me coming but he seemed anxious and reluctant to greet me. A sedan pulled up beside him – just eased in between us – and the way Boner came to attention made me veer away across the tarmac and keep going.

The last year of school just blew by. I became a school prefect, won a History prize, featured as a vicious caricature in the lower school drama production (Mae West in a mortar board, more or less).

Boner taught me to drive on the backroads. We fished occa-sionally and he showed me the gamefishing chair he'd bolted to the tray of the Land Rover so he could cast for sharks at night. His hands shook sometimes and I wondered what pills they were that he had in those film canisters on the seat. I smoked a little dope with him and then didn't see him for weeks at a time.

At second-term break Charlie arrived with some surfer mates in a Kombi. My mother watched me leave through the nylon lace curtains. As I showed Charlie and his two friends around town I sensed their contempt for the place. I apologized for it, smoked their weed and directed them out along the coast road. We cruised the beaches and got stoned and ended up at Boner's place on the lowlands road. But nobody came out to meet us. In front of the main house stood the bloodstained one-tonner, its tray a sticky mess of spent rifle shells and flyblown hanks of bracken. When Charlie's mates saw the gore-slick chainsaw they wanted out. We bounced back up the drive giggling with paranoia.

In my last term I lived on coffee and Tim-Tams and worked until I felt fat and old and crazy. Charlie didn't write or call. I remembered how short of passion I'd been with him. When he kissed me or held my breast I was more curious than excited. I wanted more but I wouldn't let him. I wasn't scared or ashamed or guilty – I just wasn't interested. There was none of the electricity I'd once felt with Boner squeezed between my thighs as a fifteen-year-old. I felt annoyed, if anything, and Charlie's puzzlement curdled into irritation. I didn't consciously compare him to Boner. Even Boner was someone I could sense in my wake. There was something shambling and hopeless about him now, something mildly embarrassing. I had got myself a driver's licence. I hardly saw him at all.

The final exams arrived. The school gym buzzed with flies. The papers made sense, the questions were answerable. I was prepared. The only exam where I came unstuck was French. I knew I'd done well at the Oral but the paper seemed mischievous, the questions arch and tricksy. It shouldn't have mattered but it made me angry and I tried way too hard to coat my answers with a sarcasm that I didn't have the vocab for. I wrote gobbledy-gook, made a mess of it. I came out reeling, relieved to have it all behind me, and there in the shade was Boner parked illegally at the kerb beneath the trees.

Ride? he murmured.

Thanks, but I'm going home to bed. That was my last exam.

Good?

All except French. I was in *beaucoup* shit today.

Bo-what?

Beaucoup. It's French. Means lots of.

I pressed my forehead against the warm sill of his door.

Made you somethin, he murmured.

I looked up and he passed me a piece of polished steel, a shark that was smooth and heavy in my hand.

Hey, it's lovely.

Friday, he said. I'm havin a bomfire. Massacre Point. Plenty piss. Bo-coo piss. Tell ya mates.

Sure, I said. But what mates did I have?

A teacher came striding down the path.

You better go, I said.

He waited until the teacher was all but upon us before he cranked the Chev into life.

I didn't tell anybody about Boner's party. I felt awkward and disloyal about it but there wasn't anybody I cared to ask. It was so unlike him to organize something like this. He was probably doing it for me and I hated to think of him disappointed.

When I got out to Massacre Point in the old man's precious Datsun, Boner's fire was as big as a house. The dirt turnaround above the beach was jammed with cars and there must have been a hundred people down there, a blur of bodies silhouetted by flames. As I made my way down in my kimono and silly gilt sandals the shadows of classmates spilled from the fire to wobble madly across the trodden sand. I thought of the shitty things these kids had said about us. They were the same people. Fuck the lot of you, I thought. I'm his friend. His only friend. And only his friend.

All of Boner's vehicles were there. At the ready was a pile of fuel – pine pallets, marri logs, tea chests, driftwood, furniture, milepegs and fence posts. Stuck in the sand in the firelight was the school sign itself with the daft motto – SEE FAR, AIM HIGH – emblazoned on it. More like FAR OUT, GET HIGH tonight, I thought.

Beyond the fire was a trailer full of ice and meat. On old doors between drums were beer kegs, bottles, cooking gear and cassettes. There were cut-down forty-fours to barbecue in and a full roasting spit with a beast on it.

Boner's Land Rover was backed down near the water and the tray of the nearby one-tonner was crammed with tubs of blood and offal that boys were ladling into the surf to chum for sharks. Boner had a line out already. I saw a yellow kero drum adrift beyond the breakers and his marlin gear racked at the foot of the game chair on the Landy. Pink Floyd was blasting across the beach. Everybody was pissed and laughing and talking all at once and I was remote from it, just watching while Boner moved from the fire to the water's edge trailing crowds like a guru. When he finally saw me he grinned.

Jesus, he said. You told everyone!

I found a bottle of rum and followed him down to the shorebreak to wait for sharks. While we stood there kids burnt kites above us and fireworks fizzed across the sand. The air was full of smoke and of the smells of scorching meat. It was the beach at Ithaca, it was Gatsby's place, Golding's island. My head spun.

About midnight the beef on the spit was ready and we hacked at it, passed it around and ate with our hands. Everyone's eyes shone. Our teeth glistened. Our every word was funny.

Then the big reel on the back of the Landy began to scream. While Boner gimped up onto the tray, a boy from the Catholic school started the engine. Boner's earrings glittered in the firelight as he took up the rod, clamped on the drag and set the hook with a heave. Line squirted out into the dark. The drum set up a spray and a wake and Boner leaned back and let it run. After a while he banged on the tray and the St Joe's boy reversed down to the water so that Boner could bullock back some line. It went on like that for hours – backing and filling, pumping and winding – until the Land Rover's clutch began to stink and the radiator threatened to boil over. The first driver was relieved by another boy whose girlfriend sprawled across the bonnet to pour beer down his neck through the drop-down windscreen. Now and then he backed up so far that there were waves crashing on the tailgate and I half expected the shark to come surfing out into Boner's lap.

He looked beautiful in the firelight, as glossy and sculpted as the steel carving he'd given me. When the shark bellied up into the shallow wash, Boner limped into the water with his inch-thick spear and drove it through the creature's head and a kind of exhausted sigh went up along the beach.

The fire burnt down. We drank and dozed until sun-up.

Within two days I was gone and it was a long time before I looked back.

During my years at university, I met my parents every Christmas in the dreary motel in the city. We had our strained little festivities, the walks through the campus and down along the foreshore. They told me stories of home but it didn't feel like home anymore. I saw a few old faces from down there but never let them think that I remembered them. I liked the expressions of hurt and confusion that came upon them. I got satisfaction from it. I heard that Erin began teacher's college, but dropped out, married young and had children. One summer afternoon she pestered me on a bus the entire length of Stirling Highway. She was fat. She wanted to catch up, to show me her brood. I got off two stops early just to be rid of her.

When I finished my Honours I drove south just the once to please my parents. The whaling station was defunct. The harbour stank of choking algae. I saw Boner parked in an F-100 outside a pub the tuna men liked. He blinked when he saw me. He was jowly and smelled nasty. He looked a wreck. His teeth were bad and his gut was bloated.

Jackie, he said.

What *are* you doing? I asked, forgetting myself enough to lay hands on his sleeve along the window sill.

Quiet life's the good life, he mumbled, detaching himself from me. Wanna ride? Go fishin?

Gotta meet my oldies in five minutes, I said. Why don't I drive out tomorrow?

I'll get you.

No, I'll drive out.

He shrugged.

When I drove out the next day the McPharlin place was even more of a shambles than I remembered. The old man sat on the verandah, frail but still fierce. I waved and went on up to Boner's shack and found him on his cot with a pipe on his chest and the ropey smell of pot in the air. He was asleep. On the walls were sets of shark jaws. The floor was strewn with oily engine parts. I almost stepped away but he sat up, startled. The little pipe hit the floor.

Me, I said.

He looked confused.

Jackie, I said.

He got off the bed in stages, like an old man.

One day I'll kill him, he said. Take me sticker down there and jam it through his fuckin head.

It's Jackie, I said.

I don't care. You think I care?

I went east for postgrad work and then left the country altogether. I did the things I dreamt of, some diplomatic stints, the UN, some teaching, a think-tank. I took a year off and lived in Mexico, tried to write a book but it didn't work out; it was like *trying* to fall in love. I was lonely and restless.

Then my father died and my mother went to pieces. I was almost grateful for the excuse to fly home to escape failure. I came back, sold their house and set my mother up in an apartment in the city. For a while I even lived with her and that's when I discovered that she was an addict. We didn't get close. We'd got a little too far along for that but we had our companionable moments. She died in a clinic of pneumonia the first winter I was back.

For several months I was lost. I didn't want to return to being a glorified bureaucrat. I had no more interest in the academy. I had an affair with a svelte Irishwoman who imported antiquities and ethnographic material for collectors. As with all my entanglements there was more curiosity from my side of it than passion. Her name was Ethna. She must have sensed that my heart wasn't in it; it was over in a matter of weeks but we remained friends and, in time, I became her partner in business.

It was 1991 when I got the call from the police to say that they had Gordon McPharlin in custody. They asked whether I could come down to help them clear up some matters relating to the death of Lawrence McPharlin.

I flew to Angelus expecting Boner to be up on a murder charge, but when I arrived I found that he was not in the lock-up but in the district hospital under heavy sedation. The old man had died in his sleep at least ten days previous and an unnamed person had discovered Boner cowering in a spud crate behind the shed. He was suffering from exposure and completely incoherent.

There's no next of kin, said a smooth-looking detective who met me at the hospital. We found you from letters he had. And we know that you went to school with him, that there'd been . . . well, a longstanding relationship.

I knew him, yes, I said as evenly as I could.

He was in quite a state, said the detective. He was naked when he was found. He had a set of shark jaws around his neck and his head and face were badly cut. His shack was full of weapons and ammunition and . . . well, some disturbing pornography. There was also a cache of drugs.

What kind of drugs? I asked.

I'm sorry, I'm not at liberty to say. Ah, there was also some injury to his genitals.

And is he being charged with an offence?

No, said the cop. He's undergone a psychiatric evaluation and he's being committed for his own good. We need to know if there's anyone else, family members we don't know about, who we might contact.

You needed me to fly here to ask me that?

I'm sorry, he murmured. I thought you were his friend.

I am his friend, I said. His oldest friend.

Good, he said. Good. We thought you could accompany him, travel with him up to the city when he goes. You know, a familiar face to smooth the way.

Jesus, I muttered, overcome at the misery and the suddenness of it. I was determined not to cry, or be shrill.

When?

Ah, tomorrow morning.

Fine, I said. Can I see him now?

The cop and a nurse took me in to see Boner. He was in a private room. There were restraints on the bed. He was sleeping. His lungs sounded spongy. His face was a mess of scabs and bruises. I cried.

That afternoon I hired a car and drove out along the lowlands road to the old McPharlin place. The main house gave off a stink I did not want to investigate. All the old cars were still there, plus a few that had come after my time. The HT van was up on blocks, the engine gone. I looked around the sheds and found broken crates, some bloodstains.

Boner's hut looked like a cyclone had been through it. The floor was a tangle of tools and spare parts, of broken plates and thrown food, as though he'd gone on a rampage, emptying drawers and boxes, throwing bottles and yanking tapes from cassette spools. His mattress was hacked open and the shark sticker had been driven into it. They were right, he'd lost his mind. A squarish set of shark jaws lay on the pillow. It took me a moment to register the neat pile of magazines beside it. On impulse I reached down to pick one off the pile but froze when I saw it. This was the porn they'd told me about. The cover featured the body of a woman spread across the bonnet

of a big American car, her knees wide. There were little holes
burnt in the paper where the woman's anus and vagina had
been, as though someone had touched the glossy paper with a
precisely aimed cigarette. On the model's shoulders, boxed in
with stickytape, was my face, my head. A black and white
image of me at sixteen. Unaware of the camera, laughing. I felt
a rush of nausea and rage. The fucking creep! The miserable,
sick bastard.

I didn't even touch it. I went outside and sucked in some air.
I felt robbed, undone. The ground was unstable underfoot. I
had to sit down while something collapsed within me.

When I left I hadn't really got myself into good enough
shape to drive but I couldn't stay there any longer. I was
halfway down the rutted drive when another car eased in from
the highway. At least it was twilight. At least I wasn't crying.
As the car got close I recognized the cop from earlier that
day. There was another detective with him, a taller man. They
pulled up beside me.

Everything alright? the cop asked.

Just wonderful, I said, wanting only for him to get out of my
way so I could get the hell off the place and find a stiff drink
in town.

You need to talk about it?

No, I don't need any talk. I'll be there in the morning. Let's
get it over with.

The cop nodded, satisfied. His mate, the tall redhead, didn't
even look my way. I wound up my window and they crept
past.

Next day I sat beside Boner in the back of an ordinary-
looking mini-van with another woman who I could only
assume was a nurse. We didn't speak. What I'd seen in Boner's
cabin made it difficult for me to sit there at all, let alone make

conversation. During the five hours, Boner mostly slept. Sometimes he muttered beneath his breath and once, for about half
an hour without pause, he sobbed in a way that seemed almost
mechanical. The only thing he said all day was a single sentence. *Eat though young.* Perhaps it was *thy* young or even
their young. I couldn't make it out. His mouth seemed unable
to shape the words. I couldn't bear to listen. I dug the Walk-
man from my bag and listened to a lecture on Buddhism.

Boner was never released. He didn't recover. Even though
I drove past the private hospital almost every day I only ever
visited at New Year. I went because I conceded that he was
sick. He hadn't been responsible for his actions. I didn't go any
more frequently than that because my disgust overrode everything else. When I went I wheeled him out into the garden
where he liked to watch the wattlebirds catch moths. He had
an almost vicious fascination for the Moreton Bay fig. He said
it looked like a screaming neck.

Over the years there were visits when he was hostile, when
he refused to acknowledge me, and occasions when I thought
he was faking mental illness altogether. He had been lame for
some time but after years of shunting himself about the ward
in a wheelchair he became so disabled by arthritis that he
relied on others to push him. His hands were claw-like, his
knees horribly distorted. When I realized how bad it had
become, I sent along supplies of chondroitin in the hope that
it might give him some small relief. I don't know that it ever
helped but he seemed to enjoy the fact that the nasty-tasting
powder was made from shark cartilage. It brought on his troll-
laugh. He'd launch into a monologue that made no sense at all.

The visits were always difficult. The place itself was quiet and orderly but Boner was a wild, twisted little man; an ancient child, fat and revolting. And of course I was busy. The import business had become my own when I bought Ethna out. I travelled a lot. I sold my house and the weekender at Eagle Bay and bought a Kharmann Ghia and an old pearling lugger. I lived on the boat in the marina and told myself that I could cast off at a moment's notice. I would not be cowed by middle age; I was my own woman. And I valued my equilibrium. I didn't need the turmoil of seeing Boner McPharlin more than once a year.

This year, on New Year's Day, I wheeled Boner out among the roses and he slumped in the chair, slit-eyed and watchful, and before we got to the tree that provoked his usual spiel about his mother's screaming neck, he began to whisper.

Santa's helpers came early for Christmas.

What's that? I said distractedly. I was hungover and going through the motions.

Four of the cunts. Same four, same cunts.

Boner, I said. Don't be gross.

Cunts are scared. Came by all scared. Big red, he's lost his hair. Frightened I'll dog him. Fuckin cunts, every one of em. Come in here like that. Fuckin think they are?

Someone visited? I asked.

Santa's helpers.

Did you know them?

Wouldn't *they* like to know? he said with a wheezy giggle.

I stopped pushing him a moment. The light was blinding. Already his hair hung in sweaty strings on his neck. The sunlight caused him to squint and he licked his cracked lips in a repulsive involuntary cycle. There were scars in his earlobes where he'd torn his earrings out years before. Despite the heat he insisted on a blanket for his legs.

So, did you? I asked. Know them, I mean.

You put me here, he said.

I'm your friend.

Friend be fucked.

Your only friend, Boner.

You see that tree? You see that tree? That tree? That's my mother's screamin neck.

Yes, you've told me.

Screamin neck, not a sound. You can hang me from that tree, I don't care, you and them can hang me, I don't care.

Stop it.

Let em do it, let em see, the pack a cunts. Never know when I might bite, eh. Even when I'm dead. Shark'll still go you when you think he's dead.

Happy New Year, Boner.

Get me out, Jack. Let's piss off.

You are out. See, we're in the courtyard.

Out! *Out*, you stupid bitch.

I'm going now.

You're old, he said mildly. You used to be pretty.

That's enough.

They said it, not me.

I have to go.

See if I fuckin care.

I really have to leave.

Well it's not fuckin right. I never said a word. Never once.

Boner, I can't stay.

Just drivin, that's all I did. Never touched anythin, anybody, and never said a word – Jesus!

I'll turn you around.

Please, Jackie. Let's ride, let's just arc it up and go.

Both of us were crying when I wheeled him into the darkness of the ward. He slumped in the chair. I left him there.

A week later he was dead. The hospital told me it was a massive heart attack. I didn't press for details. Looking back I see that I never did, not once.

There were six of us at the cremation – a nurse, four men and me. Nobody spoke but the priest. I didn't hear a word that was said. I was too busy staring at those men. They were older of course, but I knew they were the cops from back home. There was the neat one in the good suit who'd called me about Boner's breakdown. Two others whose faces were familiar. And the tall redhead who'd asked to see my arms when I was sixteen years old. His hair was faded, receding, his eyes still watchful.

I began to weep. I thought of Boner's fire, his twisted bones, his terrible silence. I got a hold of myself but during the committal, as the coffin sank, the sigh I let out was almost a moan. The sound of recognition, the sound of too late.

I walked out. The redheaded detective intercepted me on the steps. The others hung back in the shade of the crematorium.

My condolences, Jackie, he purred. I know you were his only friend.

He didn't have any friends, I said, stepping round him. You should know that, you bastard – you made sure of it.

I'm retired now, he said.

Congratulations, I said as I pushed away.

I drove around the river past my office and showrooms and went on down to the harbour. I cruised along the wharf a way and then along the mole to where the river surged out into the sea. I parked. The summer sun drove down but I was shivery.

The talk on the radio was all about the endless Royal Commission. I snapped it off and laid my cheek against the hot window.

I didn't see it whole yet – it was too early for the paranoia and second-guessing to set in – but I could feel things change shape around me. My life, my history, the sense I had of my self, were no longer solid.

All I knew was this, that I hadn't been Boner's friend at all. Hadn't been for years. A friend paid attention, showed a modicum of curiosity, made a bit of an effort. A friend didn't believe the worst without checking. A friend didn't keep her eyes shut and walk away. Just the outline now, but I was beginning to see.

They'd turned me. They played with me, set me against him to isolate him completely. Boner was their creature. All that driving, the silence, the leeway, it had to be drugs. He was driving their smack. Or something. Whatever it was he was their creature and they broke him.

I sat in the car beneath the lighthouse and thought of how I'd looked on and seen nothing. I was no different to my parents. Yet I always believed I'd come so far, surpassed so much. At fifteen I would have annihilated myself for love, but over the years something had happened, something I hadn't bothered to notice, as though in all that leaving, in the rush to outgrow the small-town girl I was, I'd left more of myself behind than the journey required.

Immunity

THERE WAS THIS BOY I LIKED. It was the war that made me think of him and the time we rode south together on the train, in the days when the trains still ran. He sat right up the front of the carriage in an army uniform. He was alone. His hair was so long that it hung out of his beret like Che Guevara's. The boots and webbing, the stripes on his arm, they looked incongruous. He was fifteen years old.

It took me three hours to work up the nerve to go and sit beside him. Although it was the last day of the holidays the carriage wasn't even half full. There were some old people, a couple of kids in batik shirts and a few other rowdy boys in khaki who I had to pass on my way down the aisle. When I plumped down beside him he looked up from his book a moment and smiled politely. He smelled of starch – yes, of Juicy Fruit and Fabulon.

He went back to reading with a solemn expression. The book was something called *Saturday Night and Sunday Morning*.

Any good? I asked.

Nah, he said. Kinda boring.

What's with the uniform?

Cadet camp, he said. We were up at Northam.

Oh. How was it?

Hot as buggery. In winter it's worse. Tin barracks, camp stretchers, awful food.

Geez, I said. Sounds grouse.

We rode along without talking for a while. It was kind of awkward. He was by the window and when I looked out at the paddocks and the hills and the dry January bushland rolling by, it must have seemed like I was staring at him.

What? he said, half-grinning.

The uniform and everything. The army stuff. I don't get it.

He shrugged.

We're out of Vietnam now, I said.

Lucky us.

I mean, didn't you worry? That they might send you?

I'm at school, he said.

But later. If it had kept going.

We're not really in the army.

Almost, though. They're training you for war.

He looked out the window.

Will you join up? I asked. When you finish school?

The army? No, it's foul.

I don't get it, I said. Being in the cadets.

There's good stuff, he said, looking around him now as if to see who might be listening in. Bivouacs, hikes. We build things.

And shoot guns, I murmured.

Yeah, he said with a grin. That's the best part.

Right.

Appalled as I was, I found myself smiling with him. He had slightly girlish lips. Beneath the crisply rolled-up sleeve and the sergeant's stripes the skin of his arm was tanned and I wanted to press against it.

You going to Angelus? he asked, looking at his hands. One of his thumbnails was black. I thought of it coming off when school got back.

Yeah, I said.

Ever been before?

That's when I realized that he didn't know me at all. We went to the same high school, where he was a year above me. I'd been watching him for eighteen months now, finding excuses to idle past him at lunchtime where he sat outside the library with some boys who didn't seem to care about him one way or the other. I had assumed that my face was familiar at the very least. But he didn't have a clue who I was.

I shook my head.

Sorta crappy town, he said.

I'm from City Beach, I lied.

Posh, he said.

Not really.

Is it a girls' school?

No, I said. I didn't know anything about City Beach. I went there once for a swim and got stung by a jellyfish. My father said I was a bloody sook.

Behind us, a baby began to cry. I pulled my hair behind my ear. I had lovely hair then. He seemed to grow more conscious of me there beside him, to shrink somehow because of it. I knew all about him. I knew he was lonely. I saw him ride down on the wharf some Sundays. I used to picture myself walking on the beach with him. He didn't have that ugliness, the sporting cruelty that boys are supposed to have. Which is why the uniform and the talk of guns upset me.

Well, I think it's stupid, someone like you, being an army cadet.

Well, that's your opinion.

It's dangerous. Reckless.

Nah.

Playing soldiers, I said scornfully.

I bit my lip then. He was fingering his book. I'd lost him.

The wheels clattered beneath us. His boots squeaked as he moved in the seat beside me.

Last year, he said, this kid got electrocuted. That's what they reckon. He was signalman. Carrying the radio, you know? It's got a huge thing on it, a whip aerial. He was climbing over something. The aerial touched some powerlines.

God, I said. And he died?

That's what they reckon.

That's horrible.

Yeah.

You ever think about stuff like that?

He burred the pages of the book against his palm.

Sometimes.

Death, I mean.

He nodded.

This week I had this weird thing. I was in the butts. At the rifle range? You have to take turns being down behind the bank. You know, putting the targets up and down, marking hits and stuff. You wave a flag for a washout, a total miss. It's boring as hell. Anyway, I'm down there and all this crap's going overhead, you know, and all the rounds are whacking targets and thumping into the sandbank on the other side of us. And there's this ricochet. It doesn't sound anything like on TV. You know, on cowboy shows. This was like some kind of moan – really scary-sounding – and then suddenly, next to me on the bench, there's this white thing like a star and it's spinning and spinning, hot as hell and just standing up on one of its points next to me leg.

A bullet?

Yep.

And I'm just sittin there with me eyes out on sticks, staring at it.

What happened?

He looked at me. He seemed to be looking at my knees.

Nothing, he said. It just ran out of puff. It slowed down and fell over. Right there, like where you are. Right next to my leg.

Did you keep it? Have you got it?

No. I didn't wanna touch it. But it was kind of like a sign. It made me feel weird. Kind of immune. Death right there beside me and I'm immune.

God, I said.

Yeah.

We were close to home now. The ranges were in view. The air had that southern chill to it again.

I'm going to school here this year, I said.

Really?

Yeah. Hell, if you're immune to death I'm gunna hang around with *you*.

He laughed and I could have torn my tongue out from sheer embarrassment. I was hurling myself at him. It was worse than walking past his house five times in one afternoon which I did one Sunday. That time I saw him at the window. He had a broom in his hand or maybe a hockey stick. He was looking but not seeing. It made me wonder about him.

We sat quietly the last few minutes as if both of us were trying to figure out what was going on between us. I breathed in
the smell of him, looked at his hands on the unread book. I
thought of him crossing the quad to see me next week. People
around us pulled down their luggage.

When we came into the station there was a cop car there
with its light going.

Shit, he said.

I knew who his father was. He grabbed his duffle bag from
the rack and pushed past me before the train had even stopped.

I never spoke to him again. This new war made me remember.

It was his little sister in hospital with meningitis. I heard all
about it later. She died.

Defender

WITH THE WINDOWS DOWN and the autumn breeze in their hair, Vic and Gail wound up through the valley past vineyards and fruit stands and ramshackle craft shops toward the scarp where the morning sun was still in the trees. She drove. He was tilted back amidst the pillows she'd wedged around him, oblivious to her sidelong glances, the way she chewed her lip. He was preoccupied with memories. After three weeks in a darkened room, they were a swarm he could neither evade nor disperse. He let out a snort.

What? said Gail, winding up her window.

I used to play basketball.

Yeah.

Wasn't any good, of course. In the city I'd always played football. Took me half a season to understand that I wasn't allowed to tackle the opposition – you know, knock blokes over. They made me a guard. I thought it was like being a full-back. Man! he said with a laugh.

A defender, said Gail. That's you all over.

Couldn't shoot for peanuts. My lay-ups were rubbish. If I somehow got a clean break toward our own basket I'd pound down the court, sick with dread, knowing that I was gonna throw a brick. But I loved stopping the other guys getting through. Always did love a zone defence, you know, a real keyway lockdown.

Ah, said Gail wryly. The old keyway lockdown.

We used to play these Aboriginal kids from St Joe's, he continued, unabashed. They always flogged us. So arrogant and graceful and hostile – just all over us – you know, and then somehow, chirpy as you like, they'd con us into walking them back to the hostel afterwards. I think they were afraid of the dark or maybe something they had to walk past.

Gail let the window down again. Her queasy sense of dread was back. Maybe this weekend wasn't such a good idea. She was convinced that they needed to be with close friends. But fond of Vic as they were, Daisy and Fenn were more her friends than his. She didn't want him to feel ambushed, outnumbered. Trouble was, he had no real friends. There were colleagues, comrades, but no one intimate.

I saw one of em again last year, said Vic. One of those boys. That school case we did in the Pilbara? He's a teacher there now. Must be the only blackfella I knew who made it through school.

That you know of, Gail said.

Teaches phys ed. He saw me and just laughed.

You didn't tell me about it.

It was kind of awkward. I mean I always liked him. I was

glad to see him. God, I almost hugged the guy and congratulated him for being a big success.

You didn't!

Just think of the odds. In our day, from that town. The others'll be dead or in jail. Making it to forty's an achievement. But, no, I didn't do anything stupid. Still, I wanted to catch up with him, buy him a drink, but I fudged it. It suddenly got too . . . complicated.

Complicated? Gail asked. What're you saying?

Vic felt her looking his way now. She had the wrong idea but he had no confidence in his ability to explain himself. His face began to tingle with a hint of neuralgia. He sank back and closed his eyes a moment.

They came into the jarrah forest, a wall of grey on either side of the road, and the air was cool and sharp with eucalyptus.

You should go back there some time, said Gail after a long silence.

The Pilbara?

No, the old town. You should deal with these things. God, last year I was down there every month.

The old town, he said bitterly.

Well, you were like a zombie.

My parents died.

Sure. But it was more than that. You know it.

Just small-town shit, Gail.

Which you haven't dealt with.

He sighed and looked at her long arms draped on the wheel, the hair licking back over her ears in the slipstream.

You should have come with me, she said fiercely. You should have.

For your sake?

Both our sakes. You're stuck, Vic. You won't admit it but

you are. Which, in case you hadn't noticed, leaves me stuck alongside you.

Stuck *with* me, you mean.

That's not what I said, she murmured. You're like someone under siege. And I know it's all these sudden memories. But are they coming because you've been sick, or are you sick from remembering? Like you've held it out too long.

You're a fundraiser, not a therapist.

Well, pretty soon you might need both!

What does that mean, Gail?

Do you realize that every vivid experience in your life comes from your adolescence? You should hear yourself talk. You're trapped in it. Nothing you do now holds your attention like the past. Not me, not even your work, these days. I feel like I'm getting less real to you by the day, that I'm just part of some long, faded epilogue to your real life. Last year I put up with it. It was lonely, Vic, but now it's worse. Shingles, twice in two months. That's a physical breakdown. How long before you cave in altogether?

She drove. He licked his chapped lips. Each of them sensed the uneasy crossing of a boundary. There was relief in it – they'd been like two people holding their breath so long, but they were fearful of where this might lead.

Why are we going away this weekend? he asked.

A change of scene.

A change of company?

That too, she said with a sigh.

You've started going to church again.

How'd you know?

I found a pew sheet.

Well, last year I went whale watching. This year I thought I'd try the Anglicans.

I'm not sure that's an evolutionary progression.

I don't think you're in a position to talk about progress, Vic.

I thought you'd never go back to all that nonsense.

Well, it's not quite the same brand of nonsense. And I'm sorry you're threatened by it.

Vic took a breath but said nothing. He put a hand to the welter of scabs on his face. He could feel the others itching at his scalp and eyelid but he resisted the impulse to claw at them. The neuralgia was well and truly back. The deep, prickling heat was, he now understood, a warning sign. He took his hand away and looked at his wife. She was crying, blinking furiously, tears streaking back across her temples in the wind.

Sorry, he said.

Doesn't matter.

I'm being a dickhead.

I have to pull over.

Gail braked and eased them onto a wedge of pink gravel. She switched the engine off and snatched up a tissue from the box on the dash. She looked away but she sensed him slumped beside her.

Last year, she said. Those weekends in Angelus. I had an affair.

Ah. Right.

It was stupid, and wrong. I didn't plan it. Lasted a few weeks. I'm so sorry.

That's why I should have come?

No. Well, part of me thinks so, but I know that's not fair.

Well, Jesus.

Gail gripped the wheel until her hands burned. She hadn't meant to tell him yet and not nearly as bluntly. For someone in his condition the timing was about as bad as she could have managed. She'd wanted to tell him so she'd be free of it, not to spit it up in a moment of anger.

He opened the door and got out. The forest sighed. There was a mineral whiff of gravel. For a moment she thought of him bolting out into the blur of trees and leaving her there by the roadside. Could it be that she wanted it? A scene? An end, even?

But he went no further than the drainage ditch, round-shouldered, hands in pockets, blowing like a man who'd already run a good distance.

When they bounced up the long winding drive and came to the house, Fenn was out on the grass with the hose and the kids were in an old cattle trough, squealing as he sprayed them down. Capering about in his floral boardshorts, the ginger beard dripping, that chest hair plastered awry, Fenn looked so huge and ungainly, so unselfconscious in his foolery, that Gail and Vic exchanged glances and smiled despite themselves.

God, she said. Look at that.

Daisy came down off the verandah. She was barefoot and her cotton dress only contained her breasts intermittently.

Don't mind my husband, she said pulling open the driver's-side door. His idea of farming is to water the children.

We were just admiring his movements, said Gail.

Ever seen such a physique?

Like a Greek god, said Gail.

How are you, Daisy? said Vic.

Better than you two by the looks of things.

How do things look, then? he said.

That poor face of yours? Like she dragged you behind the car the first fifty miles.

What about *my* face, Daise? asked Gail.

Like you drove the second fifty miles feeling guilty about it.

Vic and Gail caught each other's eye a second time. Daisy saw it. He realized then that Fenn and Daisy were already privy to Gail's secret.

C'mon, said Daisy. Or do I have to haul you both out?

Daisy made an enormous pot of tea and set down a tray of anzacs by the window from which they could keep an eye on the children. Fenn weighed a biscuit on his upturned palm and raised his impossible eyebrows.

Anzac, he said. Now there's a biscuit with the ballast of history.

They're perfectly good biscuits, said Gail. She's getting good at them.

And even if I'm not, said Daisy, he still eats them. Behold, Vic, the weight of loyalty.

Yeah, said Fenn, slapping his belly. The waist of loyalty.

Daisy and Fenn were both vets. They'd sold a thriving sub-urban practice to come here. Daisy had grown up on the place and took it on when her father grew too frail to keep up with the orchards. Vic looked out at the hard noon light on the hills and the almost shadowless lines of trees and he wondered how Fenn and Daisy would manage here. Fenn was alarmingly impractical. Animals and children loved him but he knew nothing about horticulture or even simple gardening. Daisy, who'd been away from the place since she was seventeen, had plans for an organic operation and maybe biodynamic poultry as well, but they seemed out of reach at present. There had been hidden debts, unforeseen expenses. Vic thought there was something manic about Fenn and Daisy's optimism. At times they struck him as just plain careless with their energies. Still, he admired them for striking out in a new direction, for having dreams. They were barely ten years his junior. So why did they seem so fresh?

Oh, look at you, said Daisy. You poor love.

He's looking so much better, said Gail. But it was frightening. Especially when it got close to his eye.

Nasty, said Fenn. You can go blind.

They *know* that, Fenn.

I was thinking aloud. I had a cousin with shingles once.

Thanks for the cuppa, said Vic. You mind if I duck up to the cabin for a bit of a lie-down?

I'll drive you up, said Gail.

No, I'll be right.

Bed's made, love, said Daisy. Listen to me, I sound like my mother.

When Vic was gone, Gail made herself another cup of tea and watched Fenn go out to the kids again.

What a goose, said Daisy settling in beside her, resting her head against her shoulder.

They're so lucky to have a father like him.

Yeah, murmured Daisy. I suppose they are.

Fenn climbed into the trough. Only his gut and his horny, white feet were visible as the kids climbed on him.

You must see the other sort too much, said Daisy. At work.

Yeah. But I was thinking about what it would be like. Being a little girl again, with a dad like that.

Speaking of fathers, tell me about this priest you're seeing. What's he like?

It's a she, actually. She's very unremarkable.

What's remarkable is you seeing her. After everything they did to you. Please tell me it's not just guilt that's sent you back.

Oh, I don't know. Maybe it was at first. It's been so awful, Daise. I've felt so horrible about it.

Well, you should have told him earlier.

He was a wreck. His parents had just died. After God knows how long, he sees them together in the same room again only to bury them both within a few weeks.

Telling him would have pulled him up, said Daisy. It would have given him something more immediate to think of.

Maybe. I dunno. I mean it's just so grotty. The bloke was the motel manager. He was such a sleaze. I kind of sank into it.

Well, Christ, you were lonely.

Stop defending me. You're worse than Vic.

He's making excuses for you?

You know him. Circling the wagons on everyone else's behalf.

It's endearing, said Daisy, swishing the dregs in the pot.

And it's a problem, Daise, a curse. You can't compensate for everyone all your life. In the end you have to demand something of people.

Listen to you, Daisy said. She got up to tip the tealeaves into a slopbucket beside the ancient wood range. Isn't that your story, too?

Gail smiled, conceding it. She thought of the long year past, of Vic finding his father after so much time and the way his past seemed to assail him. She'd tried so hard to understand his obsession that she all but entered into it. She drove to his home town and trudged its streets and beaches like a researcher imagining herself into his world and the slow wreck of his teenage years. In the end it was a kind of indulgence. There was nothing to show for it but more damage, more complication.

Vic's problem, said Daisy, is he's still the dutiful boy. Doing the right thing by his poor mother. Letting himself get screwed by the labour movement year in year out without a squeak. How long can you keep that shit up without a little bit of bad faith creeping in?

Yes, said Gail. But I suppose I could see myself in the same light. At what point are you just pretending?

Well, you've already blown *your* good-girl credentials.

Gail put a hand to her temple and managed a smile.

Will you stay together?

I don't know, she said. I love him.

Well, said Daisy, flapping her sweaty dress. He's probably worth it. All things considered.

Vic lay in the guesthouse with the windows open and the cries of birds and children drifting up the ridge. The cabin was built of corrugated iron and clad inside with local timber. There was a slate floor, a wood heater, a little bathroom. He liked it. But he was sure that Fenn and Daisy couldn't really afford it. The debts would eat them alive and the thought made his head race. Their bucolic existence was precarious. They were good people, yea-sayers to life, but they exhausted him. He supposed it was rude getting up like that, ten minutes after arriving, but he'd felt so sapped by everybody's solicitude that he had to go before he became too enfeebled to move at all. And they knew about Gail. She'd told them first. It made him more of an invalid than he could bear.

The neuralgia rattled him. It was usually the precursor to a relapse. And, God, he didn't want to return to how he was at Christmas – the searing headaches, the blisters. Gail was right to be afraid. It frightened him too, this total collapse, because he felt his mind teetering at its limit. He'd been this close before but he'd never told her. At this great distance he could still see himself, the boy behind the curtain, cradling death in his arms. He was forty-four years old but he felt just as helpless. He knew what the boy didn't, that you couldn't keep soldiering on indefinitely. But beyond that, even at this age, he still didn't know the first thing about saving himself.

When Vic woke it was the middle of the afternoon and all the shadows had moved so far across the room that it seemed he'd woken in a different cabin. The ghostly pain in his face was gone. He got up, put on his shoes and some sunglasses, and went out onto the little terrace of slates and river rocks. But for a solitary child bumping up and down on the trampoline, there was nobody visible down at the main house.

He walked out into the orchard. The air was cool. He knew he should probably go back for a jacket but he pressed on through the sloping lines of trees not wanting to interrupt this feeling of freshness, of respite.

But within a minute he was reviewing the morning's conversation in the car. His blathering about basketball. Gail's forbearance. His needling. Then her sudden news, the awful smarting shock of it. There was only the faintest trace left now. Did it mean that, deep down, he expected it, even thought he deserved it? That he forgave her already? Or that he felt so little because he was so abstracted, as far gone from her as she feared? He knew it was completely absurd, yet what had festered in his mind wasn't the adultery at all, but something Gail said before that. When he told her about the Aboriginal teacher. Her reaction to his confession that he'd wanted to take the bloke for a drink but baulked.

Even though he was used to Gail's exasperation, he'd never heard such raw dismay from her before. She thought he was a racist.

He knew it was bizarre that he could bear being cuckolded – yes, in time he probably could – but for your wife to think *that* of you? No, he couldn't take it; it was too much. Yet, Christ, what kind of a stiff did that make him? It was sort of funny, in a sick way, and so typical of him. At a time like this, still anxious about his good name. He knew what other lawyers called him behind his back. The Redeemer.

He wanted to have it out now, to explain himself, clear it up, but he knew what a self-absorbed lunatic he'd look. It would prove Gail's point that he was ensnared in the past. It would make things worse.

Anyhow he probably was a racist in other ways. He had an involuntary reaction against white South Africans. He didn't care for the shape of Slavs' heads – they tended to be flat at the back.

With his thoughts bolting away from him now, Vic tramped through regiments of trees until a child stepped out from behind a trunk and caused him to shriek.

Fenn and Daisy's little girl stumbled back onto her bum and began to cry without a sound. After some hesitation he patted her fine blonde hair that stuck out at all angles from her head. He tried to hold the child's hand but she wasn't having any of it.

We both got a fright, he said, trying to remember her name. I'm such a duffer. I'm sorry, I didn't see you coming.

She was three – no, four – years old. She took such a long time to take a breath and make a sound.

The child's name was Keira. Eventually she took his hand and they walked through the orchard in the dreamy latticework of shadows. A hundred yards away on a parallel course across the slope Daisy and Gail walked hand-in-hand along a separate row.

Are you looking forward to school? Vic asked.

I don't know, said Keira.

I suppose you'll go on a bus?

Or Daisy will drive me.

Yeah, or Daisy'll drive you.

He realized he had no idea what to say to a child. Gail had nieces but he never saw them.

What happened to your face? said the girl. Did you fall off your bike?

Yes, he lied. I came a cropper.

What's a cropper?

I . . . I really fell off bad. I stacked it. I came a cropper.

Fenn's fat, you know, said Keira. But it doesn't matter.

No, he said, his voice catching. Nothing like that matters.

He wanted to hug her but he would only frighten her.

At the end of the ridge they waited for Daisy and Gail. Daisy took the child downhill in a long tumbling run toward the house.

You should have seen the pair of you, said Gail. You looked like Charles Windsor on a meet and greet.

She held my hand, he murmured.

Maybe she thought you'd get lost.

You ever regret not having them?

Ask me when I'm too old to have them. I'm not quite thirty-four, Vic. The door hasn't shut yet.

He nodded and she saw that she'd surprised him. Something had got through. She just couldn't be sure what it was.

I want to explain about that Aboriginal bloke.

What?

The bloke I knew as a kid.

Oh, yes, she said, wearily.

And he told her again about the basketball and the walks to the hostel and how the blackfellas bounced balls off the arses of their defeated escorts. And the confusion he felt, seeing their cheerful, cocky ringleader as a grown man. It wasn't race, he said. Not quite. It was the jangling memory of a long drive to Perth when he was fourteen and not yet aware that his old man was beginning to go to pieces. There was the cough medicine he swigged and the rash of odd errands like this one, delivering a juvenile offender to Longmore. The prisoner was a dark, smouldering boy who pretended not to know Vic. His record was, according to Vic's father, as long and spattered as a painter's ladder. For five hours Vic sat beside him. The boy was uncuffed – unreachable, it seemed. And Vic was anxious, conflicted, afraid the whole time, long before the boy bolted at the last moment, at the very gate, whereupon he had to chase him down himself, dogging him like a fullback through a pine plantation until he got a tackle in and sprawled with him onto the bed of needles. The boy called him five kinds of fucking cunt while Vic held him there, not knowing what else to do until his father limped up, weeping with relief.

We never spoke about it, said Vic, and I never told Mum. I knew that I'd saved the old man's bacon somehow. That time, anyway.

You shouldn't have had to.

But the point is that when I saw that bloke again, this big

lanky bugger, and he's slapping his thigh and I'm trying to remember his name and all I can see is myself at fourteen, picking pine needles off my shirt and leading his little brother in cuffs to prison, I just felt sick. I couldn't deal with it.

Vic, you are the fucking Book of Lamentations.

Oh. Yeah. Is Job in that?

She looked at his scabby face and grimaced. She didn't know whether her rage was for him or against him.

I just needed to tell you, he said. That's all I had to say.

Good, she said curtly, despite herself.

You know, our basketball coach was a Mormon.

Vic.

Actually there were two of them, Elder Harley and Elder Wendell. Yanks, of course. We hated them. They just turned up and wouldn't go. In the end we burnt their bikes and hung them on a fence.

Hm. Novel.

Yeah, I spose it was.

Gail headed downhill at a pace she knew was uncompanionable. It was perverse to be disappointed by a lack of drama, the tears and screams and recriminations she'd dreaded, but she was strangely deflated. She would have preferred a burning bicycle, come to think of it, some straightforward conflagration.

They didn't speak. All the way back to the house he hung at her elbow, kicking stones, panting a little, not quite matching her step for step.

On the lawn Fenn had a skeet trap set up. There was a shotgun broken over his arm.

What's this? said Gail.

Dad's stuff, said Daisy. There's boxes of those clay pigeon thingies in the shed.

I'm not much good, said Fenn. But, by God, it's a lark.

Vic and Gail looked at one another.

You used to shoot, said Fenn. Didn't you, Vic?

Vic looked at Keira who lay on a warped garden bench with an *Archie* comic. Daisy held the other child, a boy, who fished out one of her breasts and began feeding. He looked too big, too old, to be breastfed. Daisy sat on the bench beside Keira whose grubby feet rested against her little brother's head.

Weren't you in the army cadets? asked Daisy.

Yeah, said Vic. Believe it or not.

You want a go? asked Fenn who looked incongruous in his floral boardshorts and khaki disposal shirt.

I haven't fired a weapon for thirty years, he said nervously. To tell you the truth I was a little creepy about it, once.

Vic remembered that Tasmanian kid a few years back, the way he calmly strolled about shooting tourists like they were some kind of sport. The chill of recognition he felt seeing the poor dumb kid's face on TV. The dull eyes, the shoulder-length hair, the total confusion. It might have been him at fourteen or fifteen, gun-happy and afraid.

Dad used to shoot birds, said Daisy. The fruit, you know.

Is that thing still registered? asked Gail.

Love, you look horrified, said Fenn heartily.

There's a rifle, too, said Daisy. Vet work, it's different in the country.

We've never had to use it, yet, said Fenn. Thank God. You wouldn't want to be the local RSPCA officer, though.

One side of the valley was dark now but the sun still lit the eastern slopes, bronzing the trees in their staggered lines.

But this, said Fenn. Trap-shooting. Nothing gets hurt but your eardrums.

You go ahead, said Vic.

Can I pull? said Keira.

Yeah, said Daisy. But you know the rules.

The little girl slid off the bench and rooted around in a box for a moment before pulling out a couple of pairs of earmuffs. She passed a set to her father and pulled some on herself. Vic felt Gail take his hand as Fenn loaded up from a carton on a rickety card table and faced out across the valley bottom.

Pull!

Two discs whirred out, climbing a while, only to sink into the valley untroubled by Fenn's shots. The noise of the gun was quite shocking but the baby fed on, untroubled.

I suppose if he was any better at it, said Daisy, we wouldn't be able to walk around next day collecting the skeet from the driveway for next time.

Still recyclers, said Fenn, stepping back to eject his shells onto the grass.

Doesn't it stop your chooks from laying? asked Gail.

Daisy smiled.

The sound of Britney Spears, said Fenn, is the only thing I've noticed that puts those fowls off their game.

Come inside for a drink, Gail, said Daisy.

Gail let go Vic's hand and went in with her. The boy, Amos, groaned sleepily, almost drunkenly, it seemed to Gail, as he lost the nipple. She closed the door behind them and let Daisy pour her a glass of homebrew. The gun went off again and again while they sat at the table beneath the window, the light dimming around them.

So what did he say? said Daisy, passing the child to Gail while she hoisted a leg of lamb from the fridge.

Nothing, actually, said Gail, looking down at the boy who watched her sombrely. It was all a bit . . . civilized.

Well, I'm sure it hurts like fuck. I know it does.

What did *you* do?

I smashed his model plane collection.

Did you . . . did you catch him or did he confess?

He came clean. I always hated those planes.

He spent all last year pining for dead people. His parents. Kids he knew at school. Some girl with a birthmark he loved. He left me behind.

So it was revenge?

No, it was an accident, a mistake.

And now you're even?

Seems vile to think so.

Oh, look, he's taken up arms.

Gail looked out at the scene on the lawn. Vic in his earmuffs. Fenn crouched behind the awkward-looking tripod. The things wheeling out across the evening sky and Vic's body pivoting smoothly. The small spattering disintegrations as he hit both. Fenn hooted.

He's good, said Daisy.

Of course he's good, said Gail, oblivious to the child tugging at her top.

Vic cleared the breech of each barrel and sniffed the old reek of cordite. His hands trembled a little. He stepped back with elaborate care and took up two more cartridges.

You mind? he asked Fenn.

Blast away, Maestro.

The little girl, Keira, looked at him with renewed interest.

Funny, he said. In all those years I never fired a shotgun.

You're a natural.

Vic wondered what that could possibly mean. As a boy he'd used rifles. Before the age of sixteen the state had trained him to shoot four kinds of automatic weapon and assemble a .762 self-loading-rifle in the dark. Until the school rules changed he'd fired at human outlines, targets with hearts. They were grooming him for war without the slightest inkling of the turmoil inside him. They didn't know that he sat by the window with his father's .22, sat there with it loaded and cocked, waiting for something to happen. He was only a breath away from something hideous. He was a ticking bomb. And when the old man ran away and took the rifle with him the fever broke. He'd never touched a weapon since.

Pull!

He led but did not fire. He thought of the boy lurking behind the curtain. The skeet hummed off into the twilight. It was important to know he could resist the urge.

Again? called Fenn.

Yeah, said Vic. Pull.

He hit both targets and felt his face crease into a smile that tested every scab. This was different. It was strangely untroubling in its pointlessness. Fenn was right. Nothing got hurt.

He stood there firing until Keira went inside and the smell of roasting lamb wafted across the grass. He blasted away, pull after pull after pull, until he was covered in sweat and they were out of ammo and he realized that darkness had fallen around him and he was happy.

Acknowledgements

Some of these stories have appeared before:

'Abbreviation' in *The Bulletin*; 'Aquifer' in *Granta, The Australian Women's Weekly,* and *The Beacon Best of 2001* (ed. Junot Diaz); 'Cockleshell' in *The Australian Women's Weekly, Prospect* and *The Harvard Review*; 'Commission' in *Harper's*; 'Family' in *Meanjin* and (as 'Leaper') in *Tracks*; 'Small Mercies' in *Heat*; 'Damaged Goods' in *The Threepenny Review*.

The author gratefully acknowledges the editors of these publications.

Special thanks to Denise, whose help made this book possible.